POKÉMON™
BLACK AND WHITE

VOL.1

Story by **HIDENORI KUSAKA**
Art by **SATOSHI YAMAMOTO**

Pokémon Black and White
Volume 1
VIZ Kids Edition

Story by HIDENORI KUSAKA
Art by SATOSHI YAMAMOTO

© 2011 Pokémon.
© 1995–2011 Nintendo/Creatures Inc./GAME FREAK inc.
TM and ® and character names are trademarks of Nintendo.
© 1997 Hidenori KUSAKA and Satoshi YAMAMOTO/Shogakukan
All rights reserved.
Original Japanese edition "POCKET MONSTER SPECIAL"
published by SHOGAKUKAN Inc.

English Adaptation / Annette Roman
Translation / Tetsuichiro Miyaki
Touch-up & Lettering / Susan Daigle-Leach
Design / Fawn Lau
Editor / Annette Roman

Printed in the U.S.A.

Published by VIZ Media, LLC
P.O. Box 77010
San Francisco, CA 94107

10 9 8 7 6 5 4
First printing, July 2011
Fourth printing, October 2011

www.vizkids.com

www.viz.com

POKÉMON

BLACK AND WHITE

VOL.1

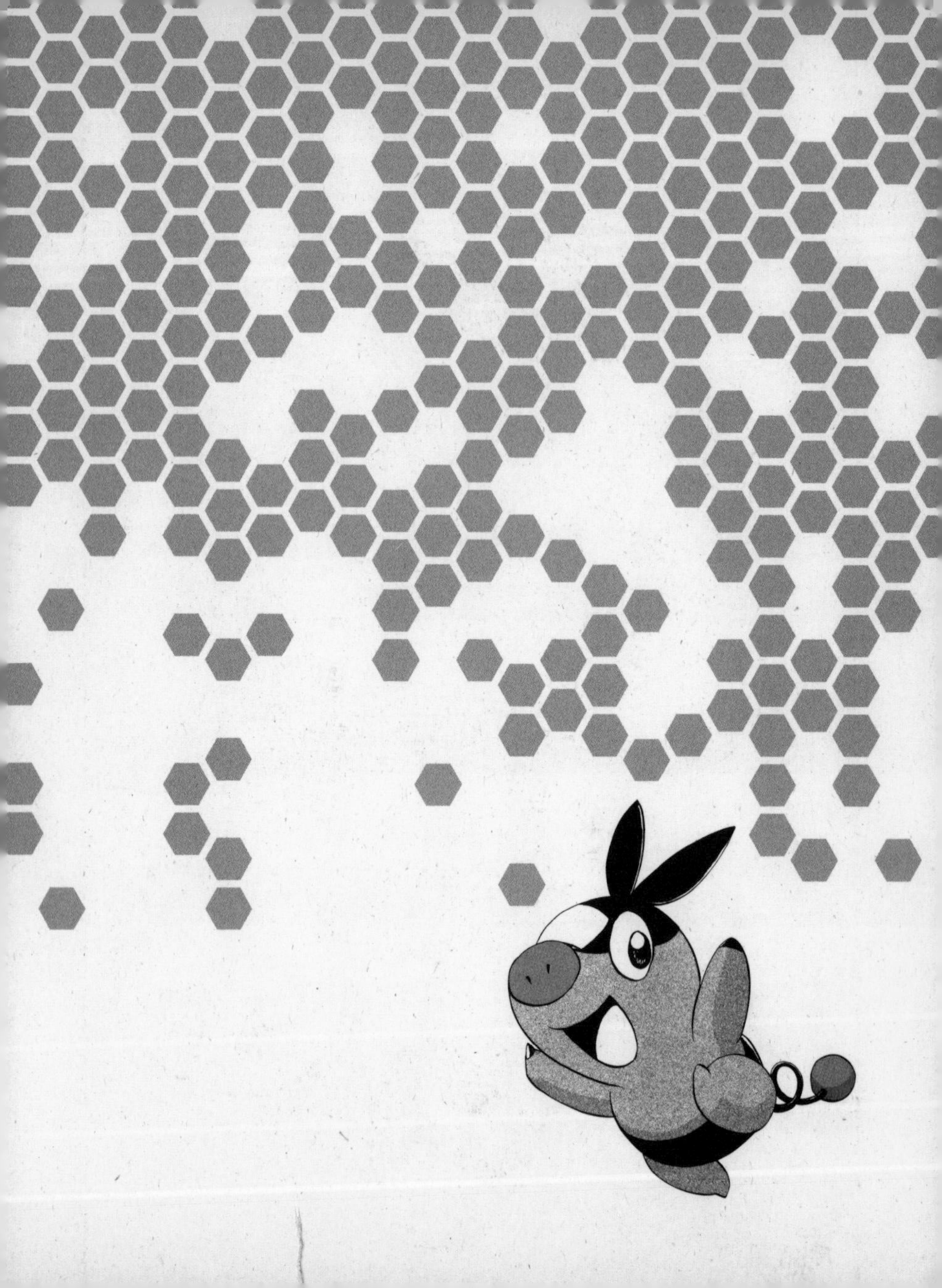

Adventure ① Fussing and Fighting

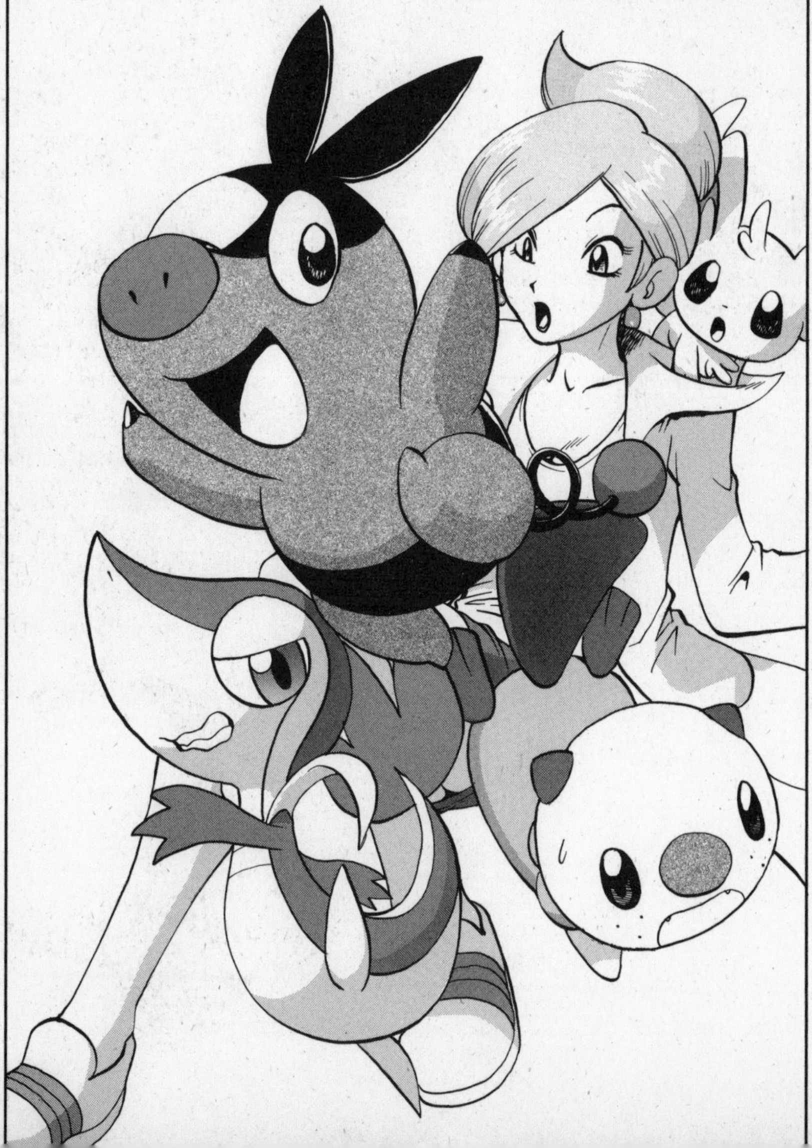

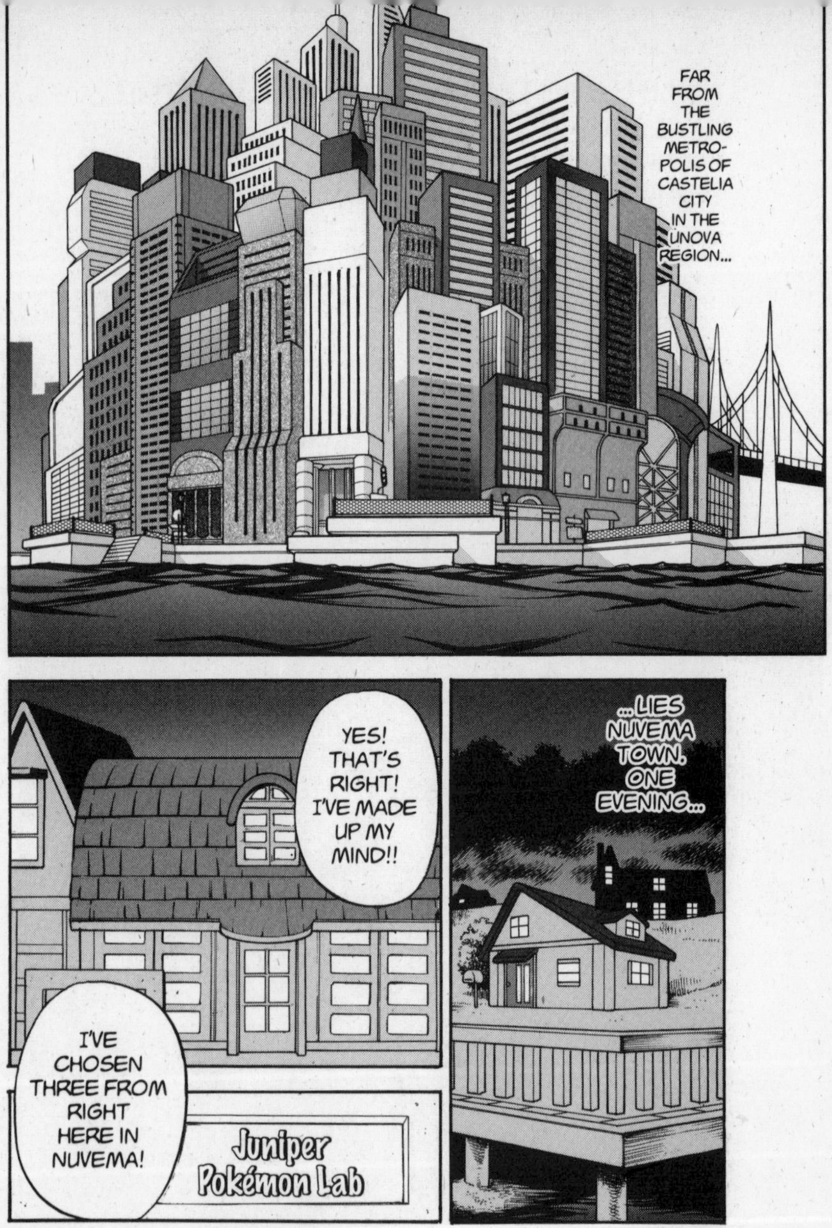
FAR FROM THE BUSTLING METRO-POLIS OF CASTELIA CITY IN THE UNOVA REGION...
...LIES NUVEMA TOWN. ONE EVENING...
YES! THAT'S RIGHT! I'VE MADE UP MY MIND!!
I'VE CHOSEN THREE FROM RIGHT HERE IN NUVEMA!
Juniper Pokémon Lab

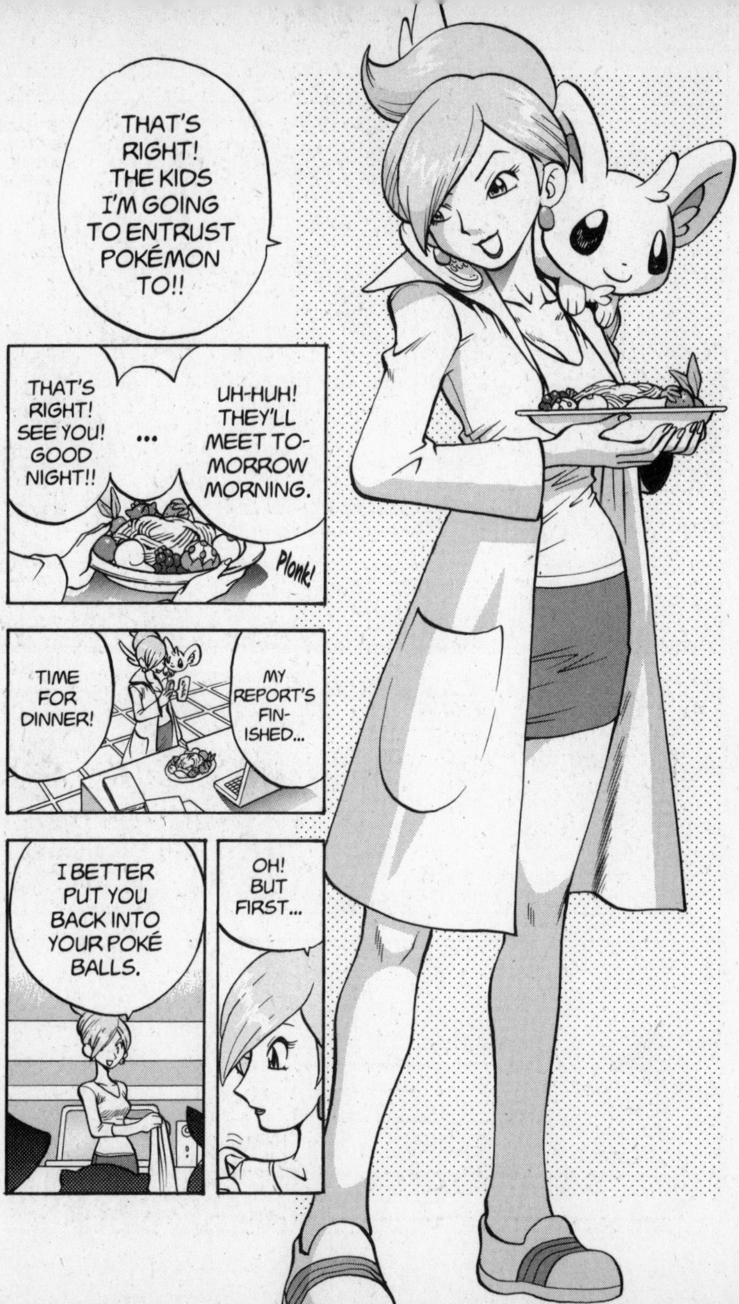

THAT'S RIGHT! THE KIDS I'M GOING TO ENTRUST POKÉMON TO!!
THAT'S RIGHT! SEE YOU! GOOD NIGHT!!
...
UH-HUH! THEY'LL MEET TO-MORROW MORNING.
Plonk!
TIME FOR DINNER!
MY REPORT'S FIN-ISHED...
I BETTER PUT YOU BACK INTO YOUR POKÉ BALLS.
OH! BUT FIRST...

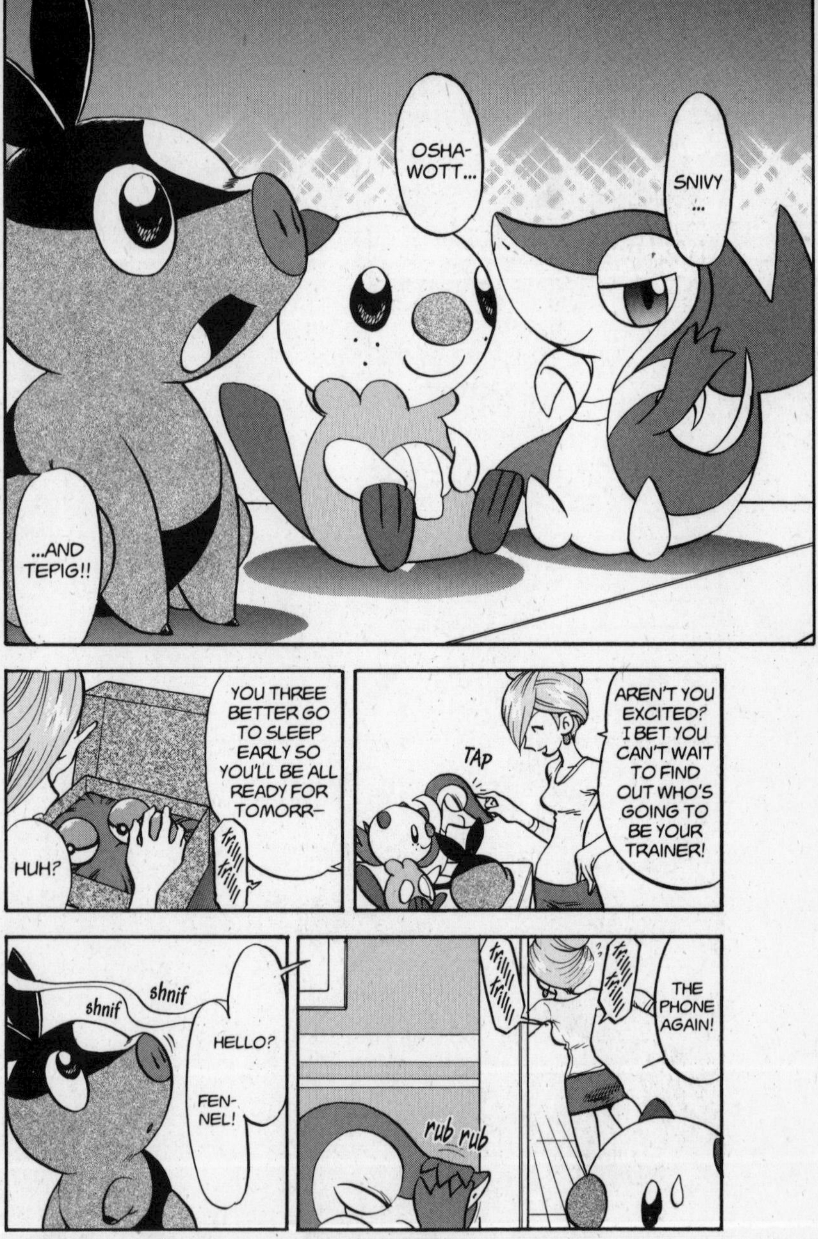
SNIVY ...
OSHA-WOTT...
...AND TEPIG!!
TAP
AREN'T YOU EXCITED? I BET YOU CAN'T WAIT TO FIND OUT WHO'S GOING TO BE YOUR TRAINER!
YOU THREE BETTER GO TO SLEEP EARLY SO YOU'LL BE ALL READY FOR TOMORR–
HUH?
THE PHONE AGAIN!
rub rub
HELLO?
FEN-NEL!
shnif
shnif

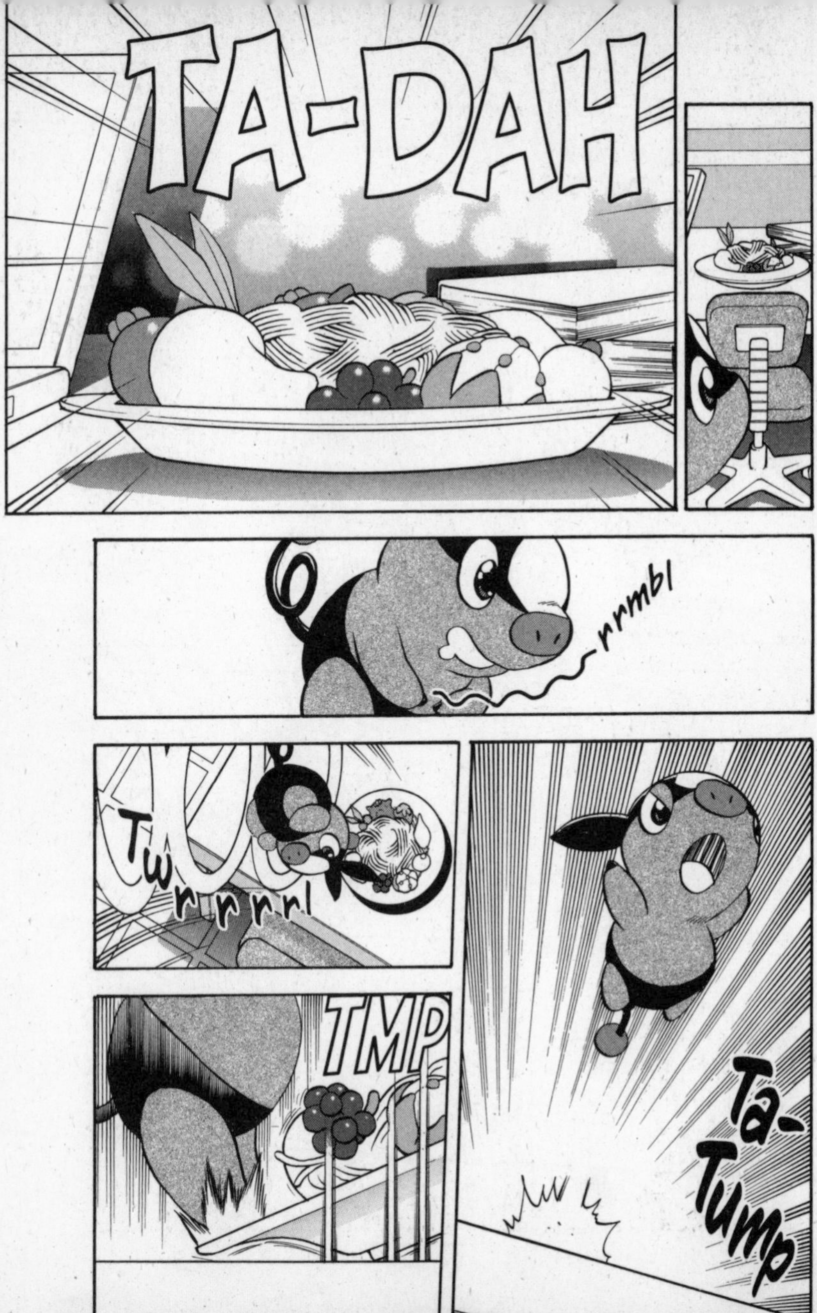
TA-DAH
rrrmbl
Twrrrrrl
Ta-Tump
TMP

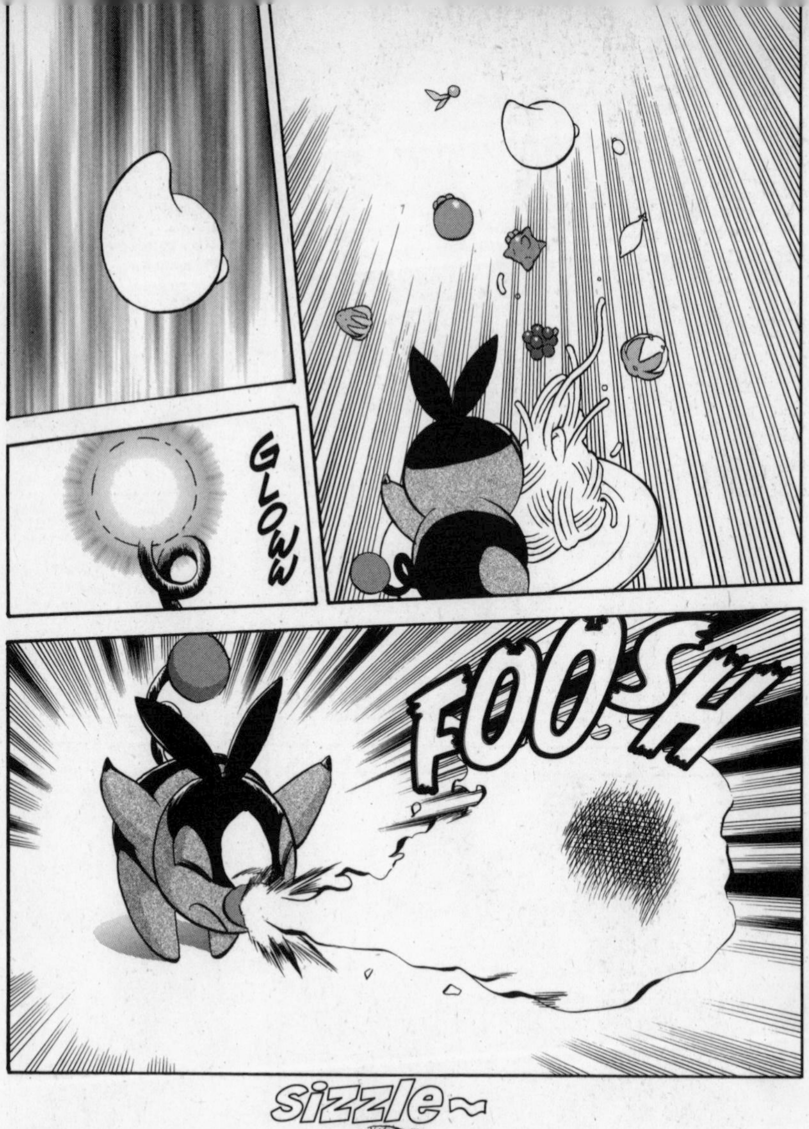
GLOWW
FOOSH
sizzle~

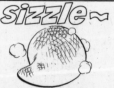

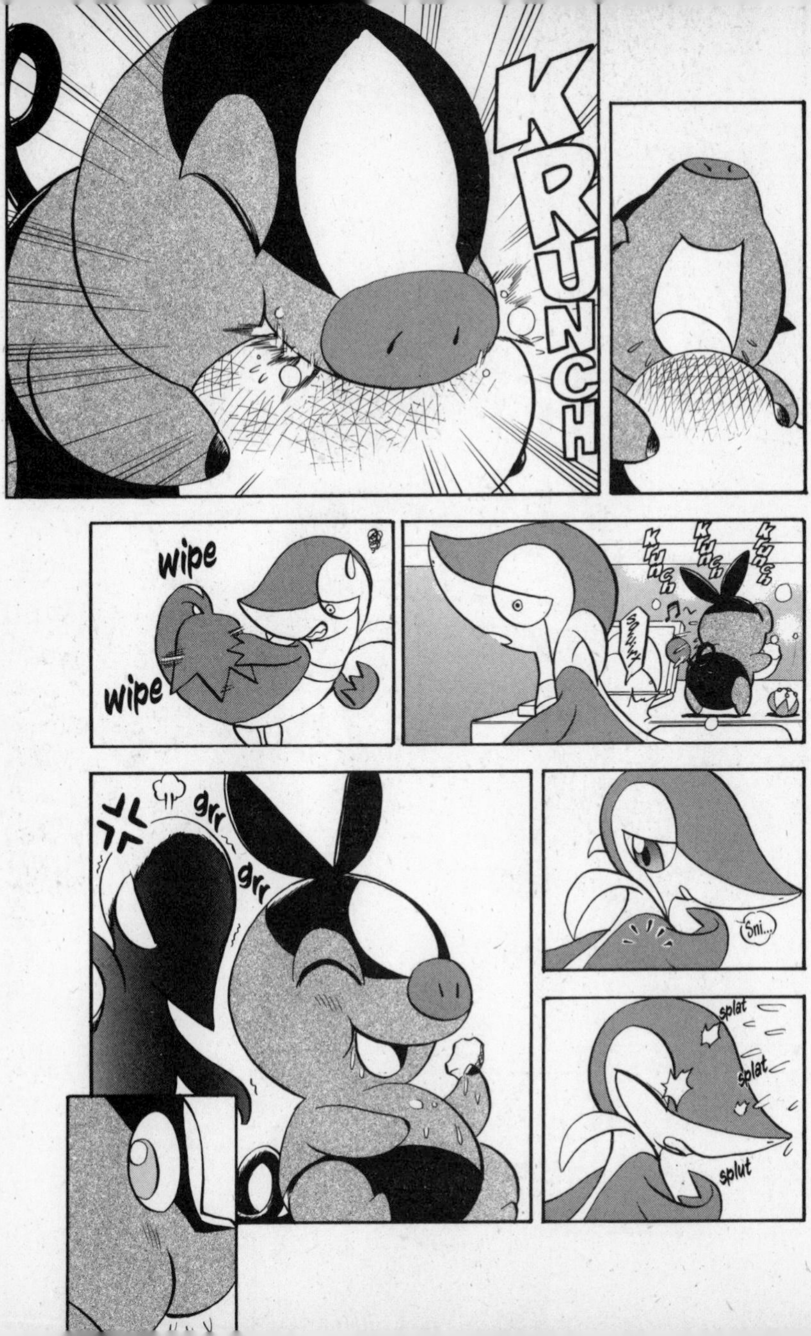
KRUNCH
wipe
wipe
krunch
krunch
krunch
grr
grr
Sni...
splat
splat
splut

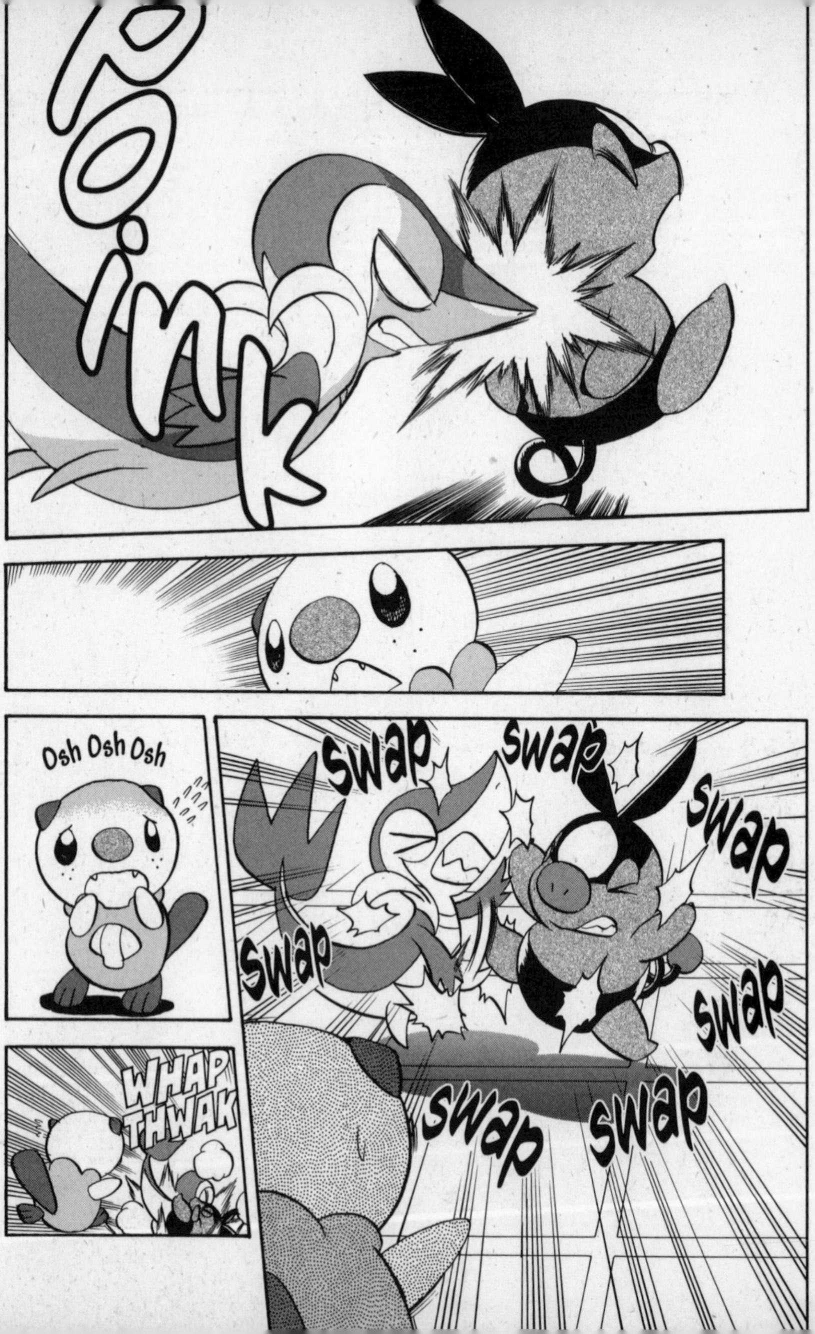
POINK
Osh Osh Osh
SWAP SWAP SWAP SWAP
SWAP SWAP SWAP SWAP
WHAP THWAK

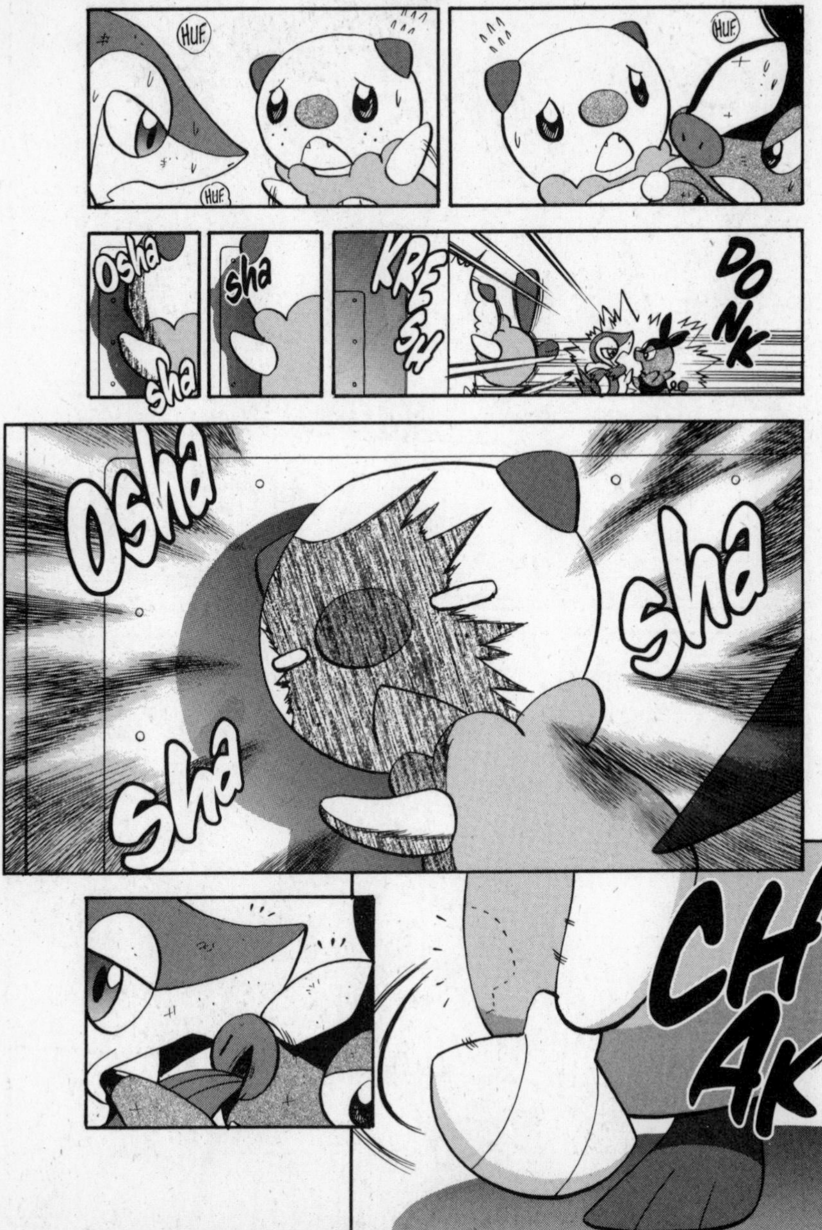
HUF.
HUF.
HUF.
Osha
sha
sha
KRESH
DONK
Osha
sha
sha
CHAK

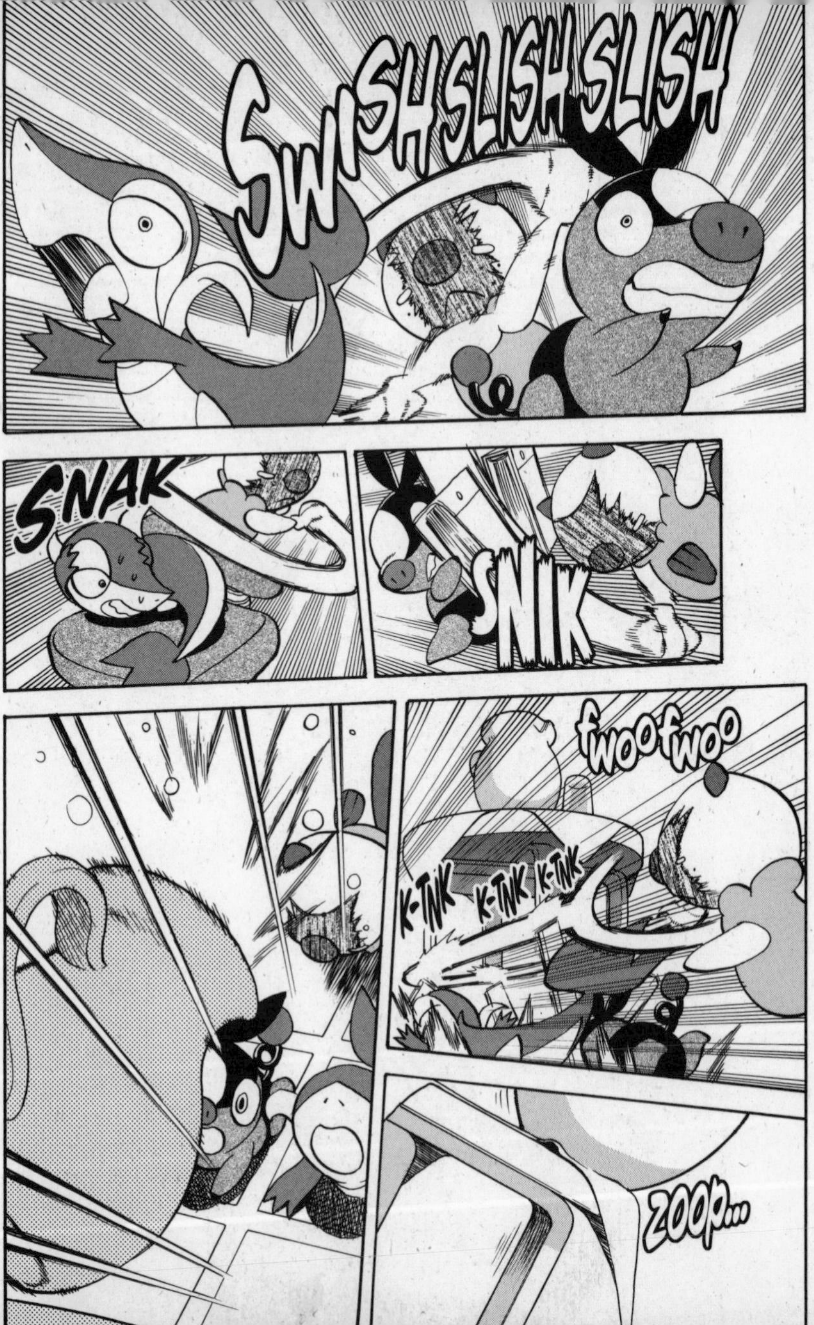
SWISH SLISH SLISH
SNAK
SNIK
fwoo fwoo
K-TNK K-TNK K-TNK
zoop...

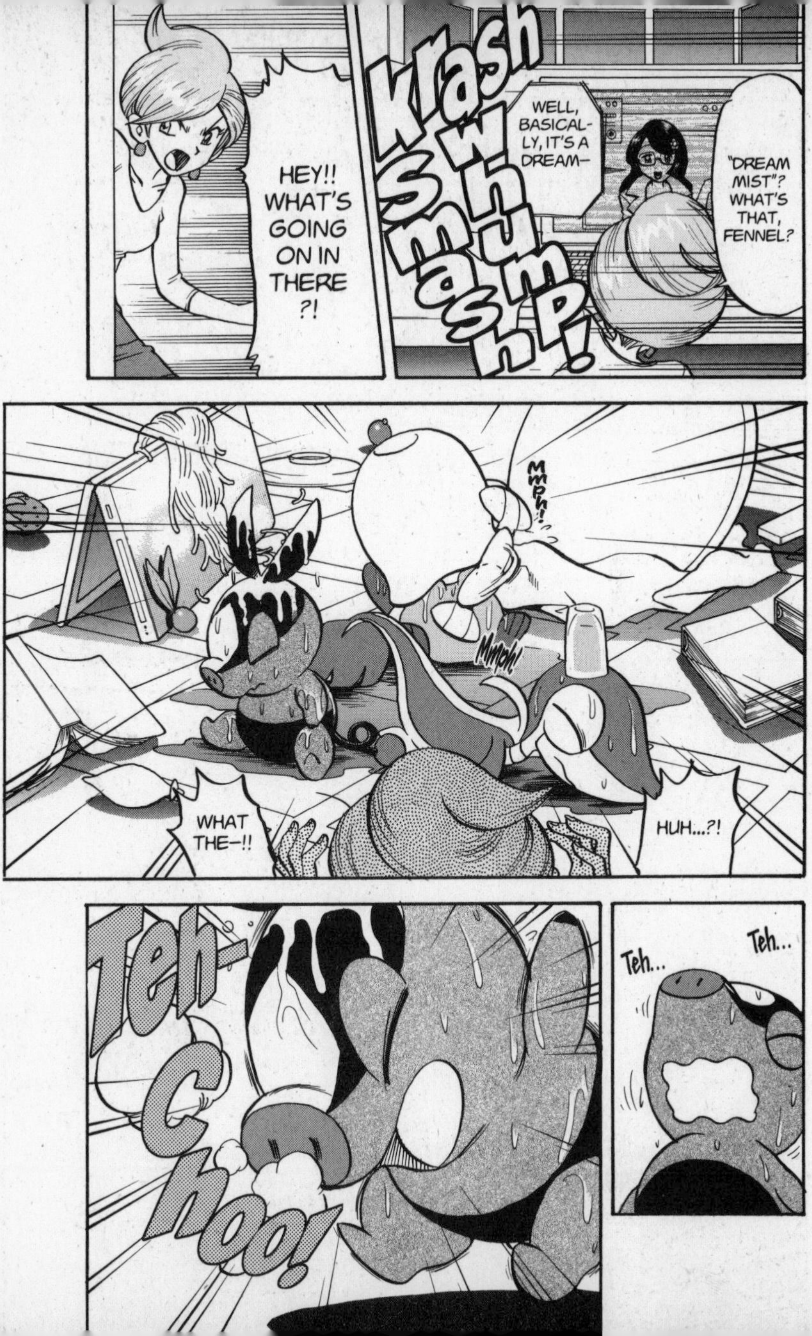
HEY!! WHAT'S GOING ON IN THERE?!
"DREAM MIST"? WHAT'S THAT, FENNEL?
WELL, BASICAL-LY, IT'S A DREAM—
Krash
Smash
Whump!
Mmph!
Mmph!
WHAT THE—!!
HUH...?!
Teh-Choo!
Teh...
Teh...

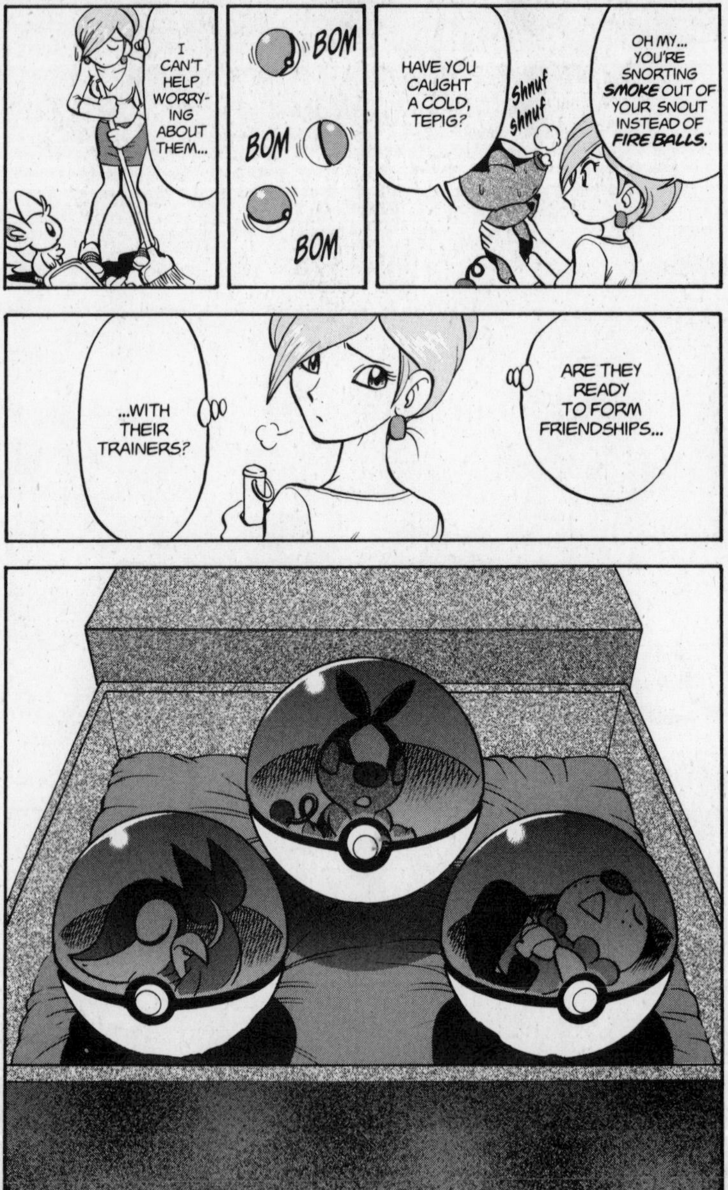
I CAN'T HELP WORRYING ABOUT THEM...
BOM
BOM
BOM
HAVE YOU CAUGHT A COLD, TEPIG?
Shnuf shnuf
OH MY... YOU'RE SNORTING SMOKE OUT OF YOUR SNOUT INSTEAD OF FIRE BALLS.
ARE THEY READY TO FORM FRIENDSHIPS...
...WITH THEIR TRAINERS?

Adventure 2 Choices

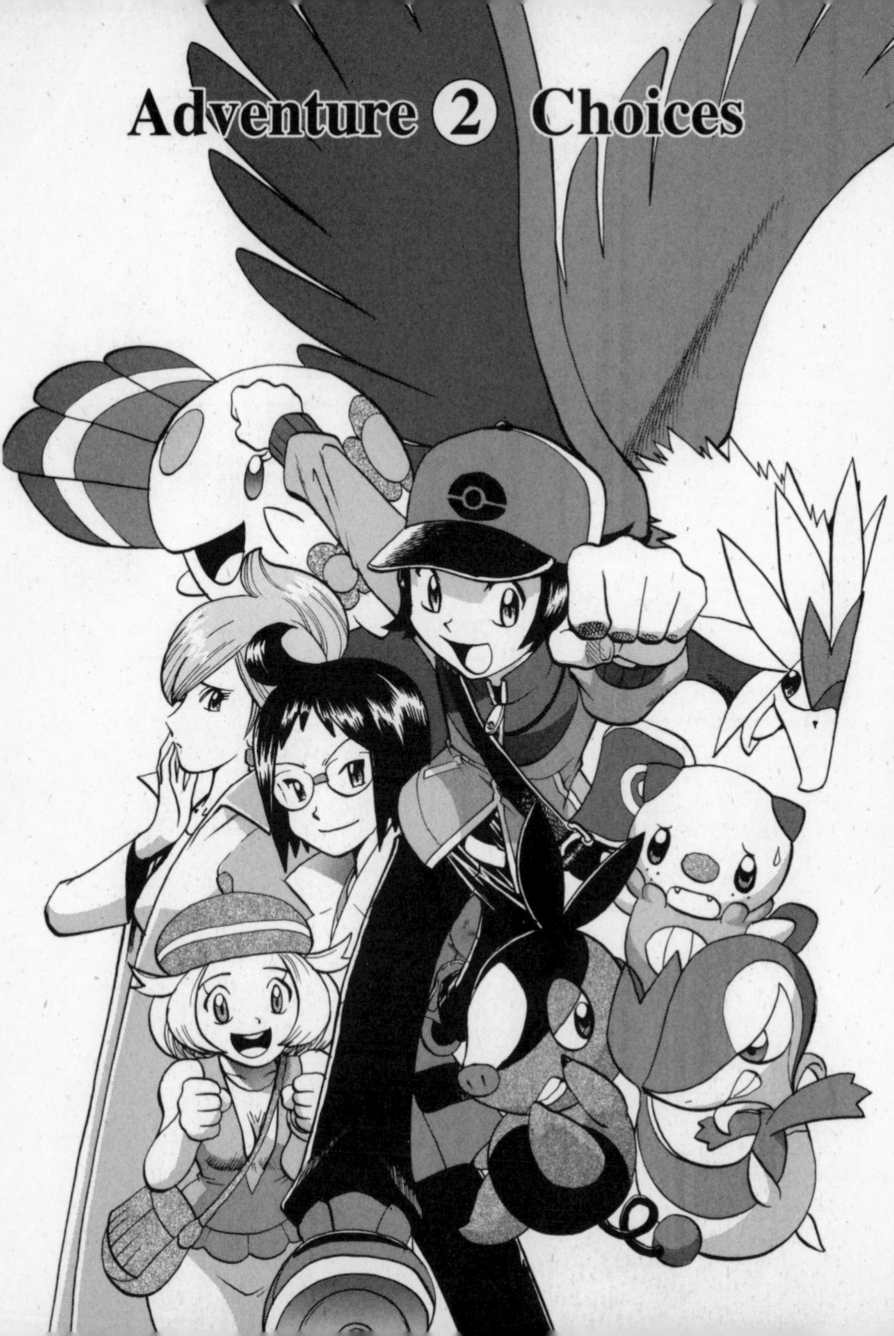

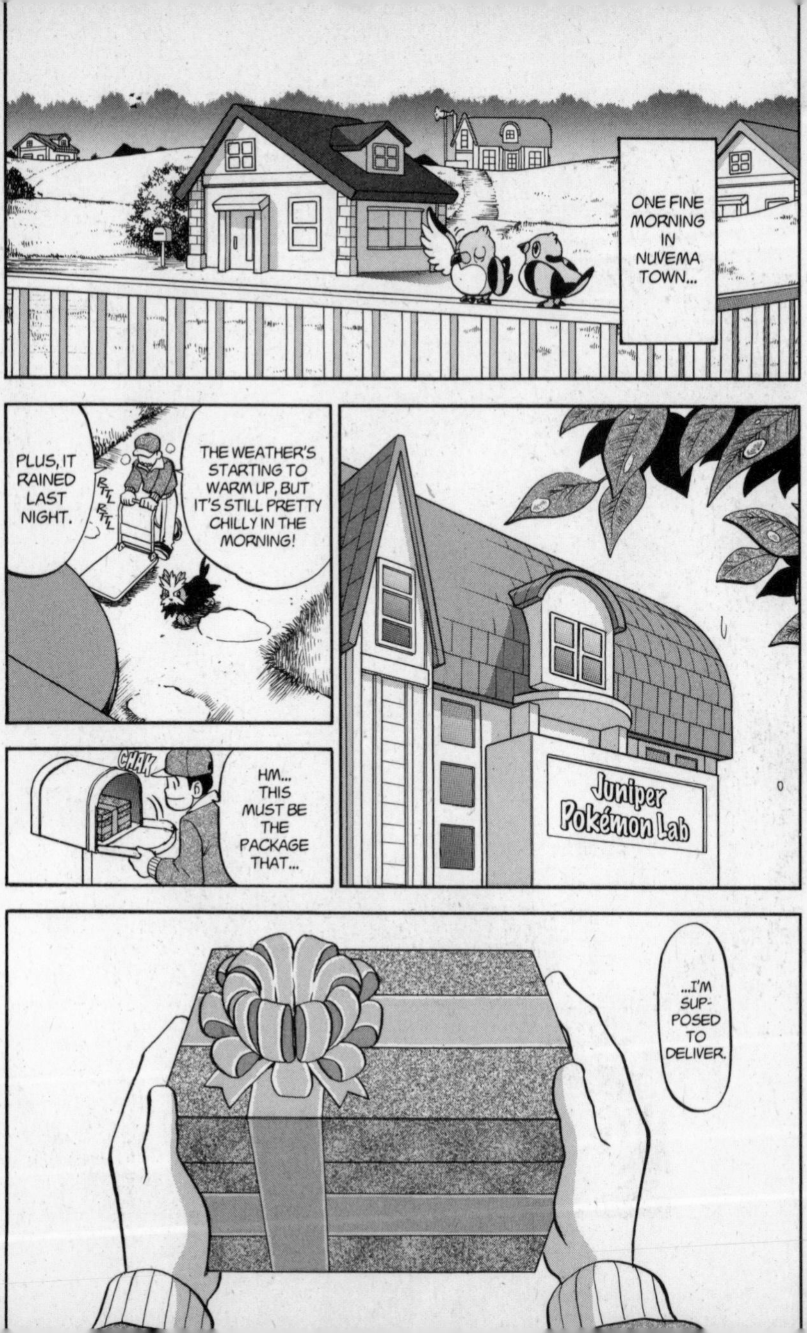
ONE FINE MORNING IN NUVEMA TOWN...
THE WEATHER'S STARTING TO WARM UP, BUT IT'S STILL PRETTY CHILLY IN THE MORNING!
PLUS, IT RAINED LAST NIGHT.
BTTL BTTL
Juniper Pokémon Lab
CHAK
HM... THIS MUST BE THE PACKAGE THAT...
...I'M SUP-POSED TO DELIVER.

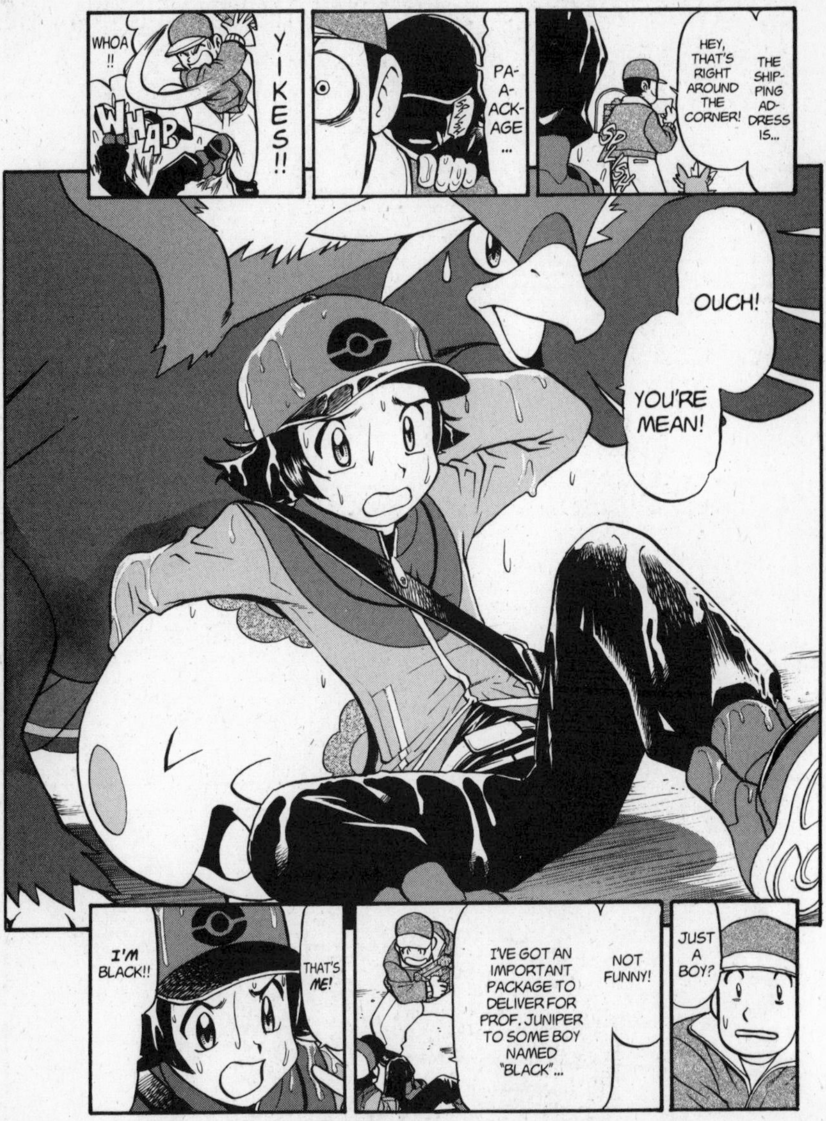
WHOA!!
WHAP
YIKES!!
PA-A-ACK-AGE...
THE SHIPPING ADDRESS IS...
HEY, THAT'S RIGHT AROUND THE CORNER!
SPLSH
OUCH!
YOU'RE MEAN!
I'M BLACK!!
THAT'S ME!
I'VE GOT AN IMPORTANT PACKAGE TO DELIVER FOR PROF. JUNIPER TO SOME BOY NAMED "BLACK"...
NOT FUNNY!
JUST A BOY?

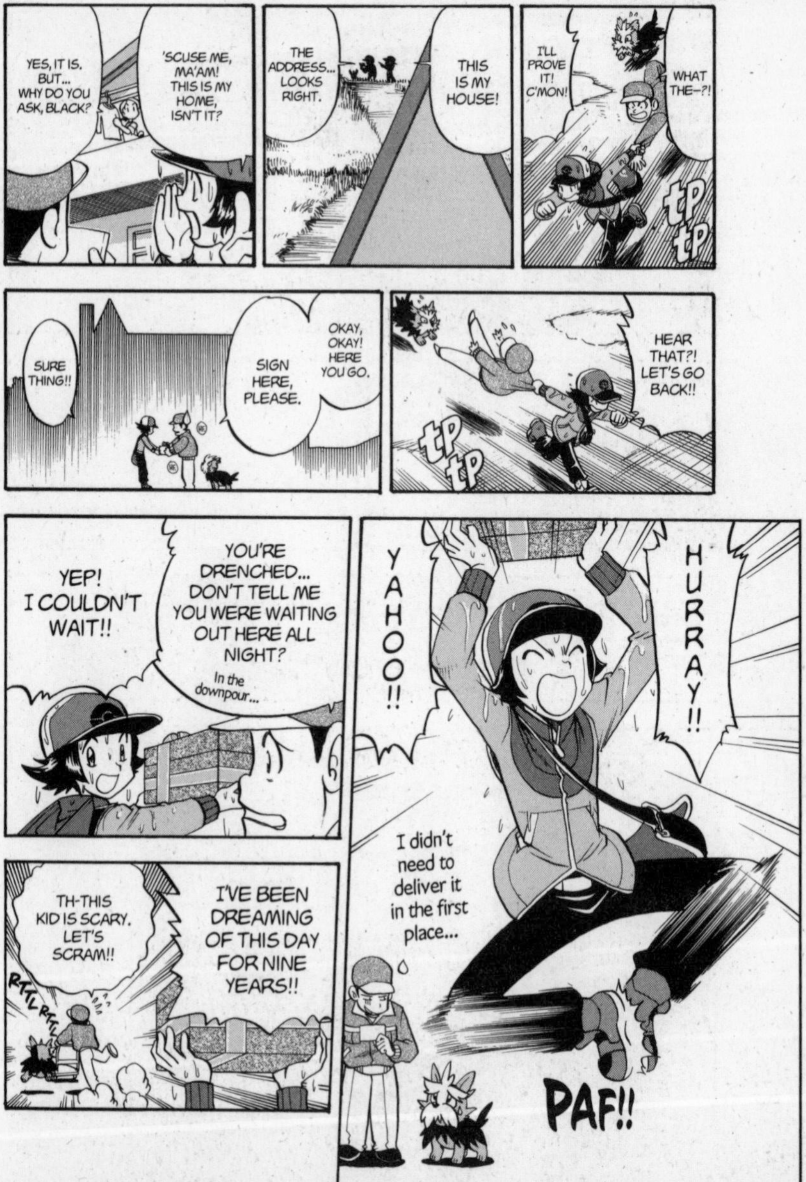
I'LL PROVE IT! C'MON!
WHAT THE–?!
tp tp
THIS IS MY HOUSE!
THE ADDRESS... LOOKS RIGHT.
'SCUSE ME, MA'AM! THIS IS MY HOME, ISN'T IT?
YES, IT IS. BUT... WHY DO YOU ASK, BLACK?
HEAR THAT?! LET'S GO BACK!!
tp tp
OKAY, OKAY! HERE YOU GO.
SIGN HERE, PLEASE.
SURE THING!!
YOU'RE DRENCHED... DON'T TELL ME YOU WERE WAITING OUT HERE ALL NIGHT?
In the downpour...
YEP! I COULDN'T WAIT!!
HURRAY!!
YAHOO!!
I didn't need to deliver it in the first place...
PAF!!
I'VE BEEN DREAMING OF THIS DAY FOR NINE YEARS!!
TH-THIS KID IS SCARY. LET'S SCRAM!!
RTTL RTTL

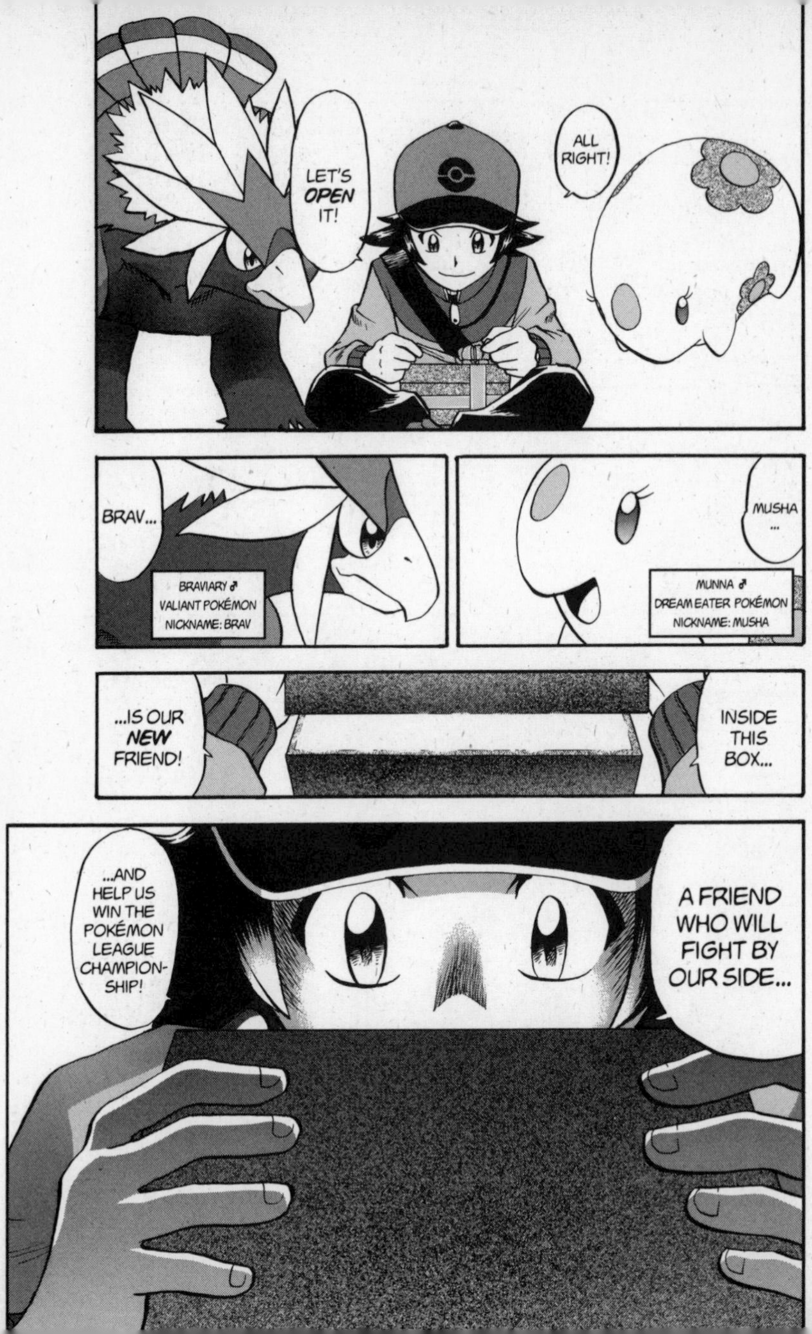
ALL RIGHT!
LET'S OPEN IT!
MUSHA ...
MUNNA ♂ DREAM EATER POKÉMON NICKNAME: MUSHA
BRAV...
BRAVIARY ♂ VALIANT POKÉMON NICKNAME: BRAV
INSIDE THIS BOX...
...IS OUR NEW FRIEND!
A FRIEND WHO WILL FIGHT BY OUR SIDE...
...AND HELP US WIN THE POKÉMON LEAGUE CHAMPION-SHIP!

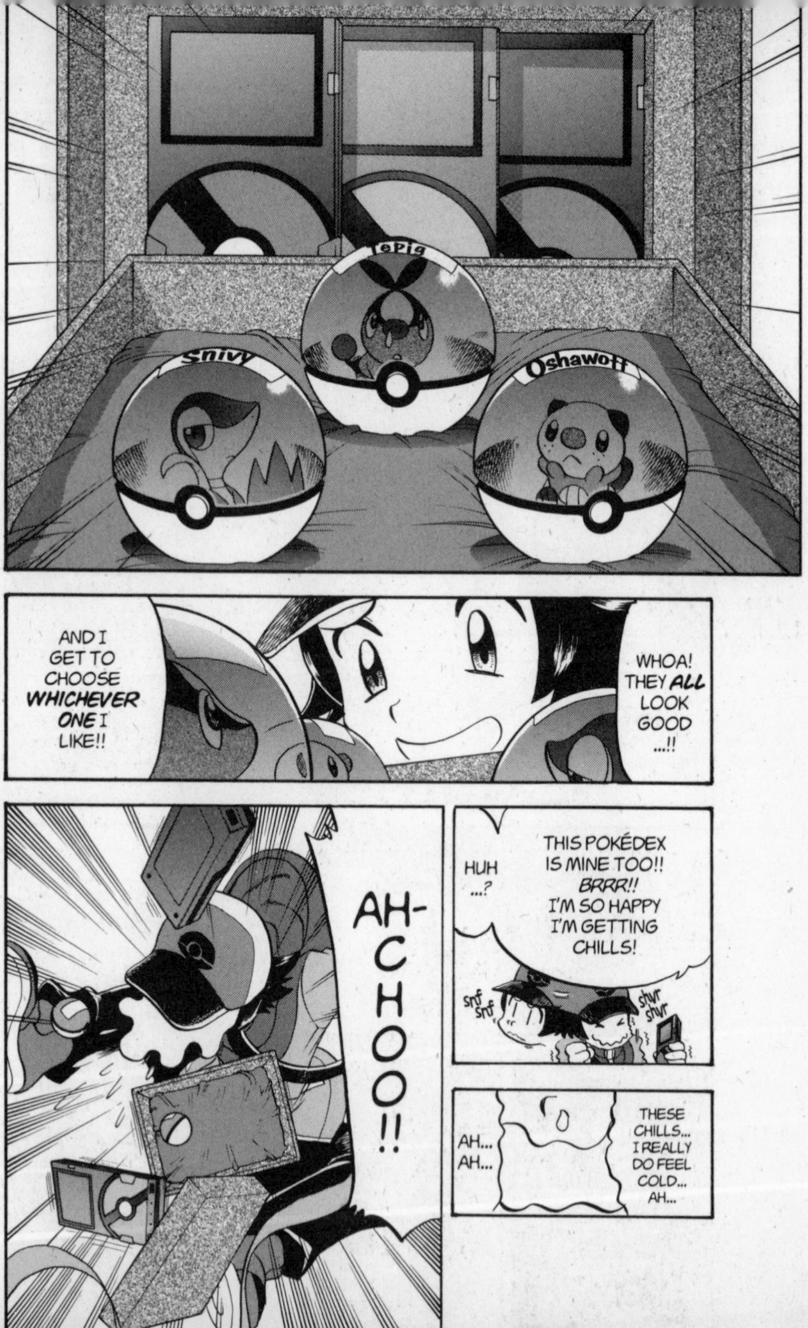
Tepig
Snivy
Oshawott
AND I GET TO CHOOSE WHICHEVER ONE I LIKE!!
WHOA! THEY ALL LOOK GOOD ...!!
THIS POKÉDEX IS MINE TOO!! BRRR!! I'M SO HAPPY I'M GETTING CHILLS!
HUH ...?
snf snf
shvr shvr
THESE CHILLS... I REALLY DO FEEL COLD... AH...
AH... AH...
AH-CHOOO!!

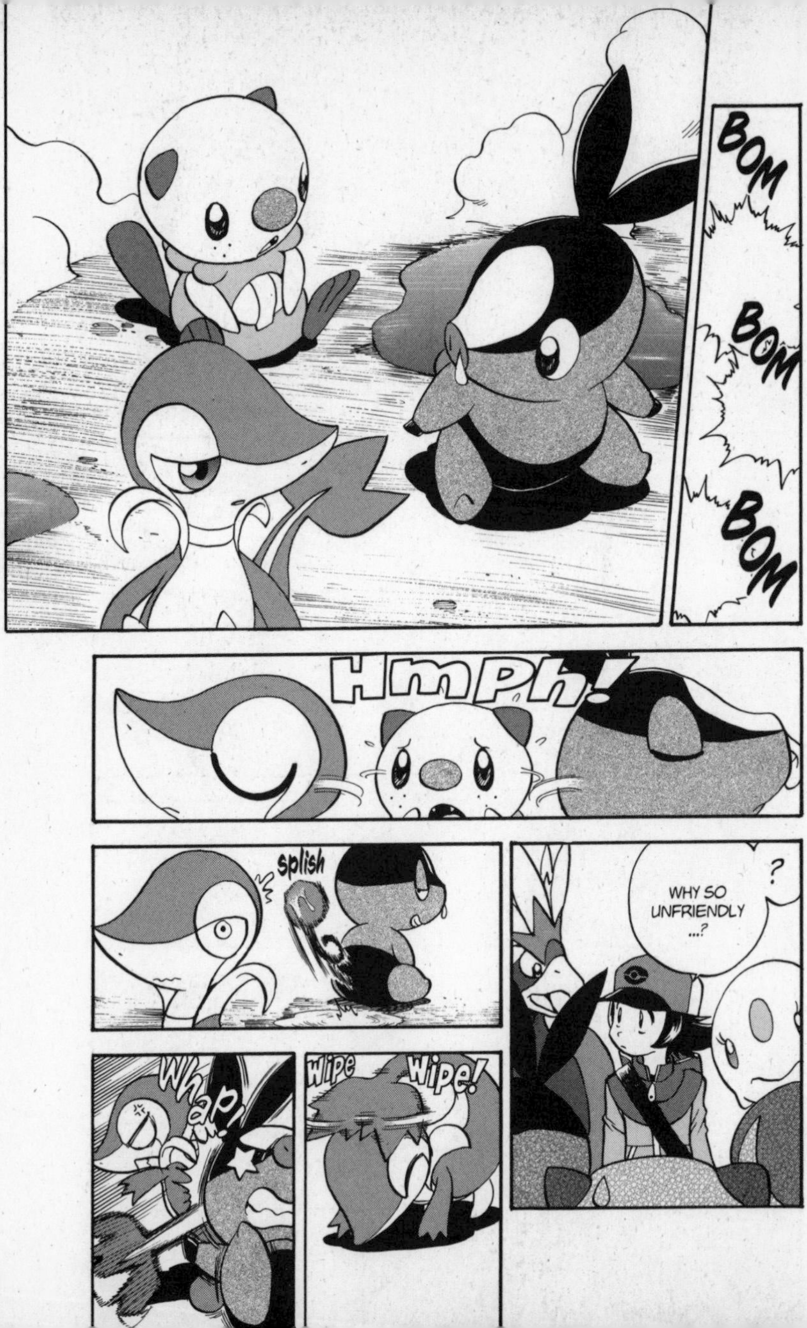
BOM
BOM
BOM
Hmph!
splish
WHY SO UNFRIENDLY ...?
?
Whap!
Wipe
Wipe!

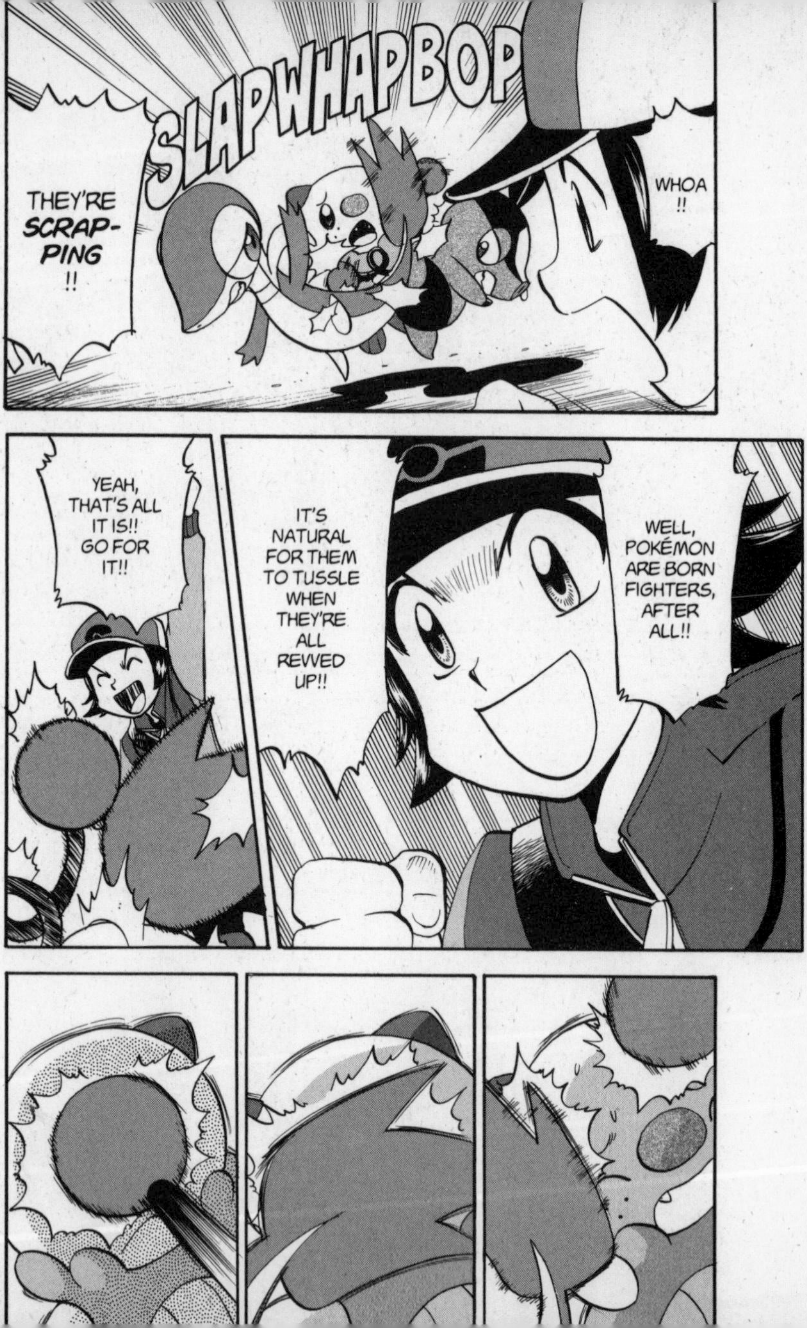
SLAPWHAPBOP
WHOA !!
THEY'RE SCRAP-PING !!
WELL, POKÉMON ARE BORN FIGHTERS, AFTER ALL!!
IT'S NATURAL FOR THEM TO TUSSLE WHEN THEY'RE ALL REVVED UP!!
YEAH, THAT'S ALL IT IS!! GO FOR IT!!

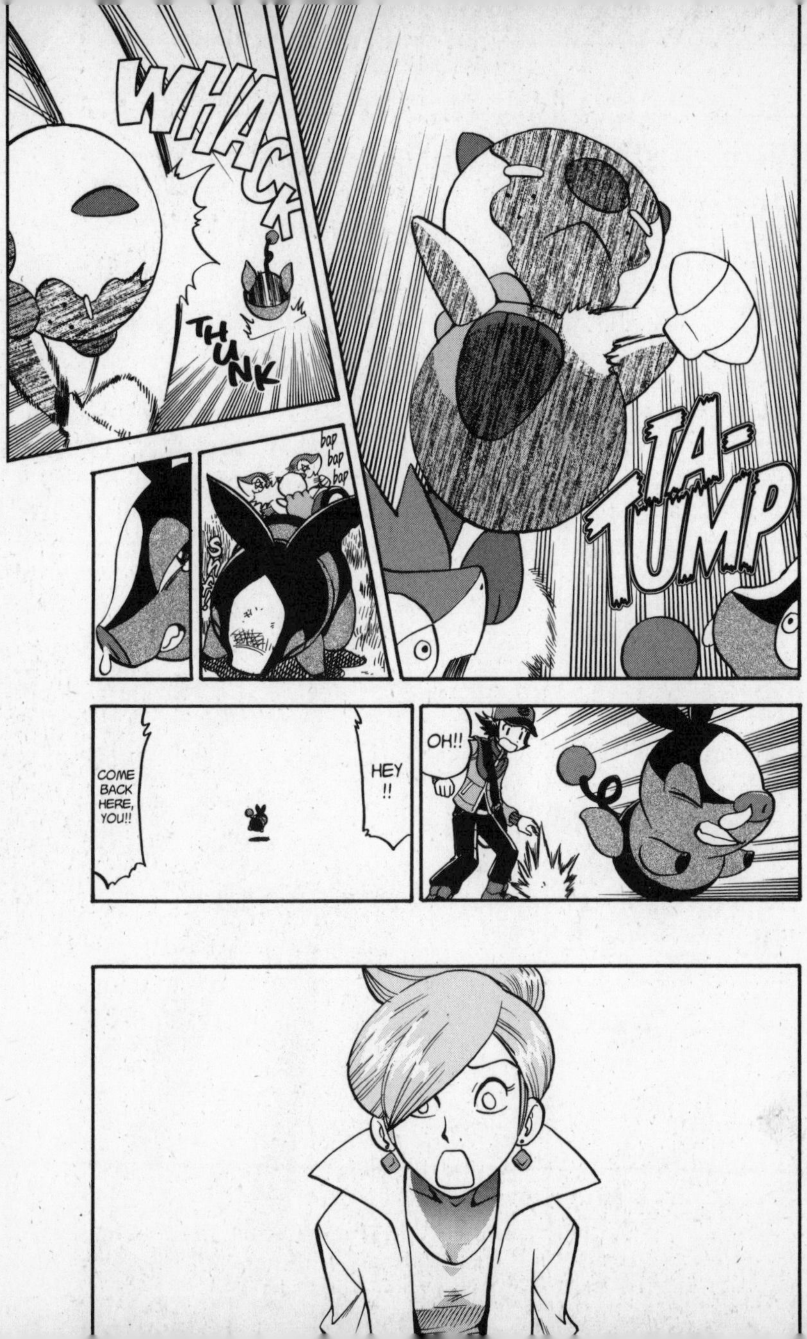
TA-TUMP
WHACK
THUNK
bap bap bap
OH!!
HEY !!
COME BACK HERE, YOU!!

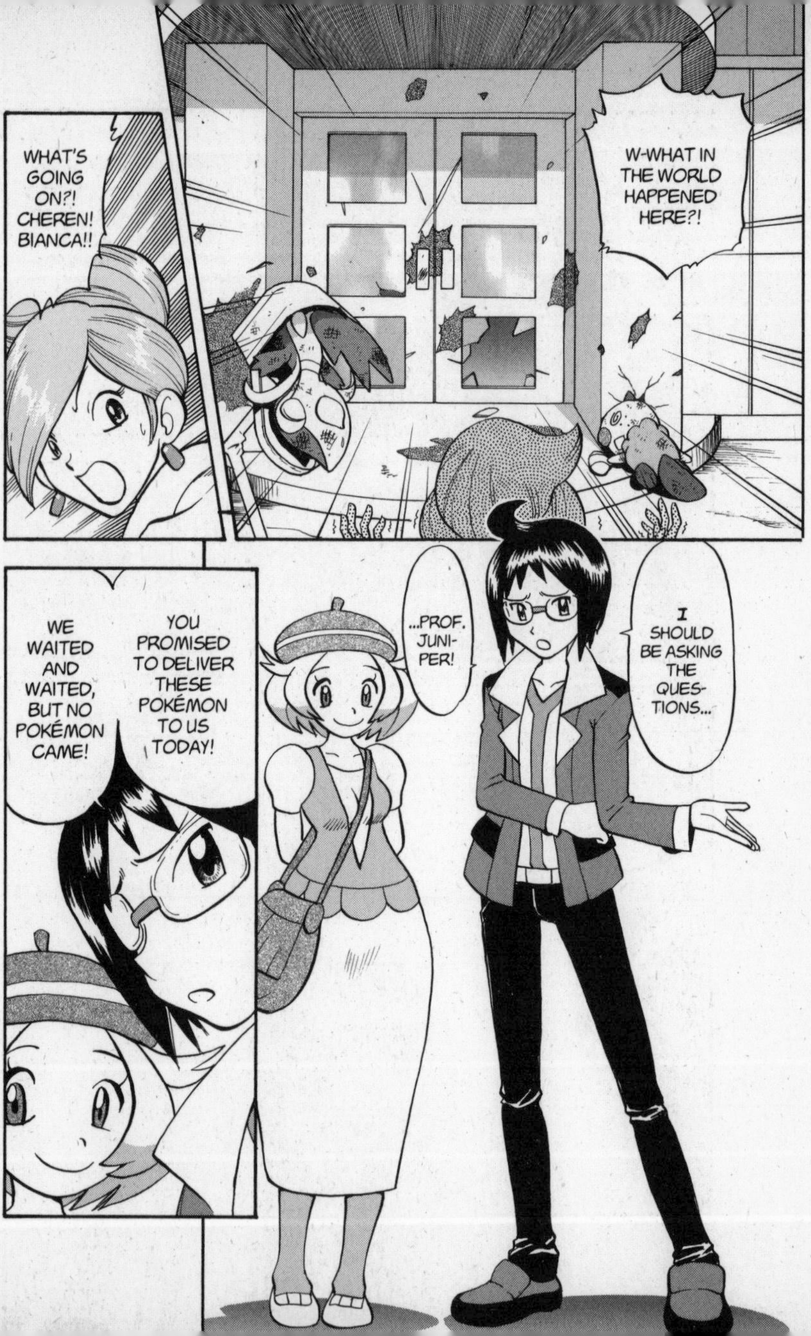
W-WHAT IN THE WORLD HAPPENED HERE?!
WHAT'S GOING ON?! CHEREN! BIANCA!!
...PROF. JUNI-PER!
I SHOULD BE ASKING THE QUES-TIONS...
YOU PROMISED TO DELIVER THESE POKÉMON TO US TODAY!
WE WAITED AND WAITED, BUT NO POKÉMON CAME!

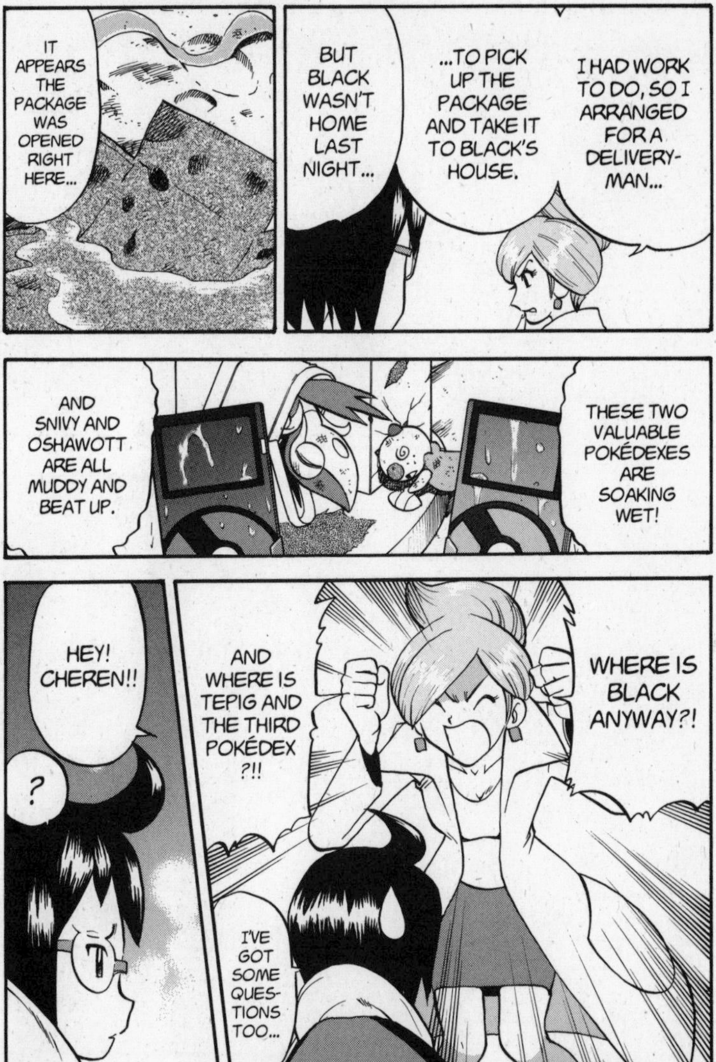

I HAD WORK TO DO, SO I ARRANGED FOR A DELIVERY-MAN...
...TO PICK UP THE PACKAGE AND TAKE IT TO BLACK'S HOUSE.
BUT BLACK WASN'T HOME LAST NIGHT...
IT APPEARS THE PACKAGE WAS OPENED RIGHT HERE...
THESE TWO VALUABLE POKÉDEXES ARE SOAKING WET!
AND SNIVY AND OSHAWOTT ARE ALL MUDDY AND BEAT UP.
WHERE IS BLACK ANYWAY?!
AND WHERE IS TEPIG AND THE THIRD POKÉDEX ?!!
I'VE GOT SOME QUES-TIONS TOO...
HEY! CHEREN!!
?

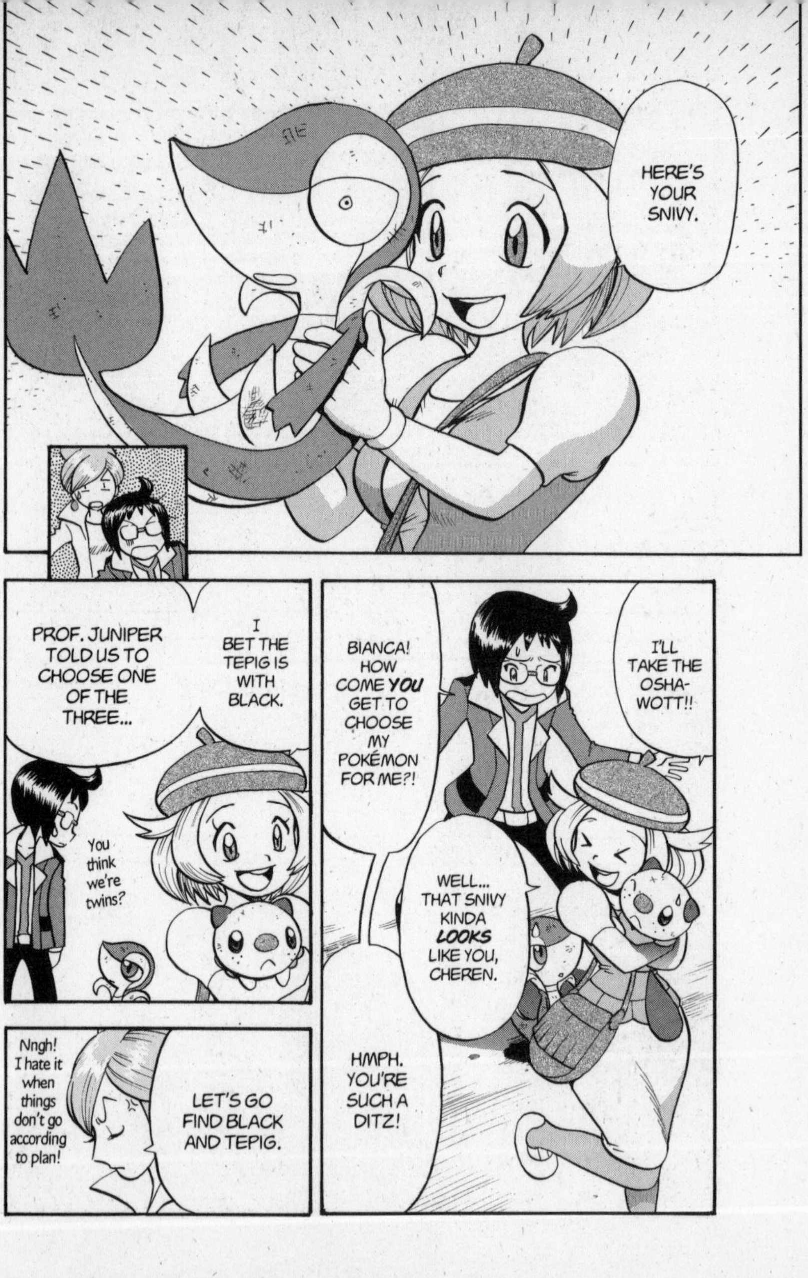
HERE'S YOUR SNIVY.
PROF. JUNIPER TOLD US TO CHOOSE ONE OF THE THREE...
I BET THE TEPIG IS WITH BLACK.
You think we're twins?
BIANCA! HOW COME *YOU* GET TO CHOOSE MY POKÉMON FOR ME?!
I'LL TAKE THE OSHA-WOTT!!
WELL... THAT SNIVY KINDA *LOOKS* LIKE YOU, CHEREN.
Nngh! I hate it when things don't go according to plan!
LET'S GO FIND BLACK AND TEPIG.
HMPH. YOU'RE SUCH A DITZ!

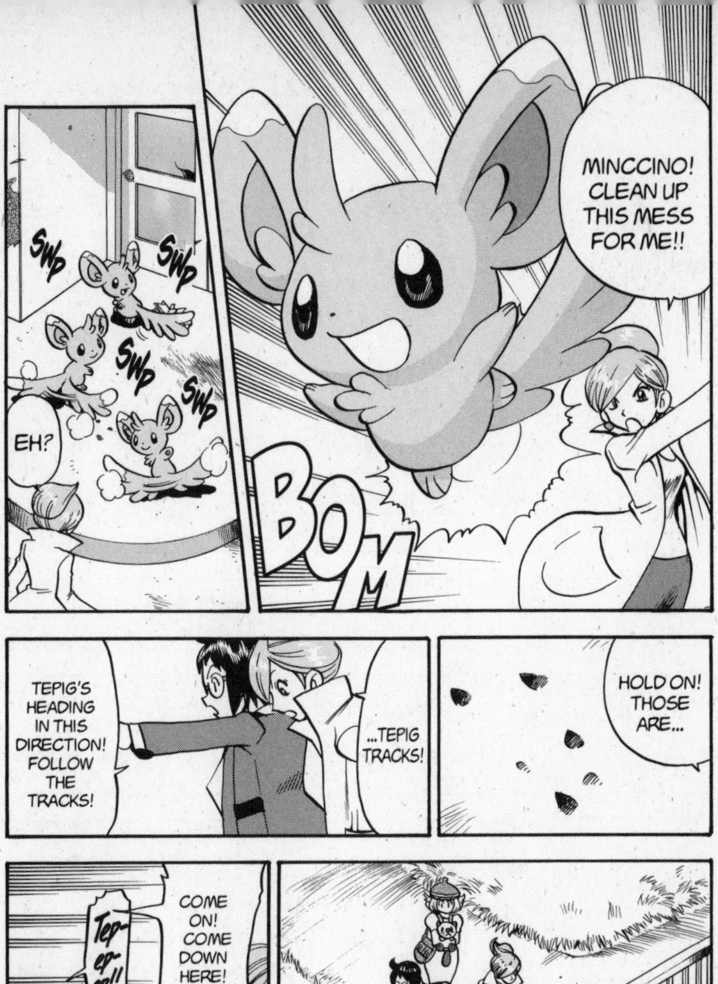
MINCCINO! CLEAN UP THIS MESS FOR ME!!
BOM
SWP
SWP
SWP
SWP
EH?
HOLD ON! THOSE ARE...
...TEPIG TRACKS!
TEPIG'S HEADING IN THIS DIRECTION! FOLLOW THE TRACKS!
COME ON! COME DOWN HERE!
Tep-ep-ep!!

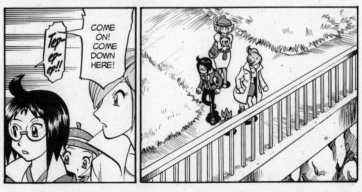

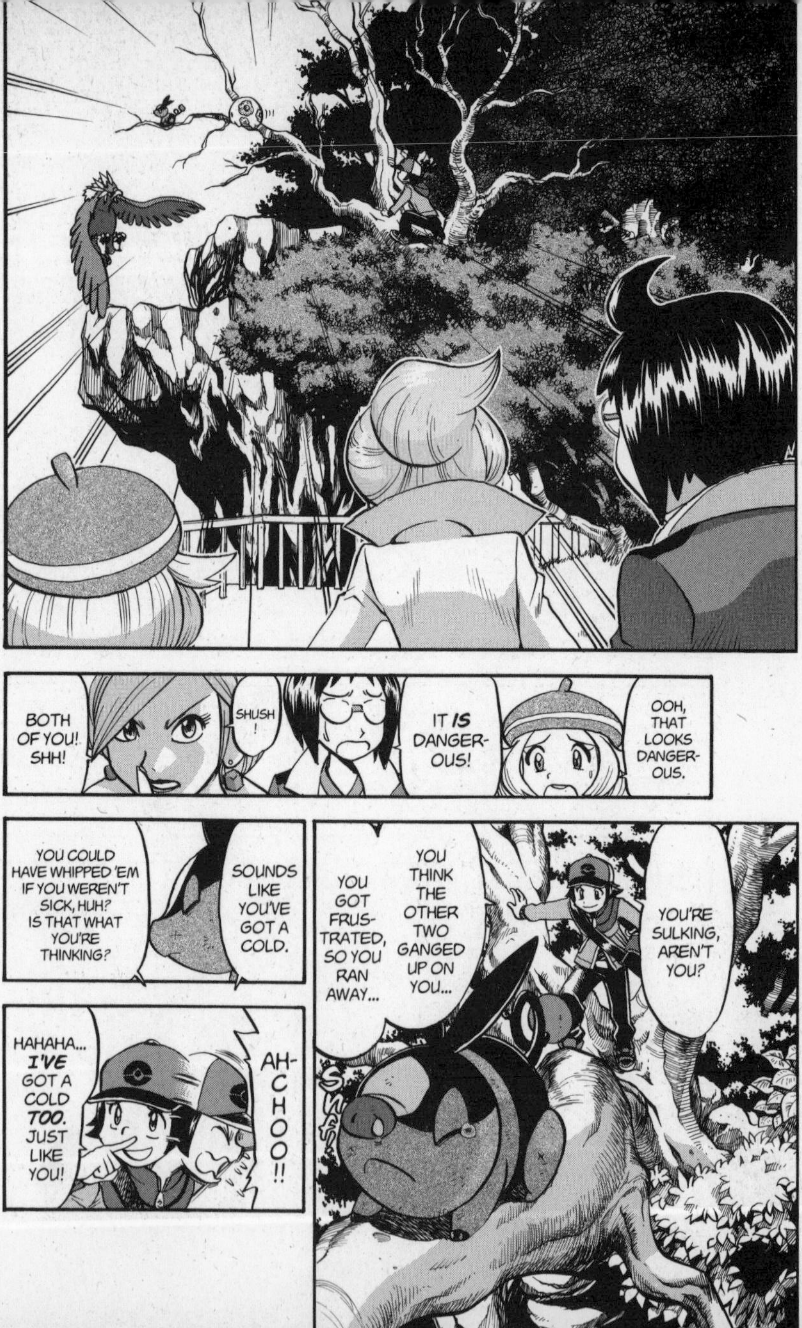
OOH, THAT LOOKS DANGEROUS.
IT IS DANGEROUS!
SHUSH!
BOTH OF YOU! SHH!
YOU'RE SULKING, AREN'T YOU?
YOU THINK THE OTHER TWO GANGED UP ON YOU...
YOU GOT FRUSTRATED, SO YOU RAN AWAY...
SOUNDS LIKE YOU'VE GOT A COLD.
YOU COULD HAVE WHIPPED 'EM IF YOU WEREN'T SICK, HUH? IS THAT WHAT YOU'RE THINKING?
AH-CHOO!!
HAHAHA... I'VE GOT A COLD TOO. JUST LIKE YOU!

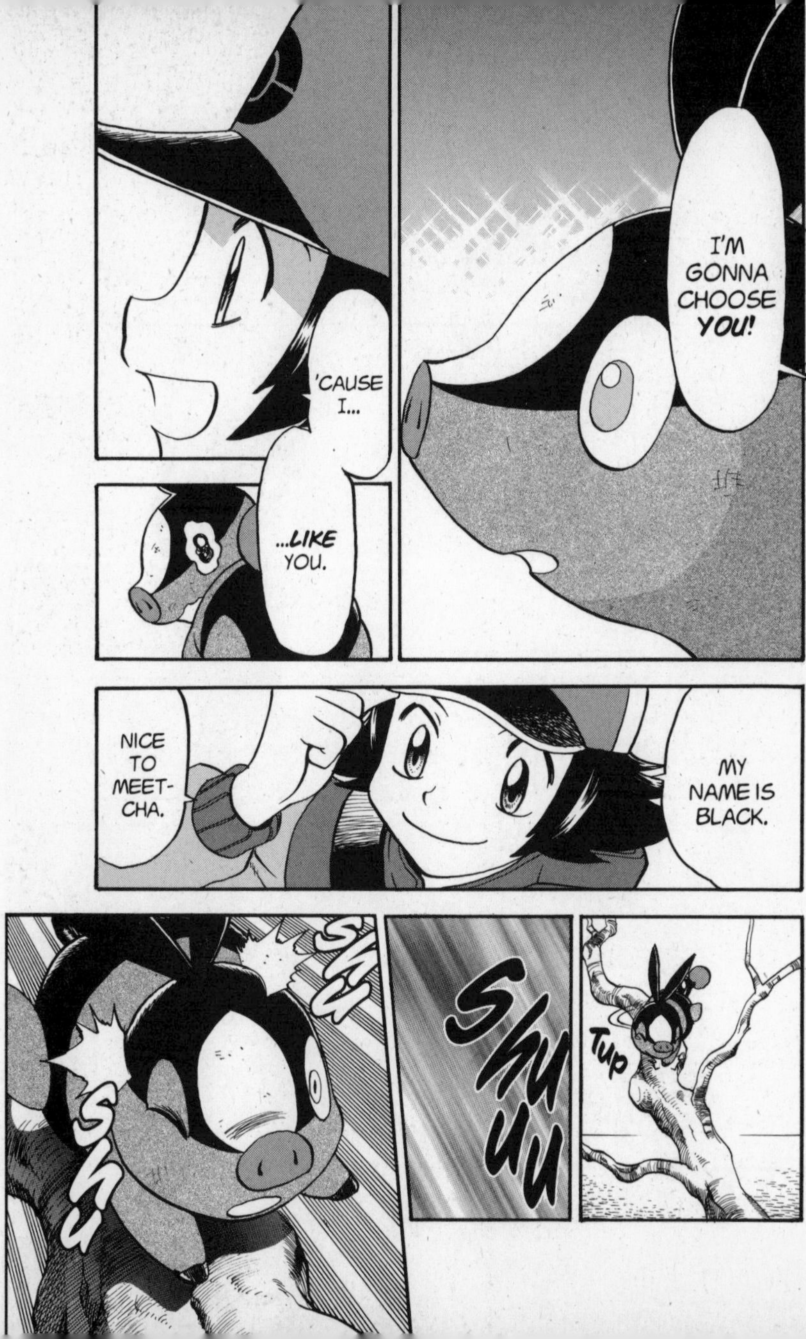

'CAUSE I...
I'M GONNA CHOOSE YOU!
...LIKE YOU.
MY NAME IS BLACK.
NICE TO MEET-CHA.
Tup
SHUUU
SHU SHU SHU

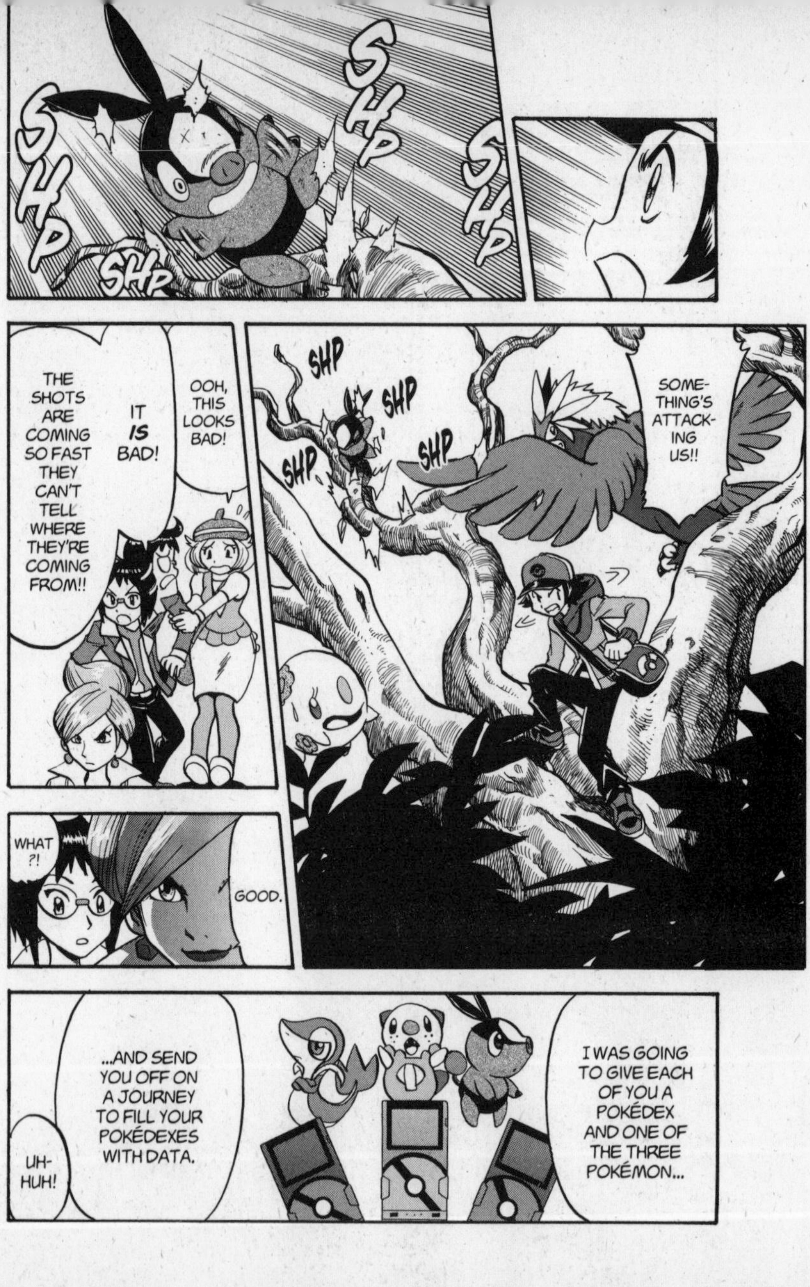

SHP
SHP
SHP
SHP
SHP
SOME-THING'S ATTACK-ING US!!
SHP
SHP
SHP
SHP
OOH, THIS LOOKS BAD!
IT IS BAD!
THE SHOTS ARE COMING SO FAST THEY CAN'T TELL WHERE THEY'RE COMING FROM!!
GOOD.
WHAT?!
I WAS GOING TO GIVE EACH OF YOU A POKÉDEX AND ONE OF THE THREE POKÉMON...
...AND SEND YOU OFF ON A JOURNEY TO FILL YOUR POKÉDEXES WITH DATA.
UH-HUH!

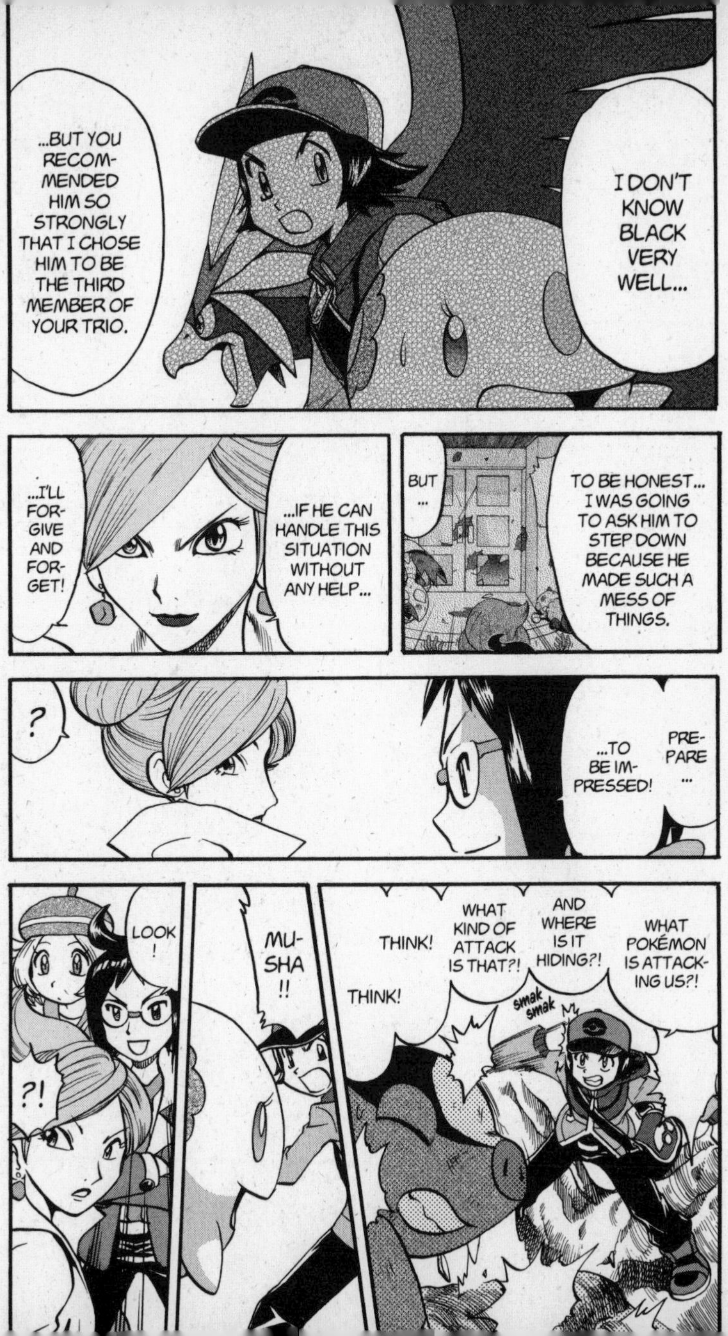

I DON'T KNOW BLACK VERY WELL...
...BUT YOU RECOMMENDED HIM SO STRONGLY THAT I CHOSE HIM TO BE THE THIRD MEMBER OF YOUR TRIO.
TO BE HONEST... I WAS GOING TO ASK HIM TO STEP DOWN BECAUSE HE MADE SUCH A MESS OF THINGS.
BUT ...
...IF HE CAN HANDLE THIS SITUATION WITHOUT ANY HELP...
...I'LL FORGIVE AND FORGET!
PREPARE ...
...TO BE IMPRESSED!
?
WHAT POKÉMON IS ATTACKING US?!
AND WHERE IS IT HIDING?!
WHAT KIND OF ATTACK IS THAT?!
THINK!
THINK!
smak smak
MUSHA !!
LOOK !
?!

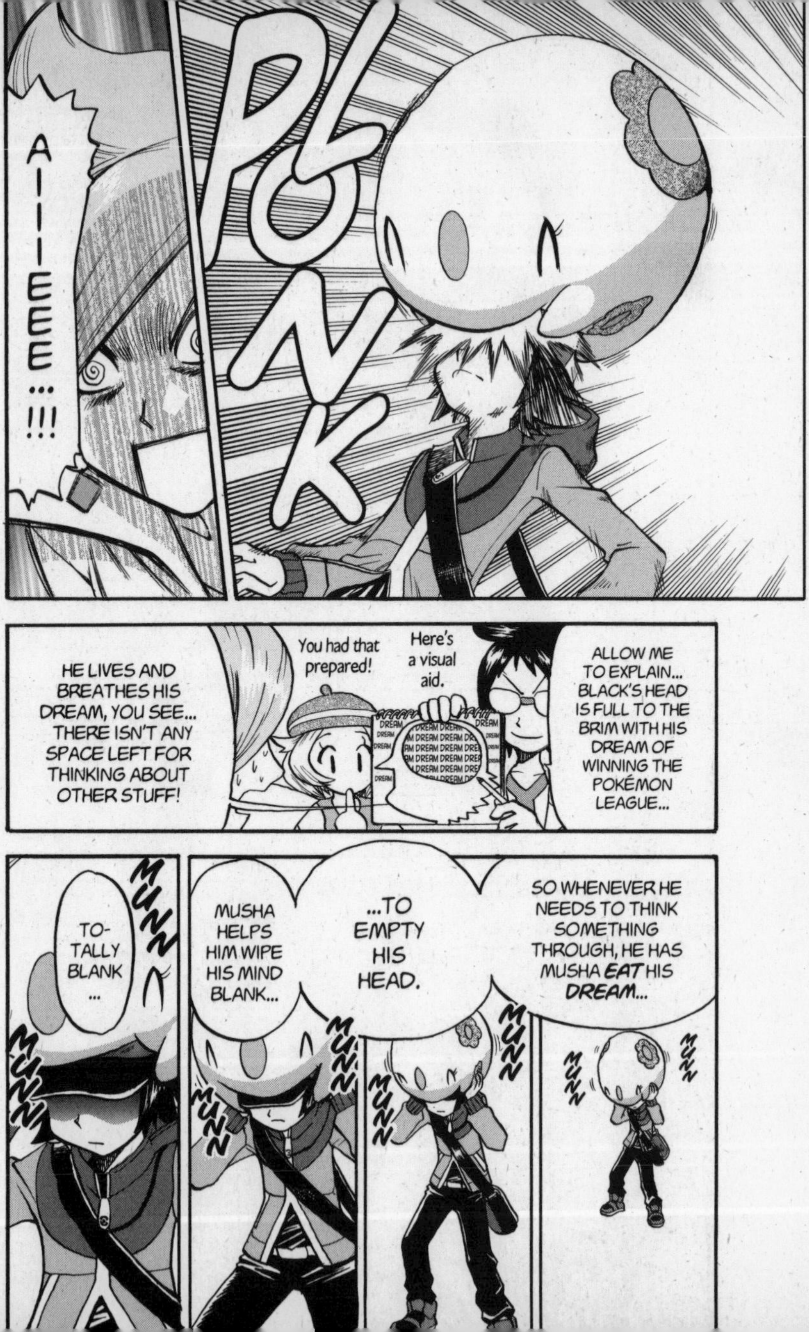

PLONK
AIIIEEE...!!!
ALLOW ME TO EXPLAIN... BLACK'S HEAD IS FULL TO THE BRIM WITH HIS DREAM OF WINNING THE POKÉMON LEAGUE...
Here's a visual aid.
You had that prepared!
HE LIVES AND BREATHES HIS DREAM, YOU SEE... THERE ISN'T ANY SPACE LEFT FOR THINKING ABOUT OTHER STUFF!
DREAM DREAM DREAM DREAM
SO WHENEVER HE NEEDS TO THINK SOMETHING THROUGH, HE HAS MUSHA EAT HIS DREAM...
MUNN MUNN
...TO EMPTY HIS HEAD.
MUNN MUNN
MUSHA HELPS HIM WIPE HIS MIND BLANK...
MUNN MUNN
TO-TALLY BLANK ...
MUNN MUNN

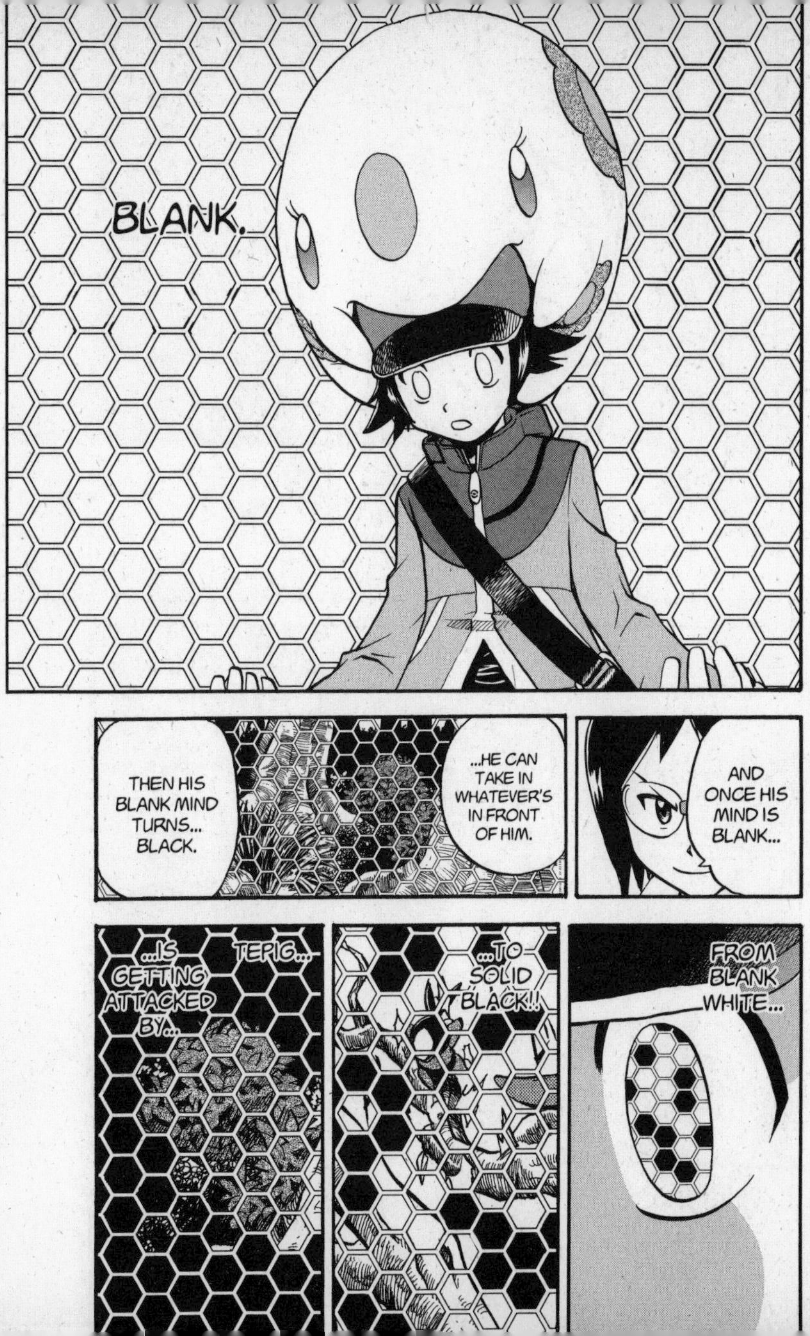
BLANK.
AND ONCE HIS MIND IS BLANK...
...HE CAN TAKE IN WHATEVER'S IN FRONT OF HIM.
THEN HIS BLANK MIND TURNS... BLACK.
FROM BLANK WHITE...
...TO SOLID BLACK!!
TEPIG...
...IS GETTING ATTACKED BY...

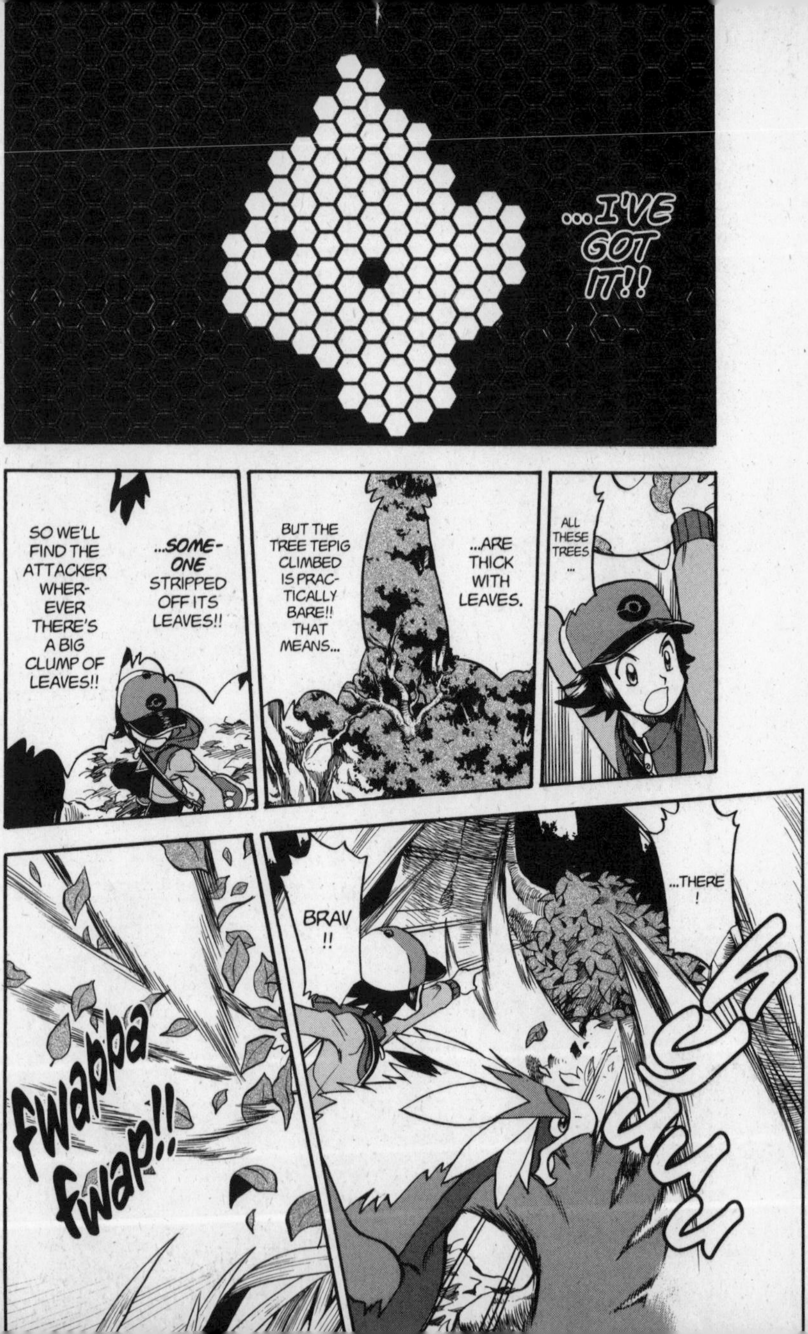
...I'VE GOT IT!!
ALL THESE TREES...
...ARE THICK WITH LEAVES.
BUT THE TREE TEPIG CLIMBED IS PRACTICALLY BARE!! THAT MEANS...
...SOMEONE STRIPPED OFF ITS LEAVES!!
SO WE'LL FIND THE ATTACKER WHEREVER THERE'S A BIG CLUMP OF LEAVES!!
...THERE!
SHUUU
BRAV!!
fwappa fwap!!

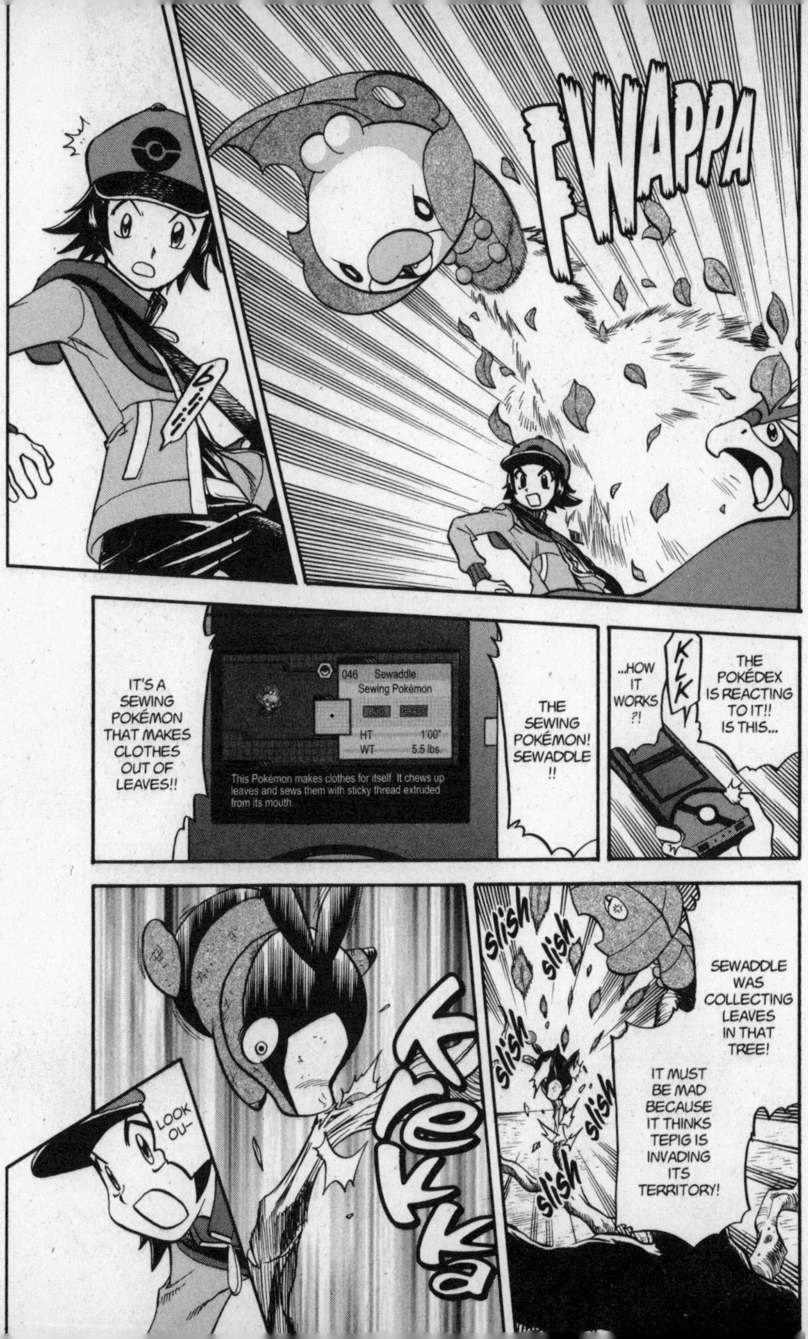
FWAPPA
THE POKÉDEX IS REACTING TO IT!! IS THIS...
KLK
...HOW IT WORKS?!
THE SEWING POKÉMON! SEWADDLE!!
046 Sewaddle
Sewing Pokémon
BUG GRASS
HT 1'00"
WT 5.5 lbs.
This Pokémon makes clothes for itself. It chews up leaves and sews them with sticky thread extruded from its mouth.
IT'S A SEWING POKÉMON THAT MAKES CLOTHES OUT OF LEAVES!!
SEWADDLE WAS COLLECTING LEAVES IN THAT TREE!
IT MUST BE MAD BECAUSE IT THINKS TEPIG IS INVADING ITS TERRITORY!
slish slish slish slish slish slish
LOOK OU—
KRAKA

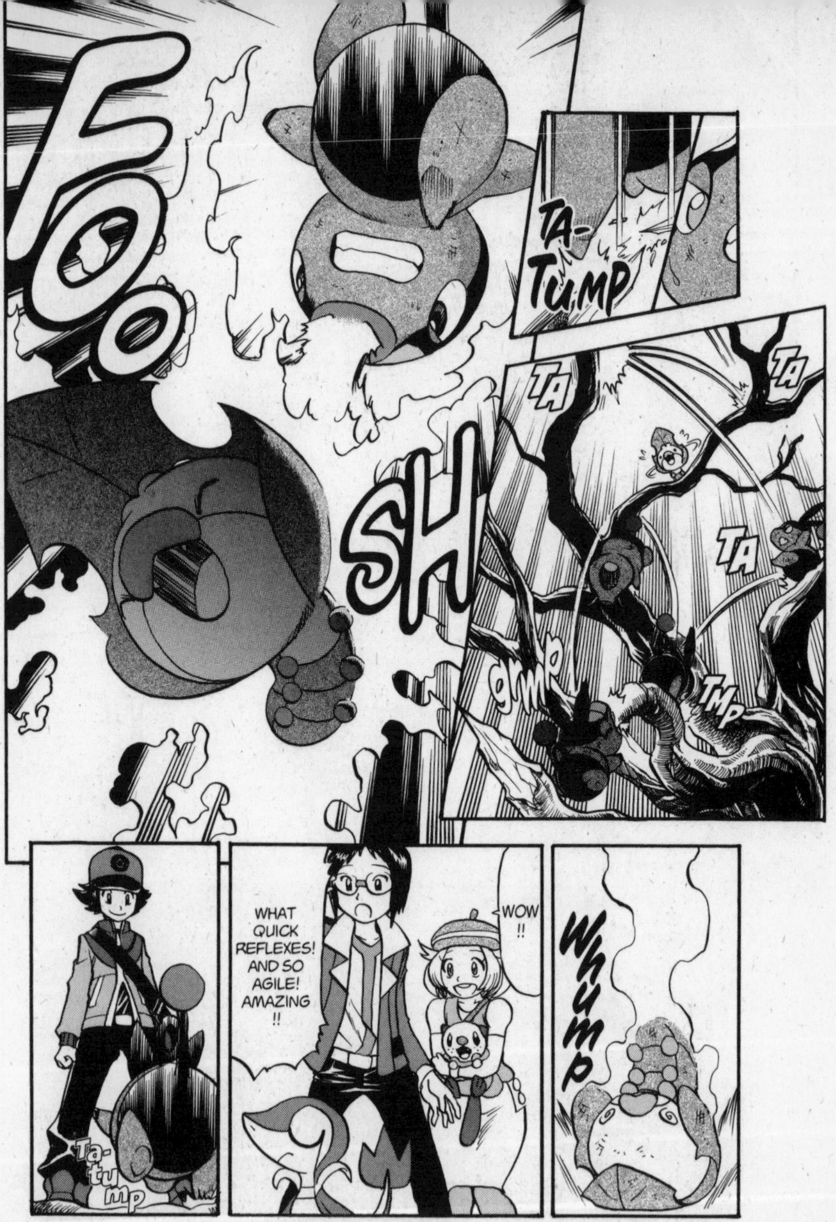
FOOO
TA-TUMP
SH
TA
TA
TA
GMP
TMP
WHAT QUICK REFLEXES! AND SO AGILE! AMAZING !!
WOW !!
WHUMP
TA-TUMP

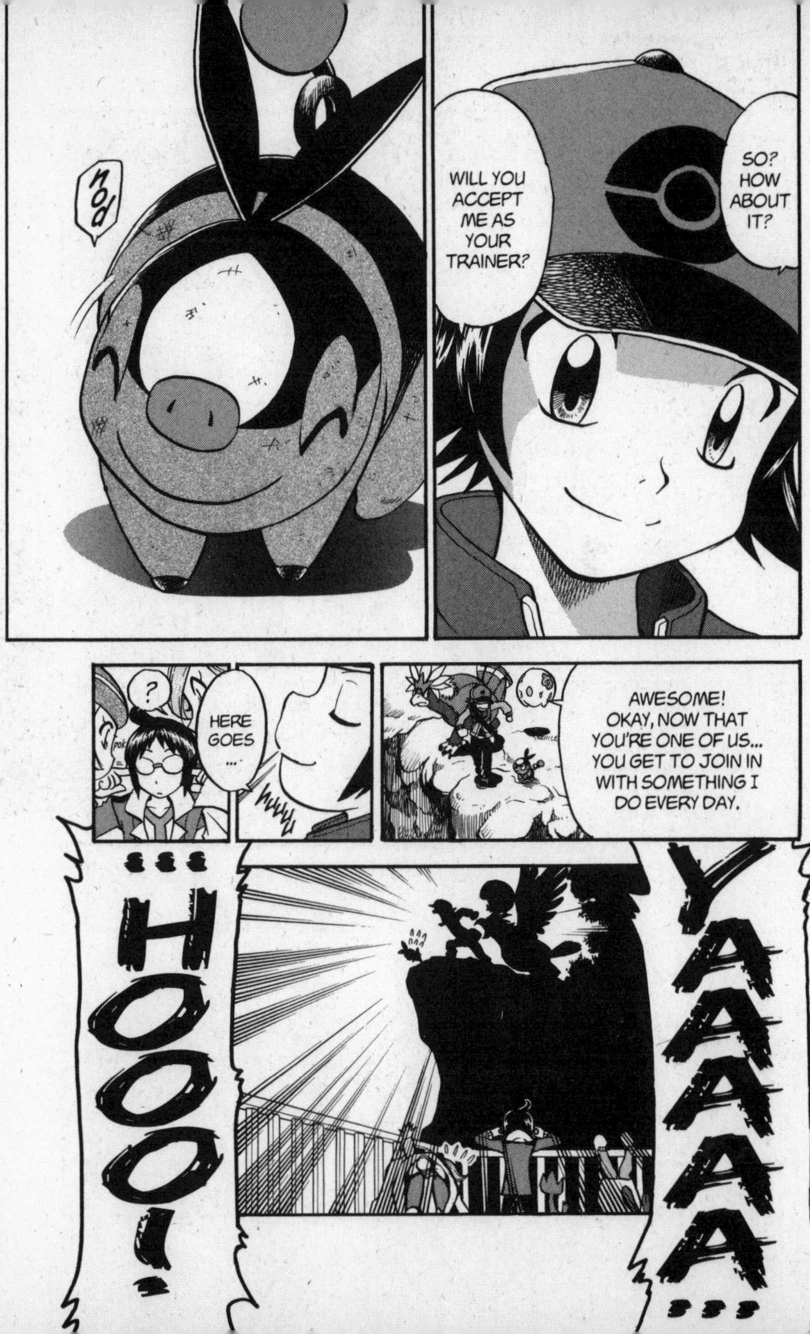
SO? HOW ABOUT IT?
WILL YOU ACCEPT ME AS YOUR TRAINER?
nod
AWESOME! OKAY, NOW THAT YOU'RE ONE OF US... YOU GET TO JOIN IN WITH SOMETHING I DO EVERY DAY.
HERE GOES...
?
pok
YAAAAA...
...HOOO!

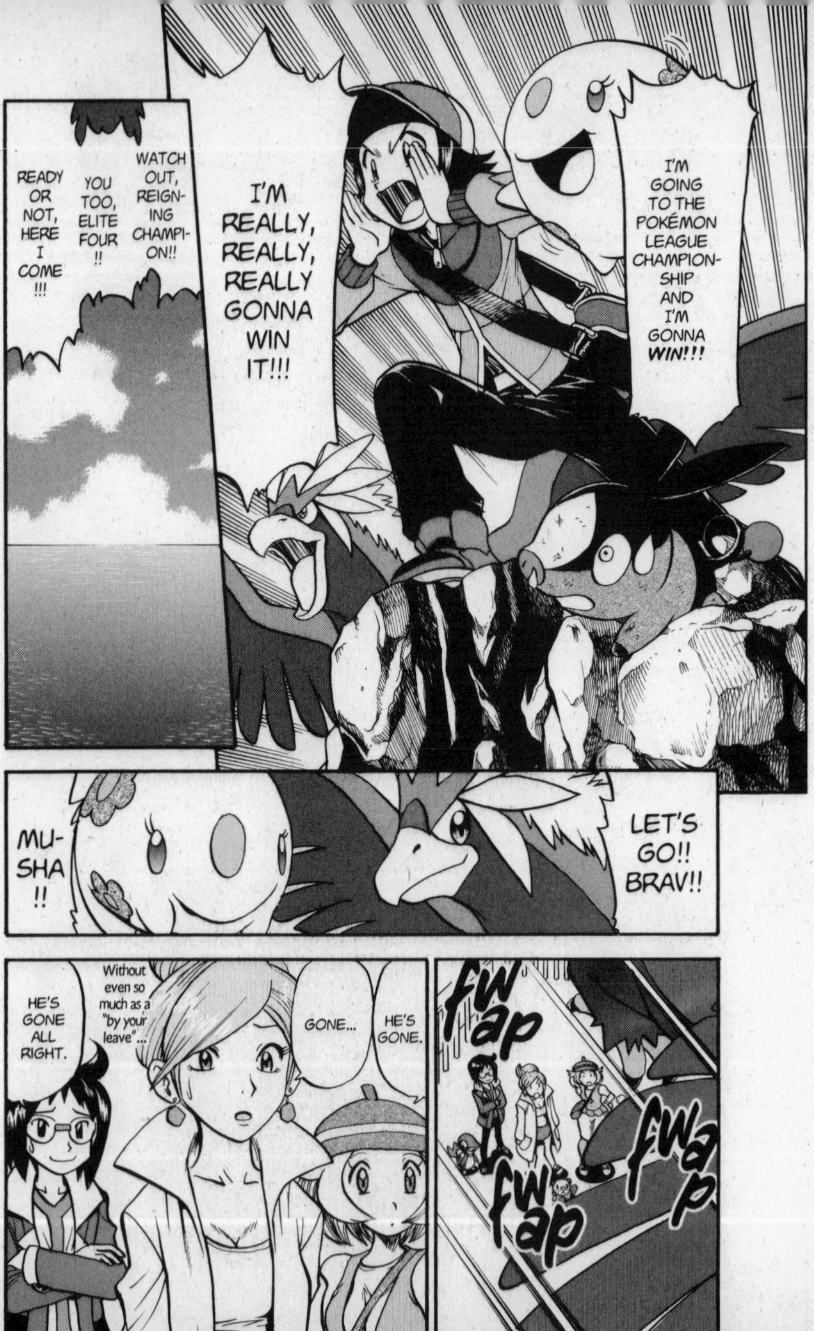
I'M GOING TO THE POKÉMON LEAGUE CHAMPIONSHIP AND I'M GONNA **WIN!!!**
I'M REALLY, REALLY, REALLY GONNA WIN IT!!!
WATCH OUT, REIGNING CHAMPION!!
YOU TOO, ELITE FOUR!!
READY OR NOT, HERE I COME!!!
LET'S GO!! BRAV!!
MU-SHA!!
HE'S GONE.
GONE...
Without even so much as a "by your leave"...
HE'S GONE ALL RIGHT.
fwap
fwap
fwap
fwap

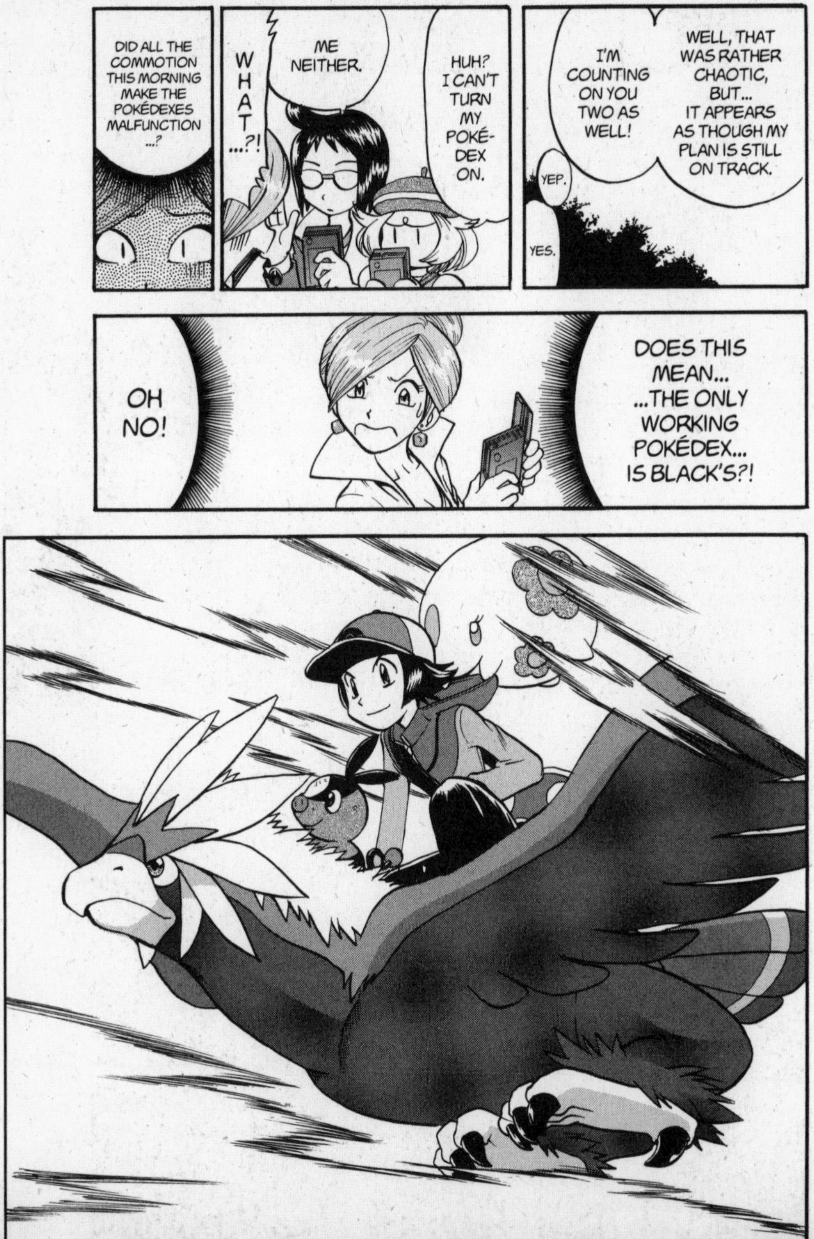
DID ALL THE COMMOTION THIS MORNING MAKE THE POKÉDEXES MALFUNCTION ...?
WHAT ...?!
ME NEITHER.
HUH? I CAN'T TURN MY POKÉ-DEX ON.
WELL, THAT WAS RATHER CHAOTIC, BUT... IT APPEARS AS THOUGH MY PLAN IS STILL ON TRACK.
I'M COUNTING ON YOU TWO AS WELL!
YEP.
YES.
OH NO!
DOES THIS MEAN... ...THE ONLY WORKING POKÉDEX... IS BLACK'S?!

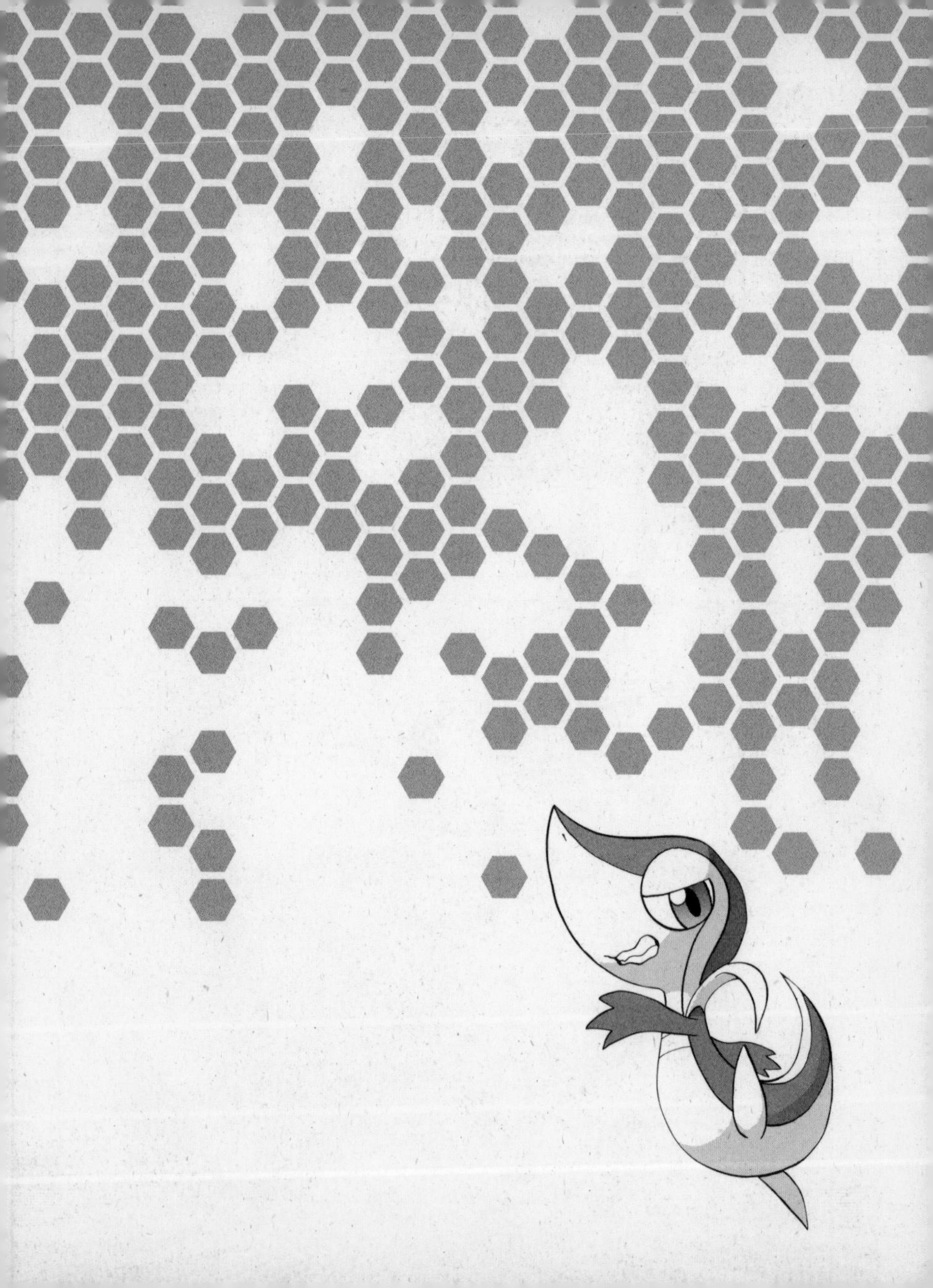

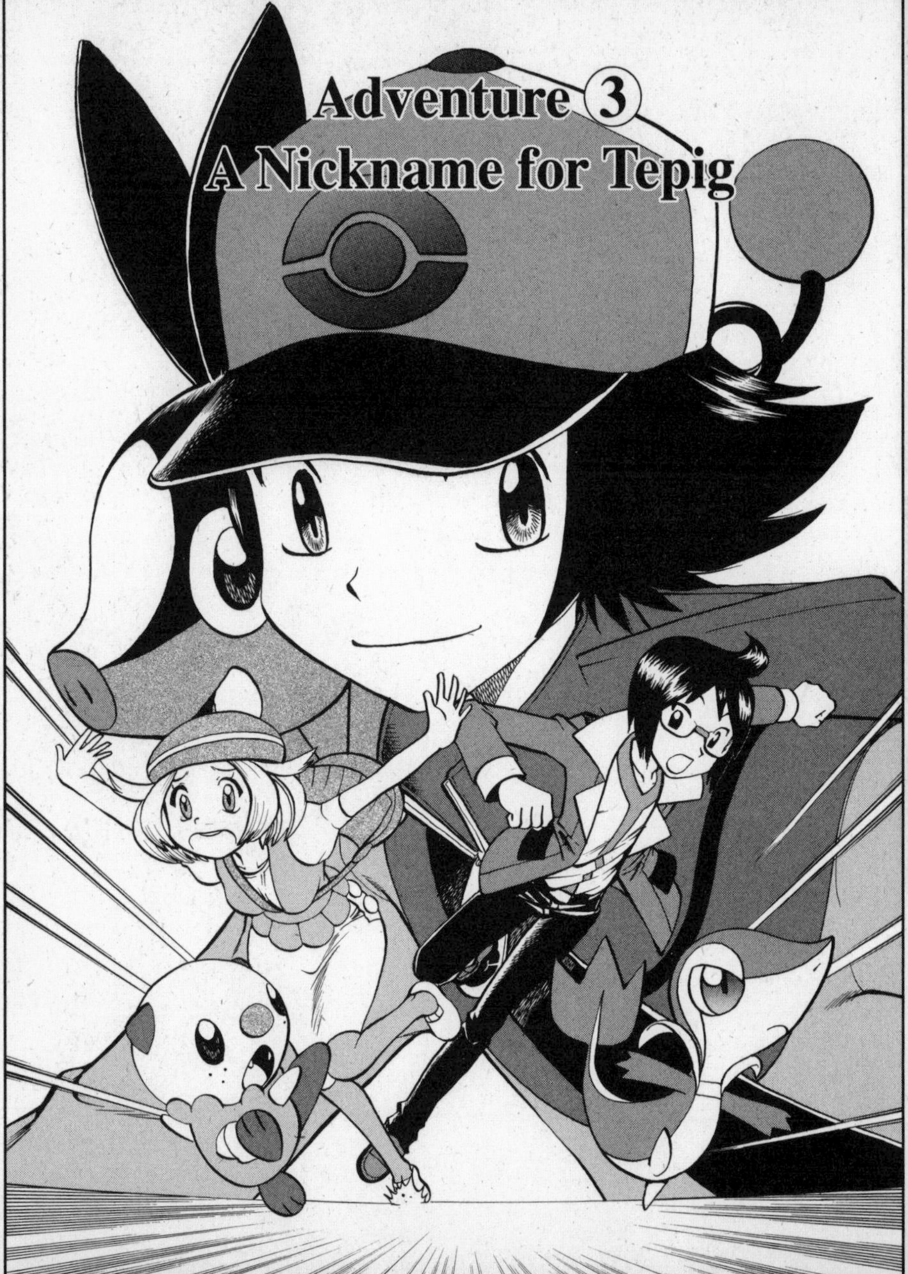
Adventure 3
A Nickname for Tepig

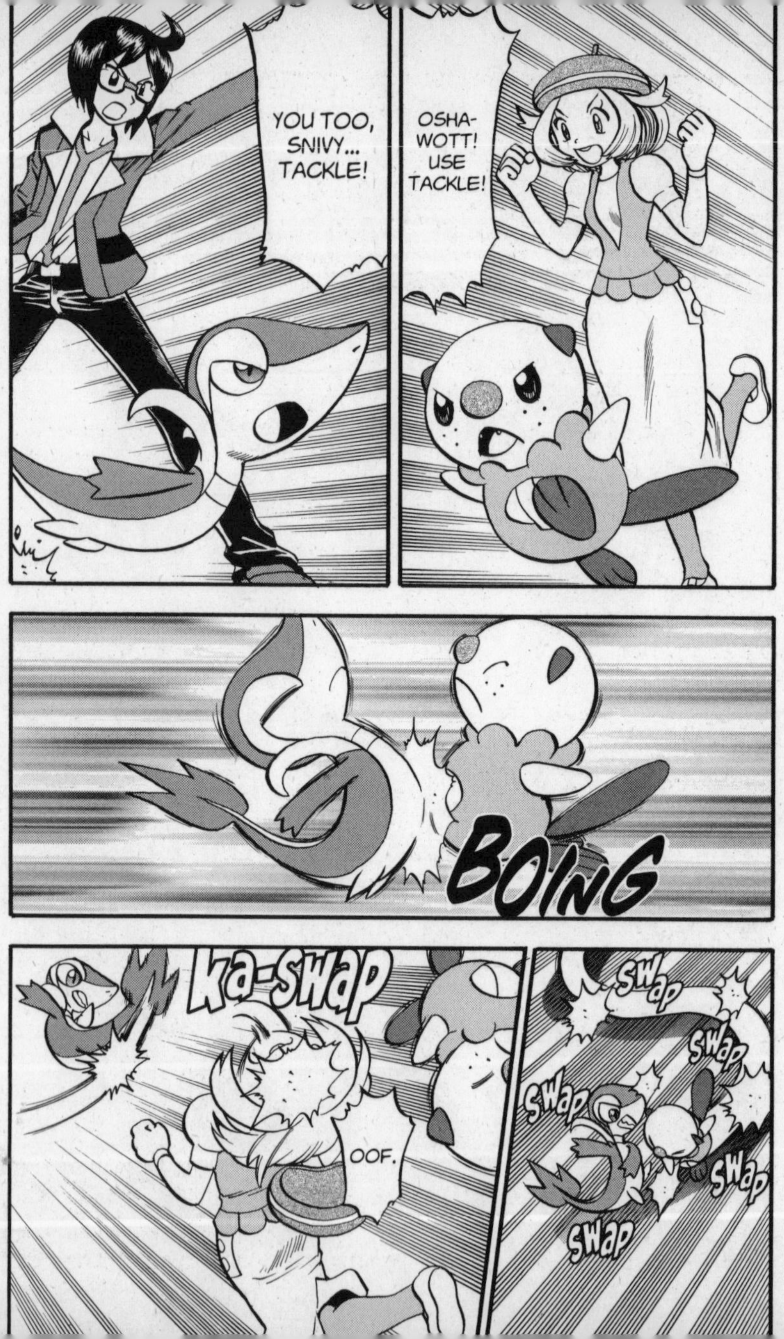
YOU TOO, SNIVY... TACKLE!
OSHA-WOTT! USE TACKLE!
BOING
KA-SWAP
OOF.
SWAP
SWAP
SWAP
SWAP
SWAP

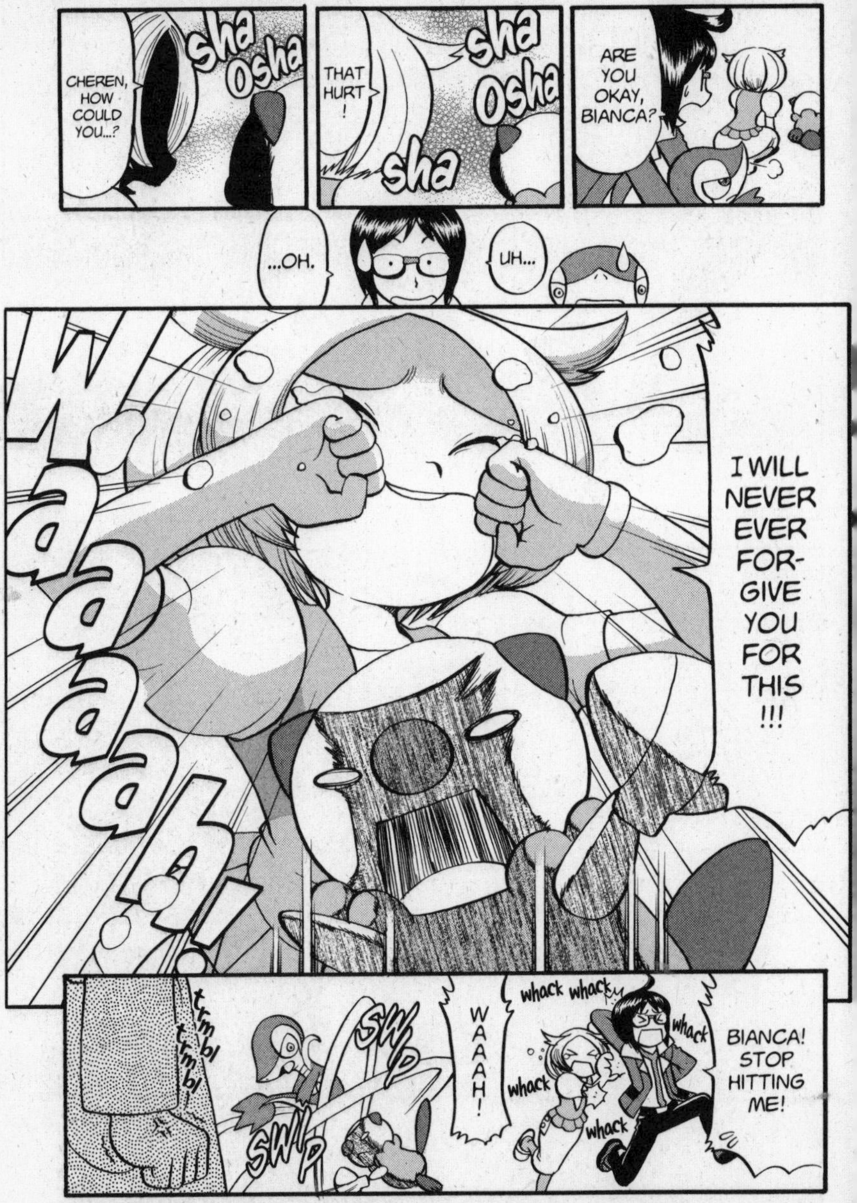
sha osha
CHEREN, HOW COULD YOU...?
THAT HURT!
sha osha
sha
ARE YOU OKAY, BIANCA?
...OH.
UH...
Waaaaah!
I WILL NEVER EVER FOR-GIVE YOU FOR THIS!!!
trmbl trmbl
swp
swp
WAAAAH!
whack whack
whack
whack
whack
BIANCA! STOP HITTING ME!

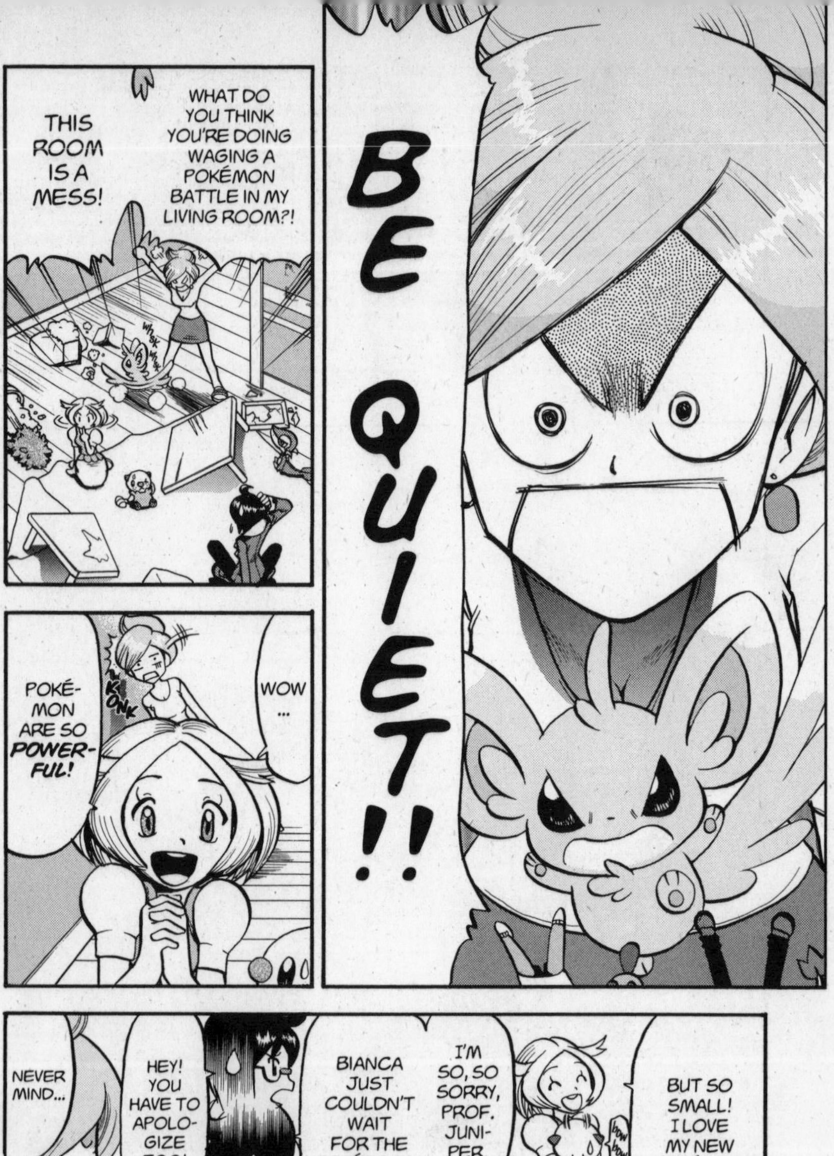

BE QUIET!!
WHAT DO YOU THINK YOU'RE DOING WAGING A POKÉMON BATTLE IN MY LIVING ROOM?!
THIS ROOM IS A MESS!
WOW...
POKÉMON ARE SO POWERFUL!
BUT SO SMALL! I LOVE MY NEW POKÉMON FRIENDS!
I'M SO, SO SORRY, PROF. JUNIPER.
BIANCA JUST COULDN'T WAIT FOR THE POKÉDEXES TO BE FIXED...
HEY! YOU HAVE TO APOLOGIZE TOO!
NEVER MIND...

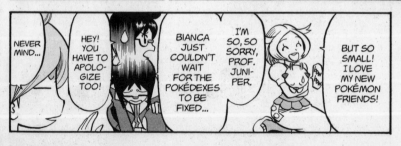

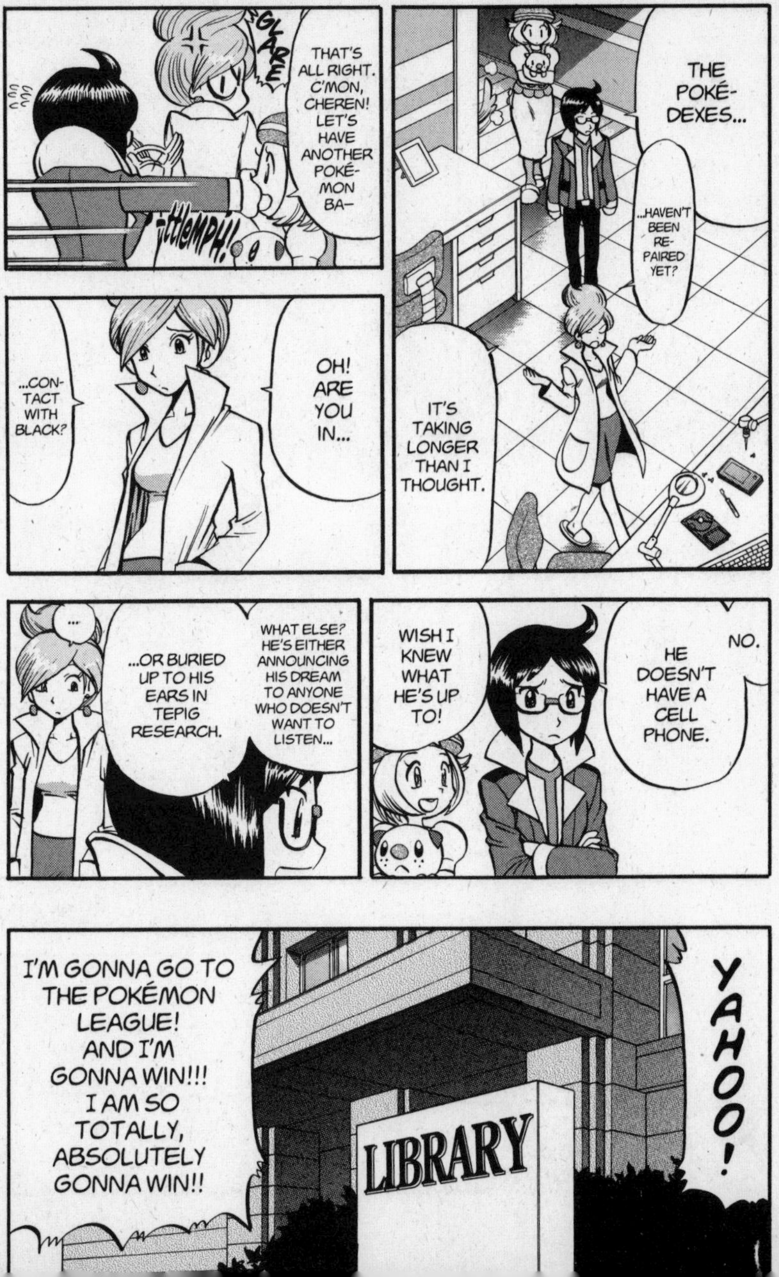
THE POKÉ-DEXES...
...HAVEN'T BEEN RE-PAIRED YET?
IT'S TAKING LONGER THAN I THOUGHT.
GLARE
THAT'S ALL RIGHT. C'MON, CHEREN! LET'S HAVE ANOTHER POKÉMON BA-
-ttlemPH!!
OH! ARE YOU IN...
...CONTACT WITH BLACK?
NO.
HE DOESN'T HAVE A CELL PHONE.
WISH I KNEW WHAT HE'S UP TO!
...
WHAT ELSE? HE'S EITHER ANNOUNCING HIS DREAM TO ANYONE WHO DOESN'T WANT TO LISTEN...
...OR BURIED UP TO HIS EARS IN TEPIG RESEARCH.
YAHOO!
I'M GONNA GO TO THE POKÉMON LEAGUE! AND I'M GONNA WIN!!! I AM SO TOTALLY, ABSOLUTELY GONNA WIN!!
LIBRARY

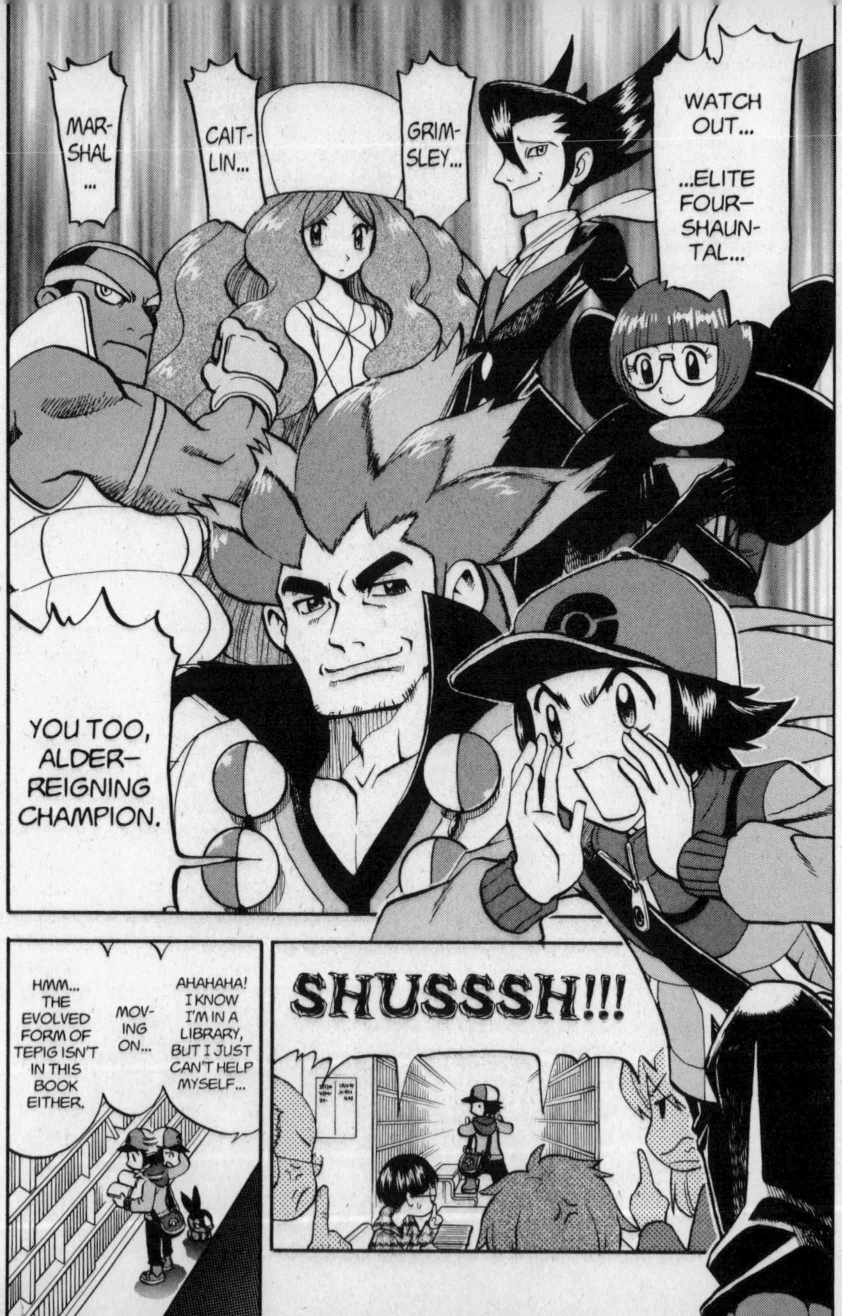
MAR-SHAL...
CAIT-LIN...
GRIM-SLEY...
WATCH OUT...
...ELITE FOUR-SHAUN-TAL...
YOU TOO, ALDER-REIGNING CHAMPION.
HMM... THE EVOLVED FORM OF TEPIG ISN'T IN THIS BOOK EITHER.
MOV-ING ON...
AHAHAHA! I KNOW I'M IN A LIBRARY, BUT I JUST CAN'T HELP MYSELF...
SHUSSSH!!!

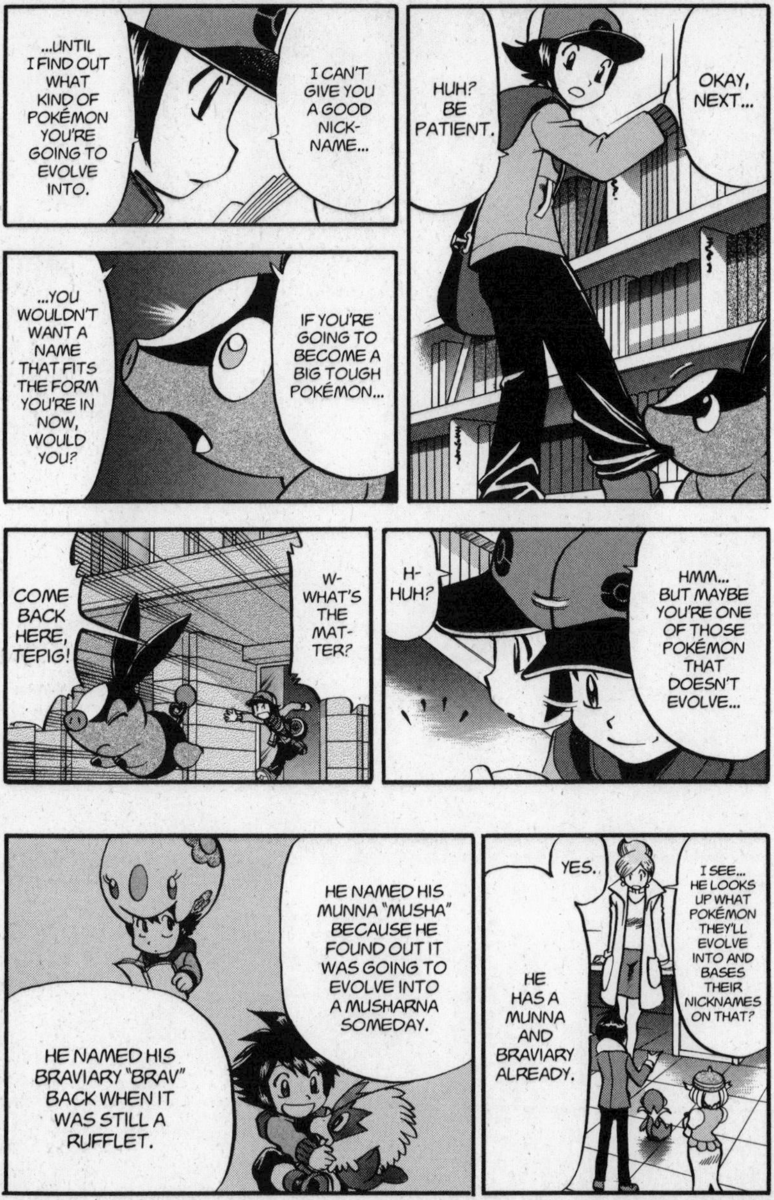
OKAY, NEXT...
HUH? BE PATIENT.
I CAN'T GIVE YOU A GOOD NICK-NAME...
...UNTIL I FIND OUT WHAT KIND OF POKÉMON YOU'RE GOING TO EVOLVE INTO.
IF YOU'RE GOING TO BECOME A BIG TOUGH POKÉMON...
...YOU WOULDN'T WANT A NAME THAT FITS THE FORM YOU'RE IN NOW, WOULD YOU?
HMM... BUT MAYBE YOU'RE ONE OF THOSE POKÉMON THAT DOESN'T EVOLVE...
H-HUH?
W-WHAT'S THE MAT-TER?
COME BACK HERE, TEPIG!
I SEE... HE LOOKS UP WHAT POKÉMON THEY'LL EVOLVE INTO AND BASES THEIR NICKNAMES ON THAT?
YES.
HE HAS A MUNNA AND BRAVIARY ALREADY.
HE NAMED HIS MUNNA "MUSHA" BECAUSE HE FOUND OUT IT WAS GOING TO EVOLVE INTO A MUSHARNA SOMEDAY.
HE NAMED HIS BRAVIARY "BRAV" BACK WHEN IT WAS STILL A RUFFLET.

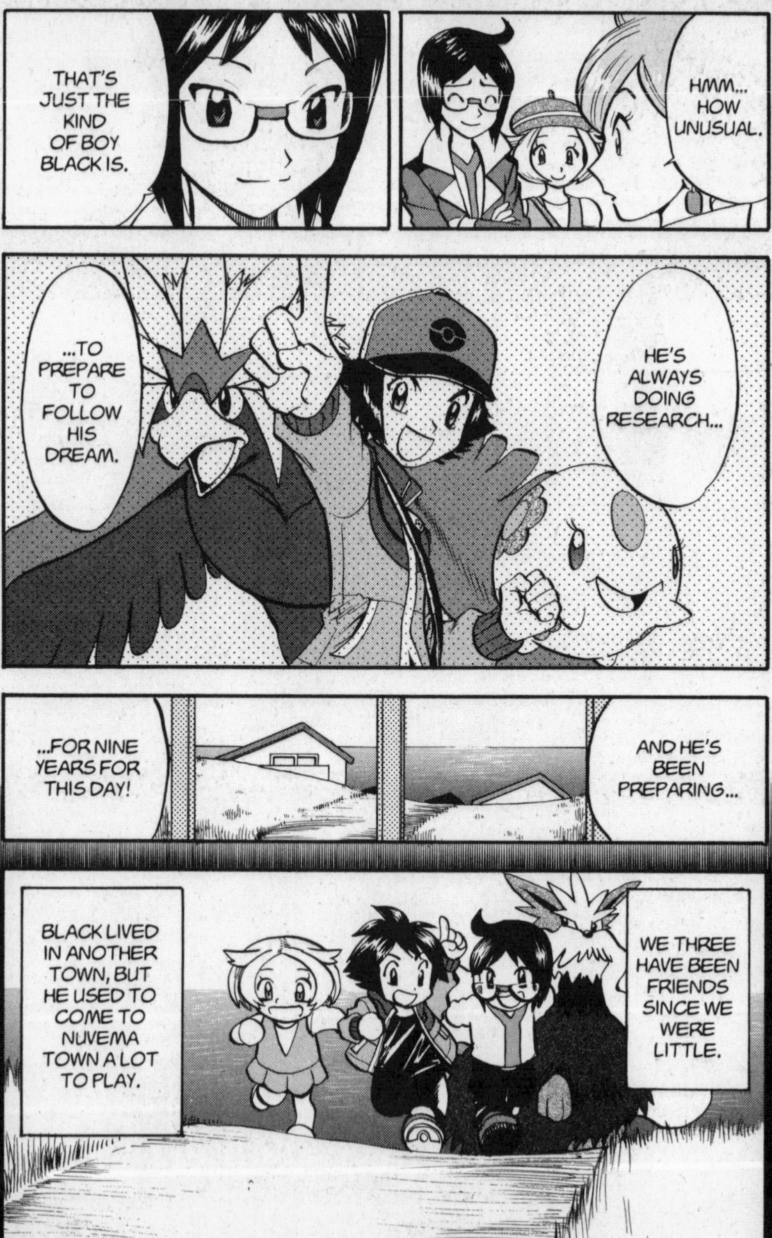
HMM... HOW UNUSUAL.
THAT'S JUST THE KIND OF BOY BLACK IS.
HE'S ALWAYS DOING RESEARCH...
...TO PREPARE TO FOLLOW HIS DREAM.
AND HE'S BEEN PREPARING...
...FOR NINE YEARS FOR THIS DAY!
WE THREE HAVE BEEN FRIENDS SINCE WE WERE LITTLE.
BLACK LIVED IN ANOTHER TOWN, BUT HE USED TO COME TO NUVEMA TOWN A LOT TO PLAY.

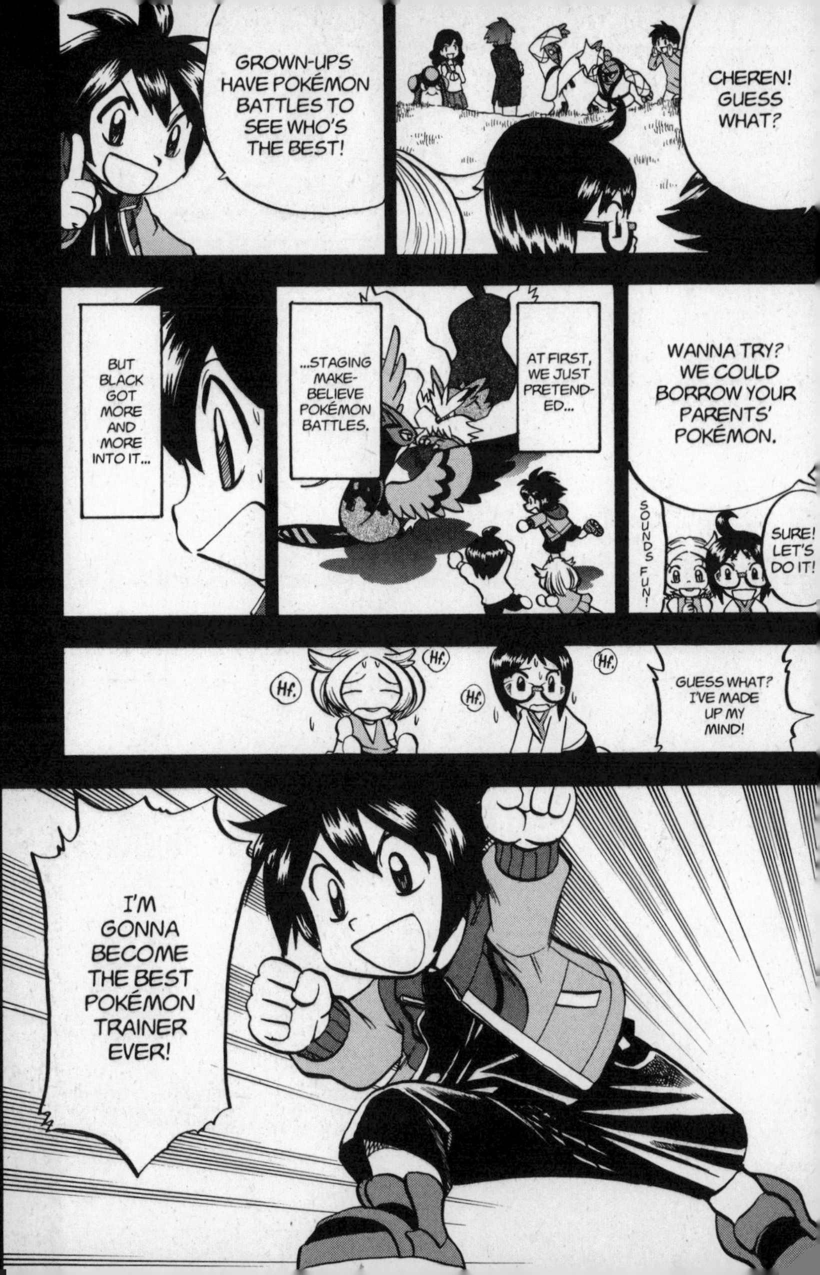
CHEREN! GUESS WHAT?
GROWN-UPS HAVE POKÉMON BATTLES TO SEE WHO'S THE BEST!
WANNA TRY? WE COULD BORROW YOUR PARENTS' POKÉMON.
SURE! LET'S DO IT!
SOUNDS FUN!
AT FIRST, WE JUST PRETEND-ED...
...STAGING MAKE-BELIEVE POKÉMON BATTLES.
BUT BLACK GOT MORE AND MORE INTO IT...
GUESS WHAT? I'VE MADE UP MY MIND!
HF.
HF.
HF.
HF.
I'M GONNA BECOME THE BEST POKÉMON TRAINER EVER!

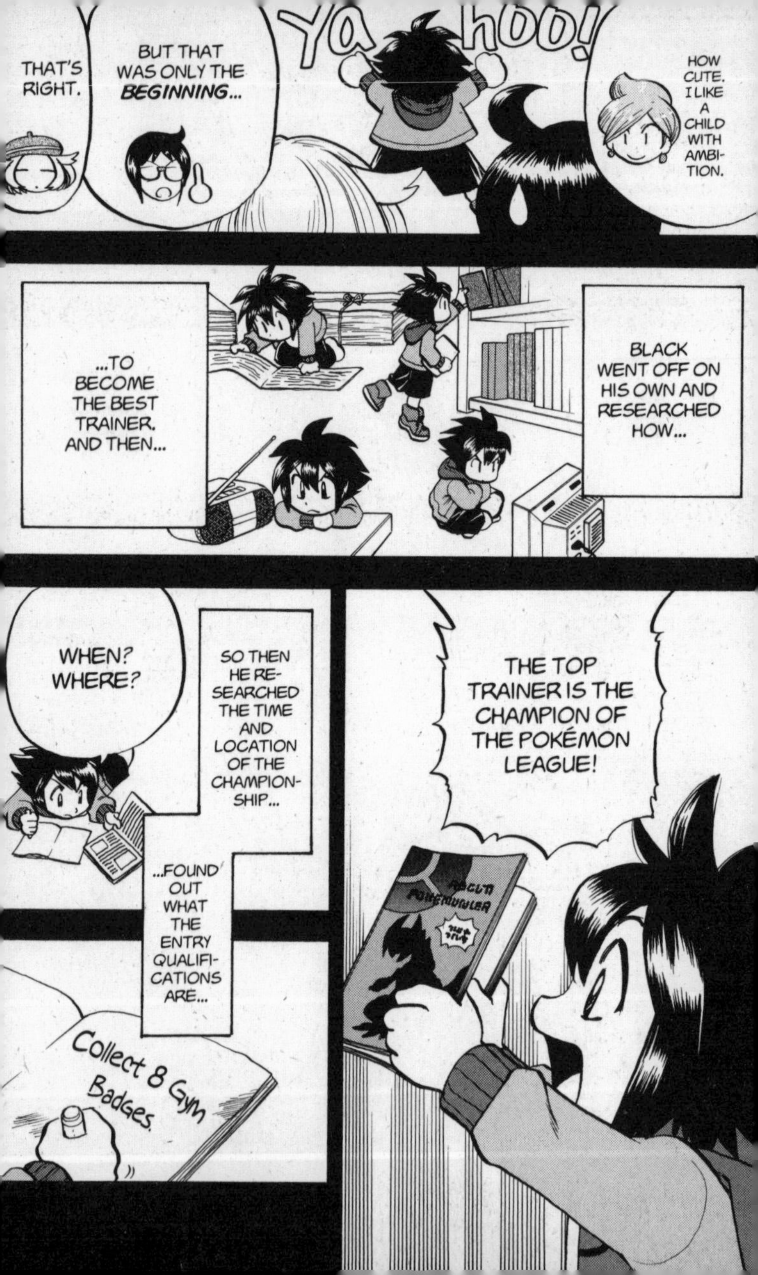
YA HOO!
HOW CUTE. I LIKE A CHILD WITH AMBITION.
BUT THAT WAS ONLY THE *BEGINNING*...
THAT'S RIGHT.
BLACK WENT OFF ON HIS OWN AND RESEARCHED HOW...
...TO BECOME THE BEST TRAINER. AND THEN...
THE TOP TRAINER IS THE CHAMPION OF THE POKÉMON LEAGUE!
SO THEN HE RE-SEARCHED THE TIME AND LOCATION OF THE CHAMPION-SHIP...
WHEN? WHERE?
...FOUND OUT WHAT THE ENTRY QUALIFI-CATIONS ARE...
Collect 8 Gym Badges.

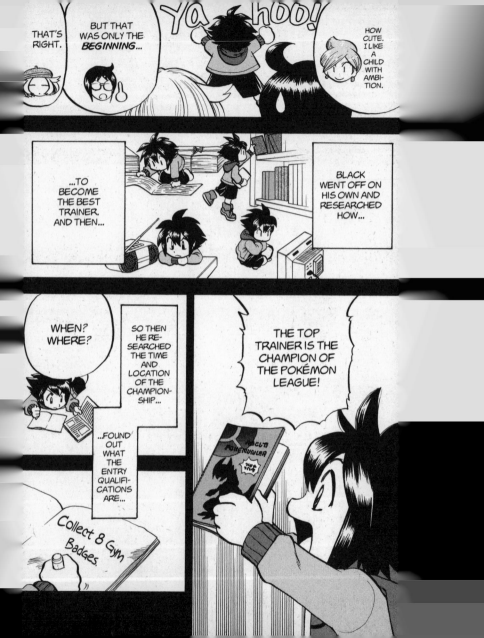

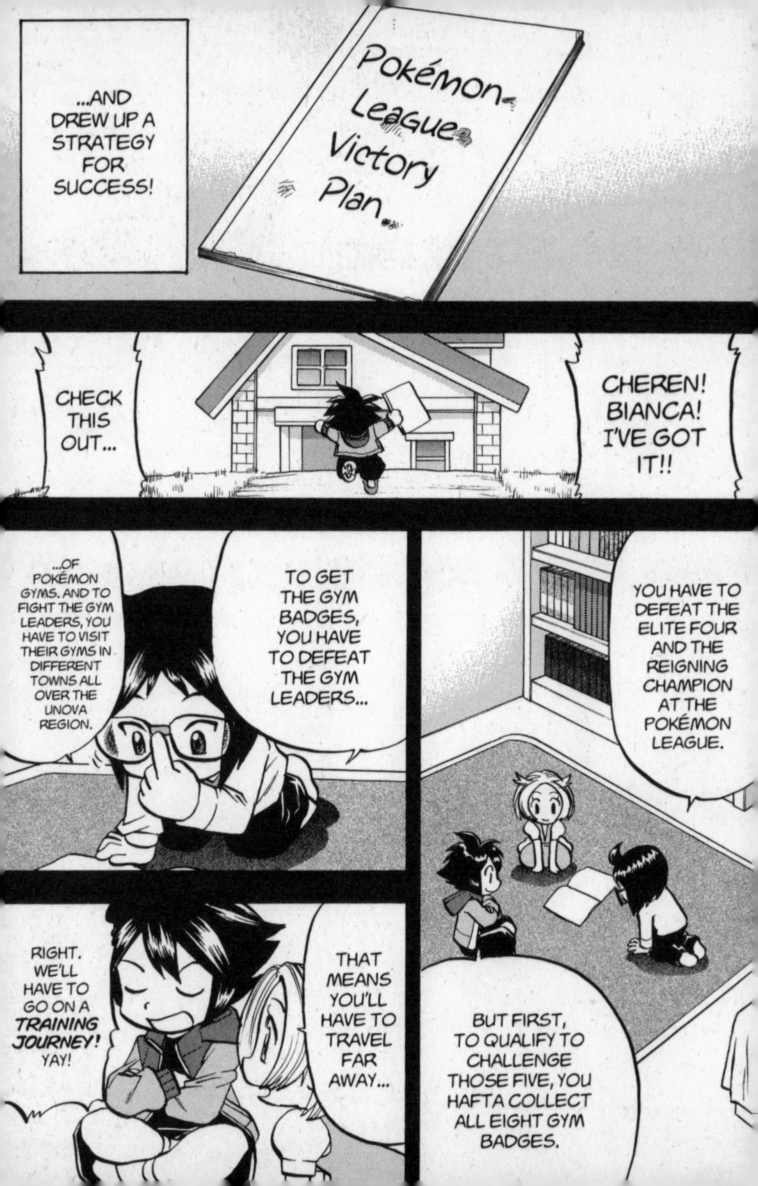

...AND DREW UP A STRATEGY FOR SUCCESS!
Pokémon League Victory Plan
CHECK THIS OUT...
CHEREN! BIANCA! I'VE GOT IT!!
YOU HAVE TO DEFEAT THE ELITE FOUR AND THE REIGNING CHAMPION AT THE POKÉMON LEAGUE.
BUT FIRST, TO QUALIFY TO CHALLENGE THOSE FIVE, YOU HAFTA COLLECT ALL EIGHT GYM BADGES.
TO GET THE GYM BADGES, YOU HAVE TO DEFEAT THE GYM LEADERS...
...OF POKÉMON GYMS. AND TO FIGHT THE GYM LEADERS, YOU HAVE TO VISIT THEIR GYMS IN DIFFERENT TOWNS ALL OVER THE UNOVA REGION.
THAT MEANS YOU'LL HAVE TO TRAVEL FAR AWAY...
RIGHT. WE'LL HAVE TO GO ON A *TRAINING JOURNEY!* YAY!

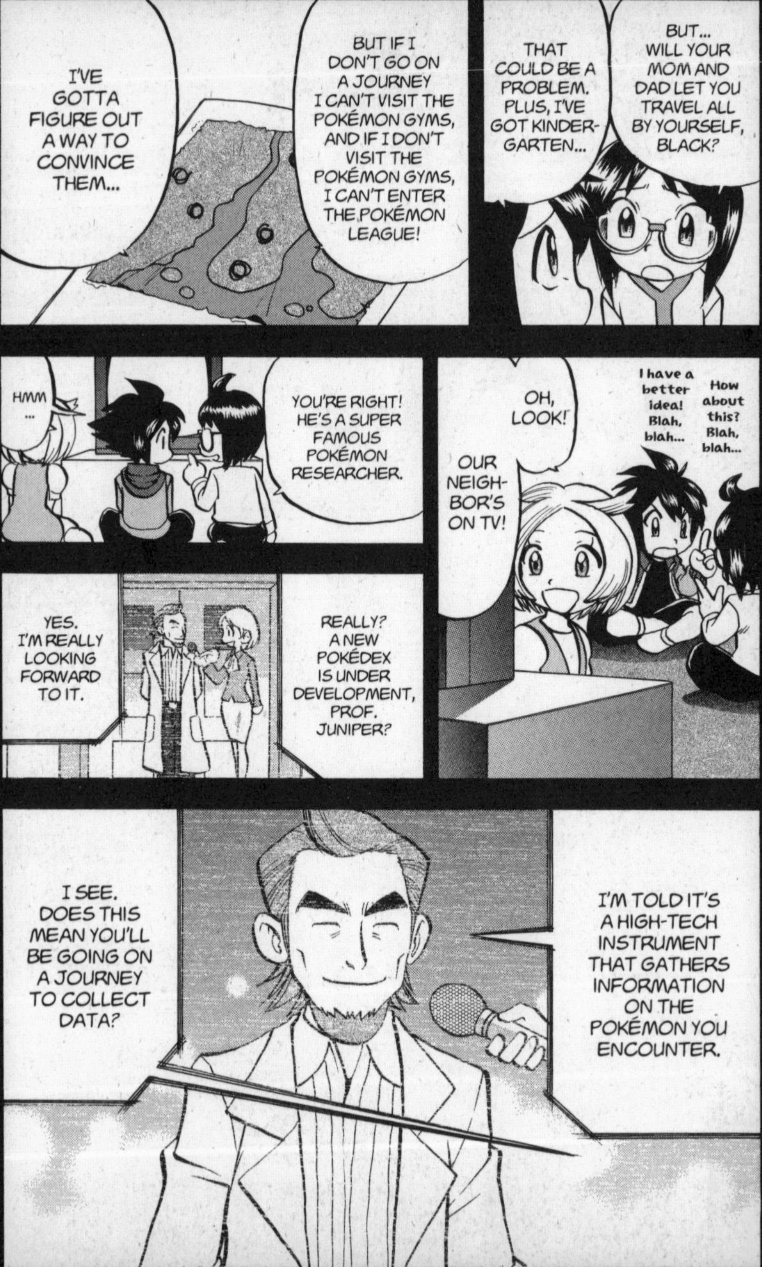
BUT... WILL YOUR MOM AND DAD LET YOU TRAVEL ALL BY YOURSELF, BLACK?
THAT COULD BE A PROBLEM. PLUS, I'VE GOT KINDER-GARTEN...
BUT IF I DON'T GO ON A JOURNEY I CAN'T VISIT THE POKÉMON GYMS, AND IF I DON'T VISIT THE POKÉMON GYMS, I CAN'T ENTER THE POKÉMON LEAGUE!
I'VE GOTTA FIGURE OUT A WAY TO CONVINCE THEM...
How about this? Blah, blah...
I have a better idea! Blah, blah...
OH, LOOK!
OUR NEIGH-BOR'S ON TV!
YOU'RE RIGHT! HE'S A SUPER FAMOUS POKÉMON RESEARCHER.
HMM...
REALLY? A NEW POKÉDEX IS UNDER DEVELOPMENT, PROF. JUNIPER?
YES. I'M REALLY LOOKING FORWARD TO IT.
I'M TOLD IT'S A HIGH-TECH INSTRUMENT THAT GATHERS INFORMATION ON THE POKÉMON YOU ENCOUNTER.
I SEE. DOES THIS MEAN YOU'LL BE GOING ON A JOURNEY TO COLLECT DATA?

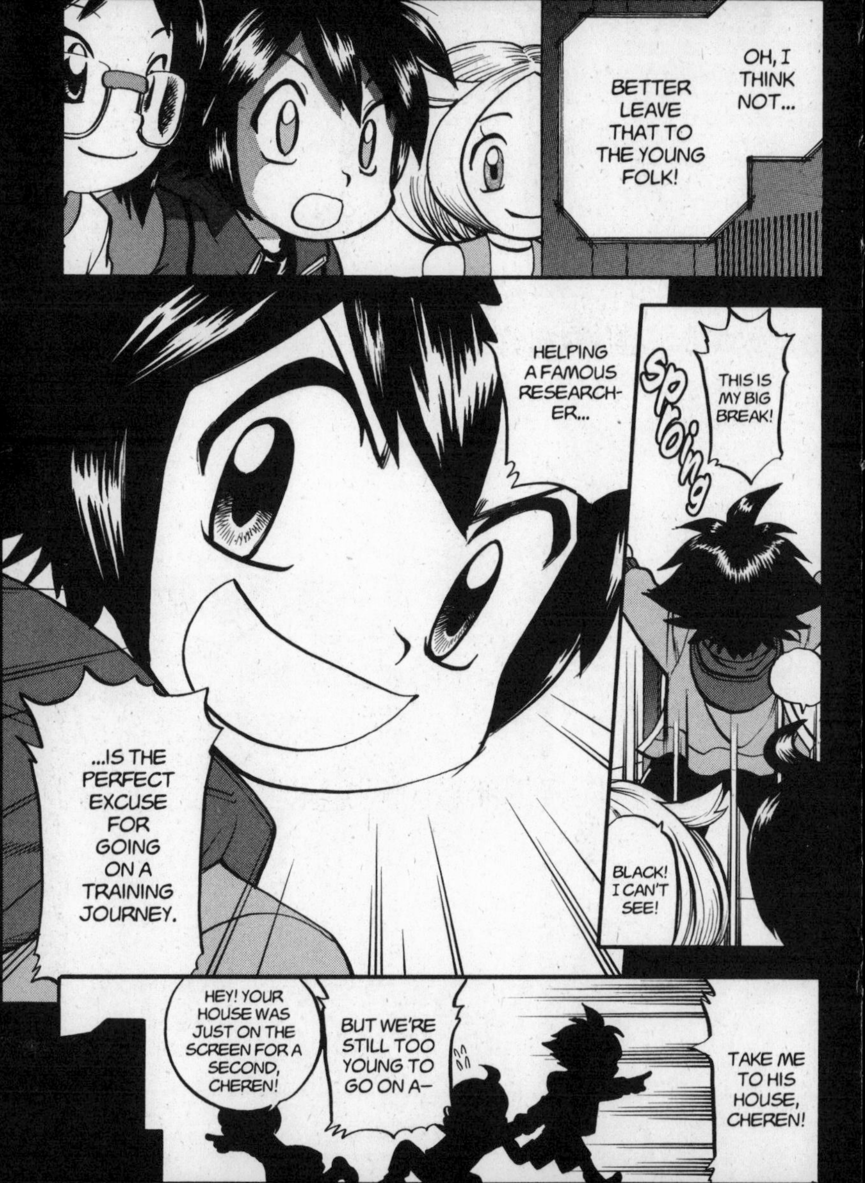

BETTER LEAVE THAT TO THE YOUNG FOLK!
OH, I THINK NOT...
HELPING A FAMOUS RESEARCH-ER...
...IS THE PERFECT EXCUSE FOR GOING ON A TRAINING JOURNEY.
THIS IS MY BIG BREAK!
SPROING
BLACK! I CAN'T SEE!
HEY! YOUR HOUSE WAS JUST ON THE SCREEN FOR A SECOND, CHEREN!
BUT WE'RE STILL TOO YOUNG TO GO ON A–
TAKE ME TO HIS HOUSE, CHEREN!

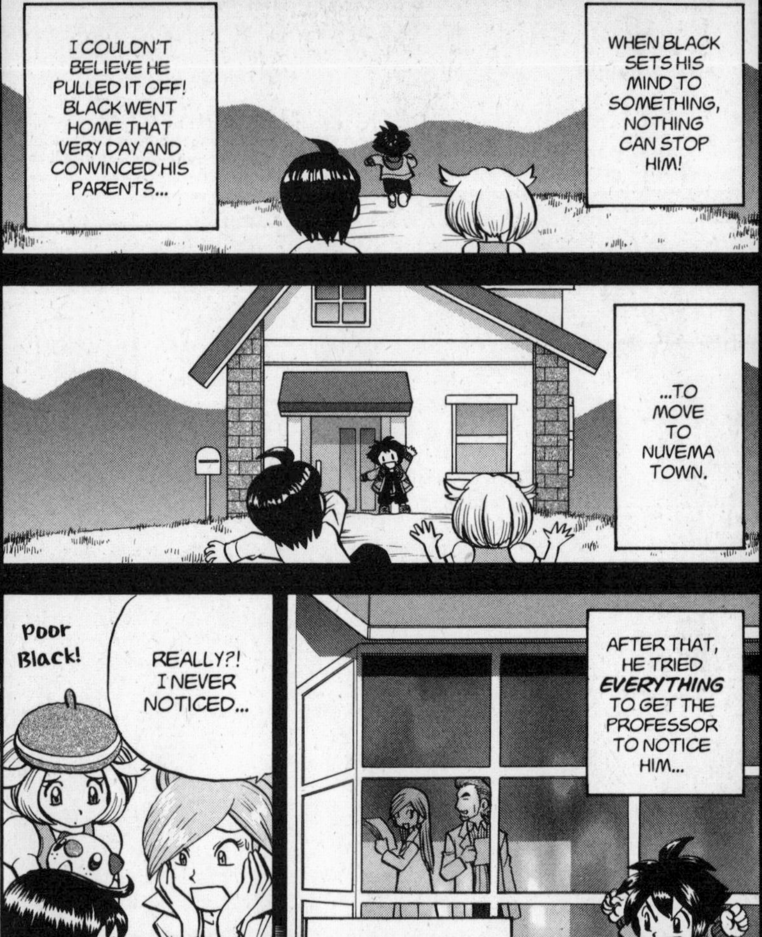
I COULDN'T BELIEVE HE PULLED IT OFF! BLACK WENT HOME THAT VERY DAY AND CONVINCED HIS PARENTS...
WHEN BLACK SETS HIS MIND TO SOMETHING, NOTHING CAN STOP HIM!
...TO MOVE TO NUVEMA TOWN.
Poor Black!
REALLY?! I NEVER NOTICED...
NEVER MIND...
AFTER THAT, HE TRIED EVERYTHING TO GET THE PROFESSOR TO NOTICE HIM...
HE STAGED POKÉMON BATTLES EVERY DAY IN FRONT OF YOUR HOUSE, PROF. JUNIPER.

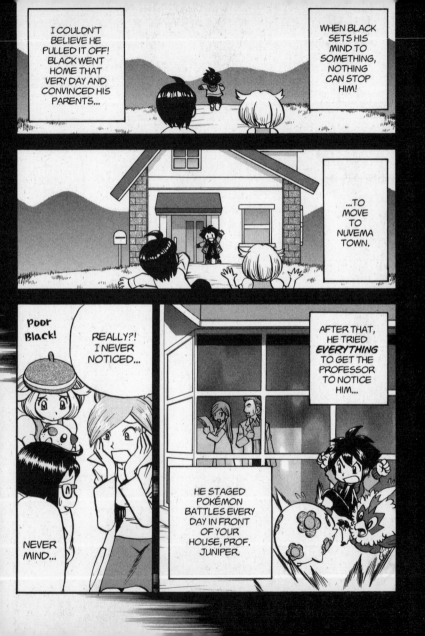

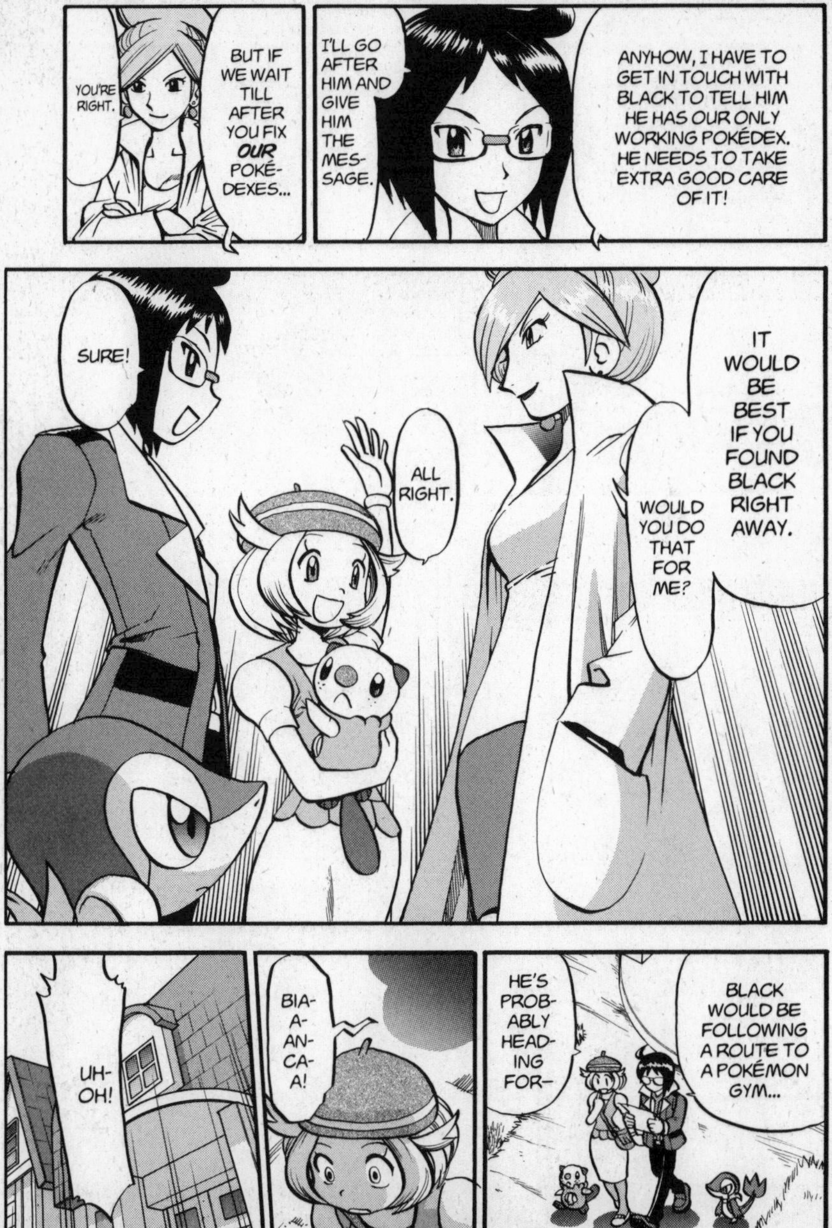
ANYHOW, I HAVE TO GET IN TOUCH WITH BLACK TO TELL HIM HE HAS OUR ONLY WORKING POKÉDEX. HE NEEDS TO TAKE EXTRA GOOD CARE OF IT!
I'LL GO AFTER HIM AND GIVE HIM THE MES-SAGE.
BUT IF WE WAIT TILL AFTER YOU FIX *OUR* POKÉ-DEXES...
YOU'RE RIGHT.
IT WOULD BE BEST IF YOU FOUND BLACK RIGHT AWAY.
WOULD YOU DO THAT FOR ME?
ALL RIGHT.
SURE!
BLACK WOULD BE FOLLOWING A ROUTE TO A POKÉMON GYM...
HE'S PROB-ABLY HEAD-ING FOR-
BIA-A-AN-CA-A!
UH-OH!

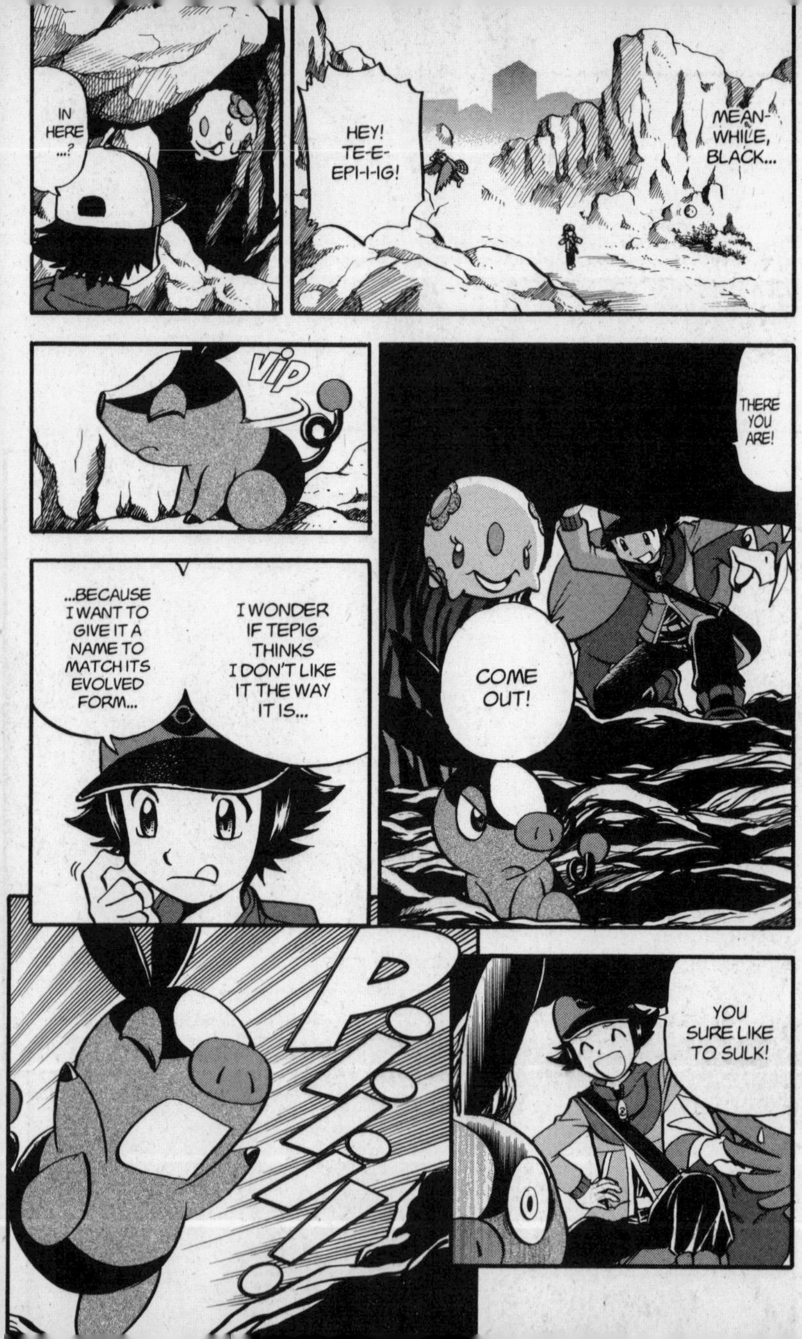
IN HERE ...?
HEY! TE-E-EPI-I-IG!
MEAN-WHILE, BLACK...
VIP
THERE YOU ARE!
COME OUT!
I WONDER IF TEPIG THINKS I DON'T LIKE IT THE WAY IT IS...
...BECAUSE I WANT TO GIVE IT A NAME TO MATCH ITS EVOLVED FORM...
YOU SURE LIKE TO SULK!
P...!!

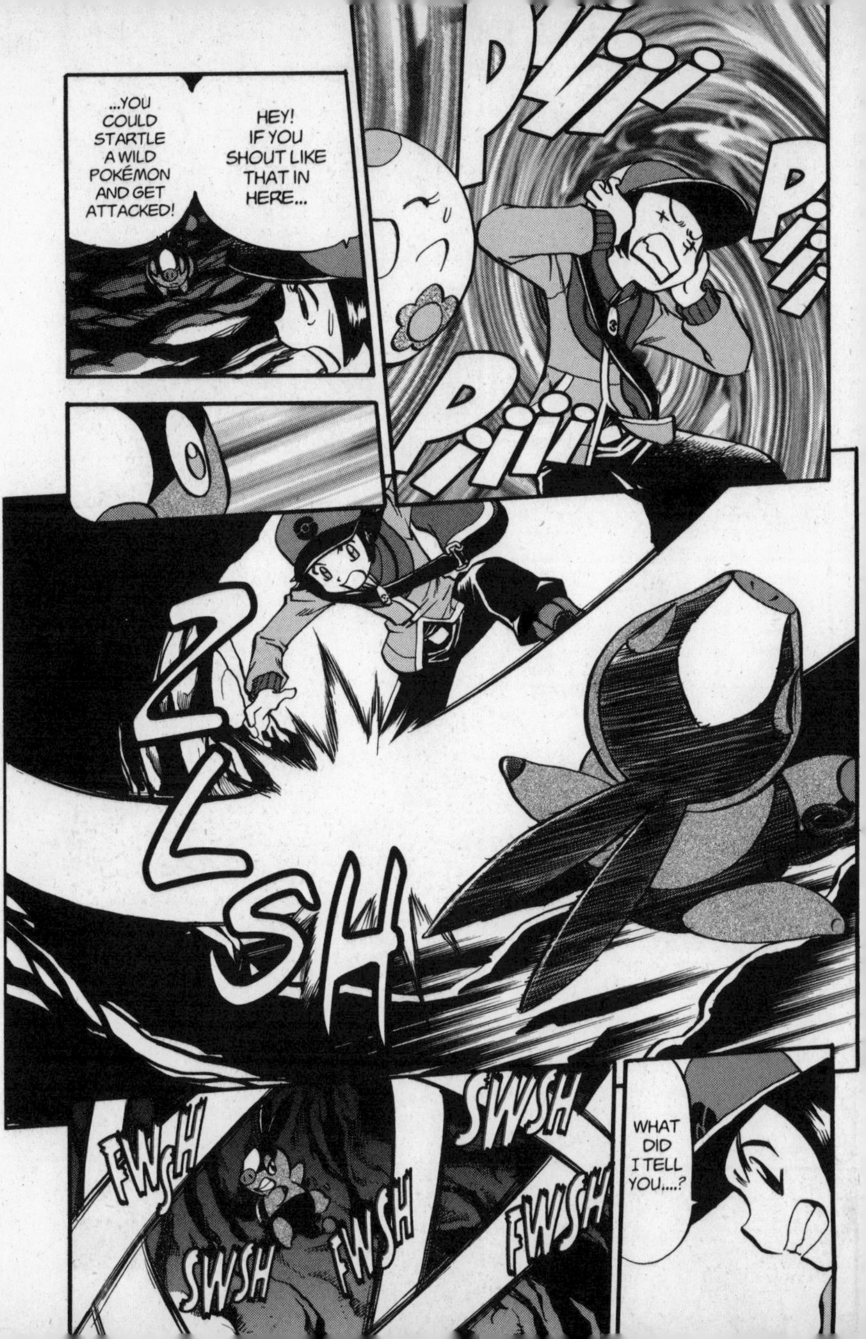

HEY! IF YOU SHOUT LIKE THAT IN HERE...
...YOU COULD STARTLE A WILD POKÉMON AND GET ATTACKED!
PIIIIII...
PIIII
PIIIIII
ZZZSH
WHAT DID I TELL YOU....?
SWSH
FWSH
FWSH
FWSH
SWSH

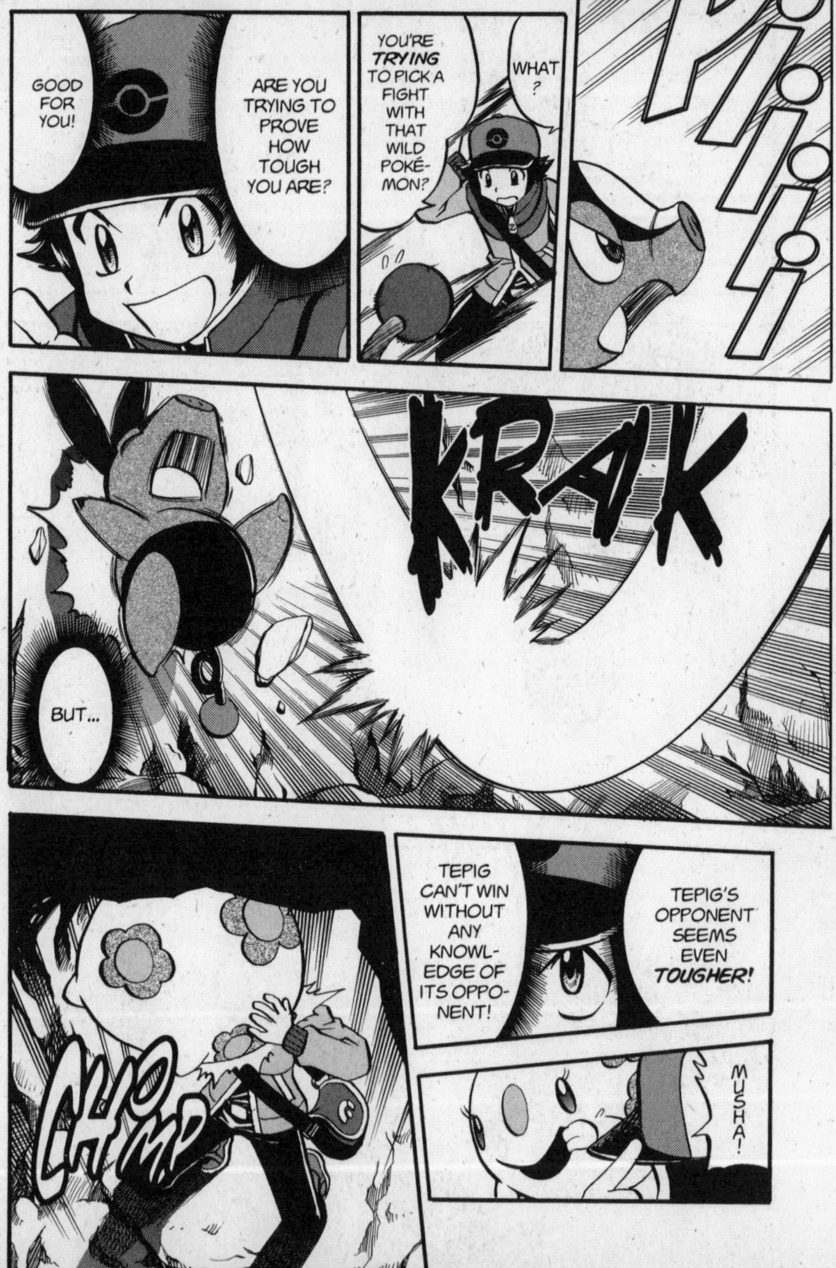
GOOD FOR YOU!
ARE YOU TRYING TO PROVE HOW TOUGH YOU ARE?
YOU'RE *TRYING* TO PICK A FIGHT WITH THAT WILD POKÉMON?
WHAT?
PIIIIII
KRAK
BUT...
TEPIG CAN'T WIN WITHOUT ANY KNOWLEDGE OF ITS OPPONENT!
TEPIG'S OPPONENT SEEMS EVEN *TOUGHER!*
CHOMP
MUSHA!

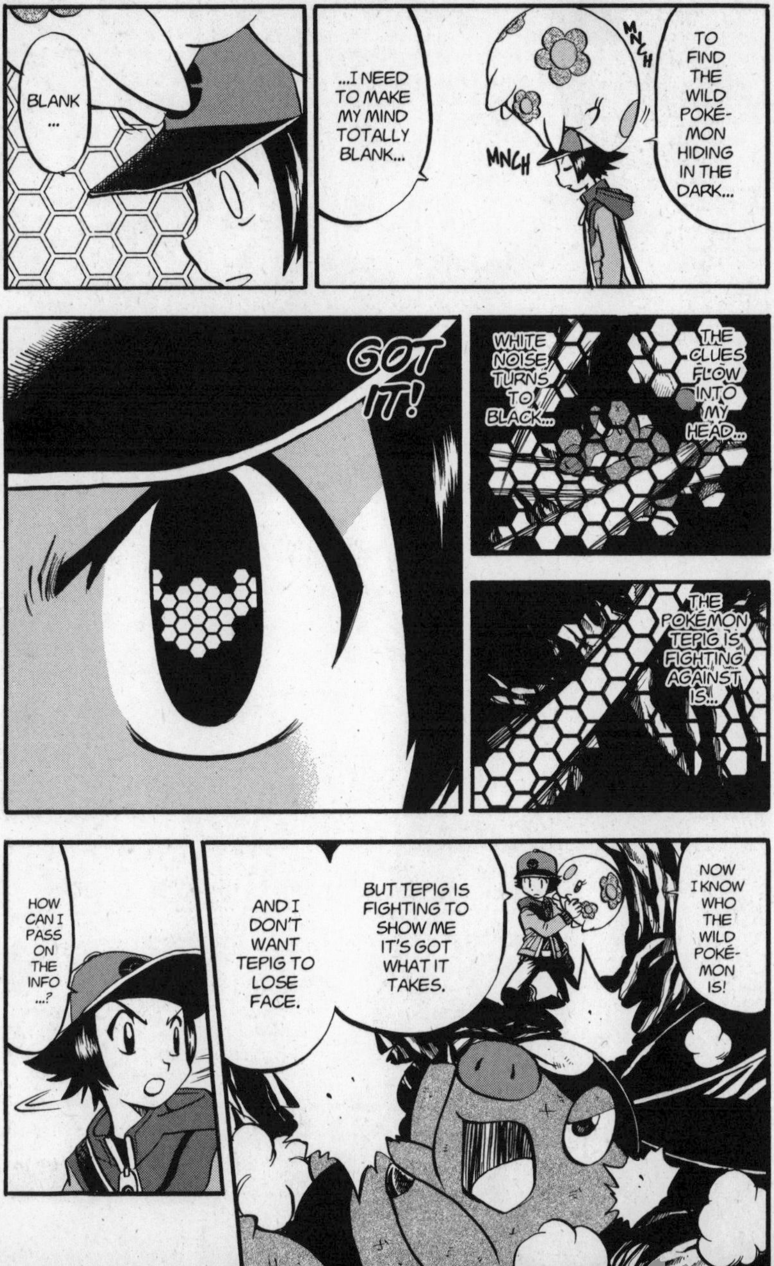

BLANK ...
...I NEED TO MAKE MY MIND TOTALLY BLANK...
MNCH
MNCH
TO FIND THE WILD POKÉMON HIDING IN THE DARK...
GOT IT!
WHITE NOISE TURNS TO BLACK...
THE CLUES FLOW INTO MY HEAD...
THE POKÉMON TEPIG IS FIGHTING AGAINST IS...
HOW CAN I PASS ON THE INFO ...?
AND I DON'T WANT TEPIG TO LOSE FACE.
BUT TEPIG IS FIGHTING TO SHOW ME IT'S GOT WHAT IT TAKES.
NOW I KNOW WHO THE WILD POKÉMON IS!

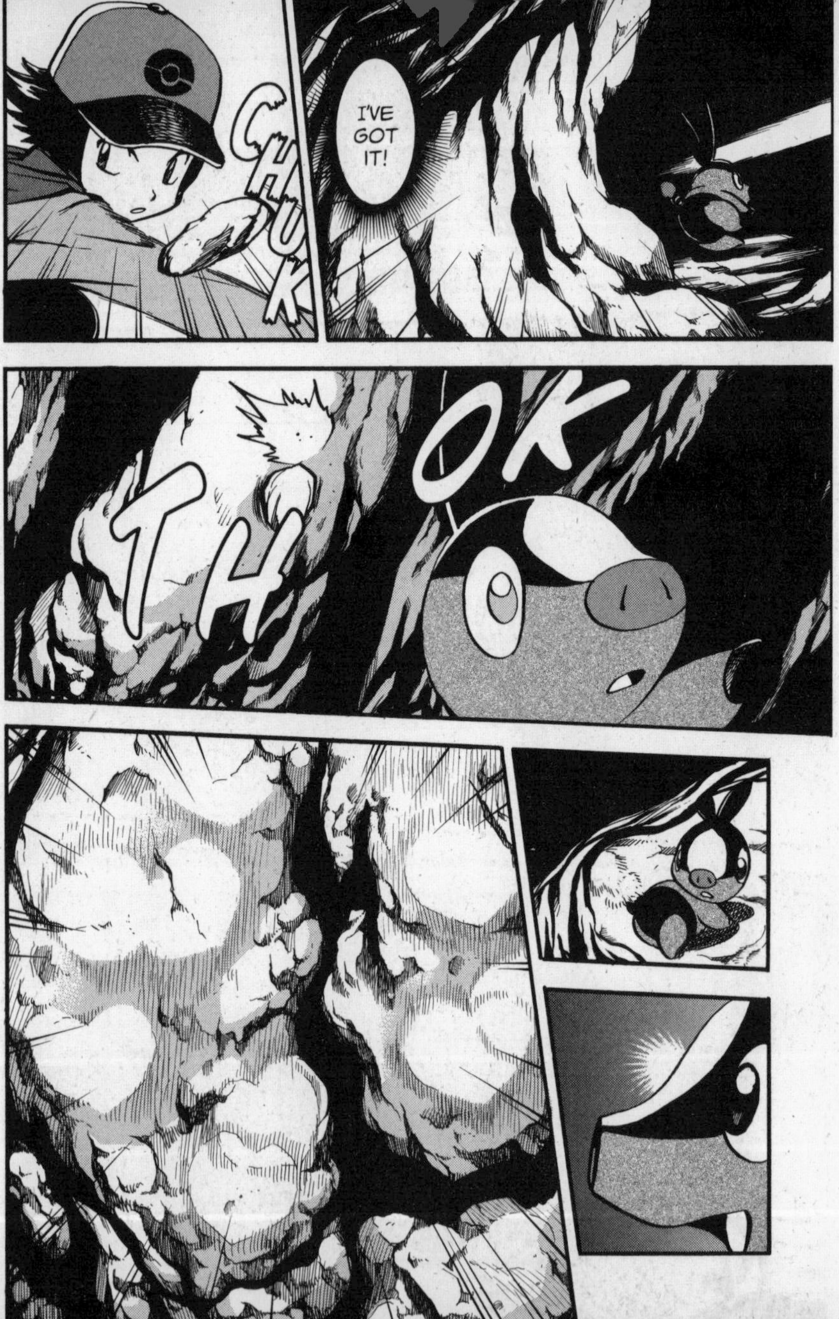
I'VE GOT IT!
CHUK
THOK

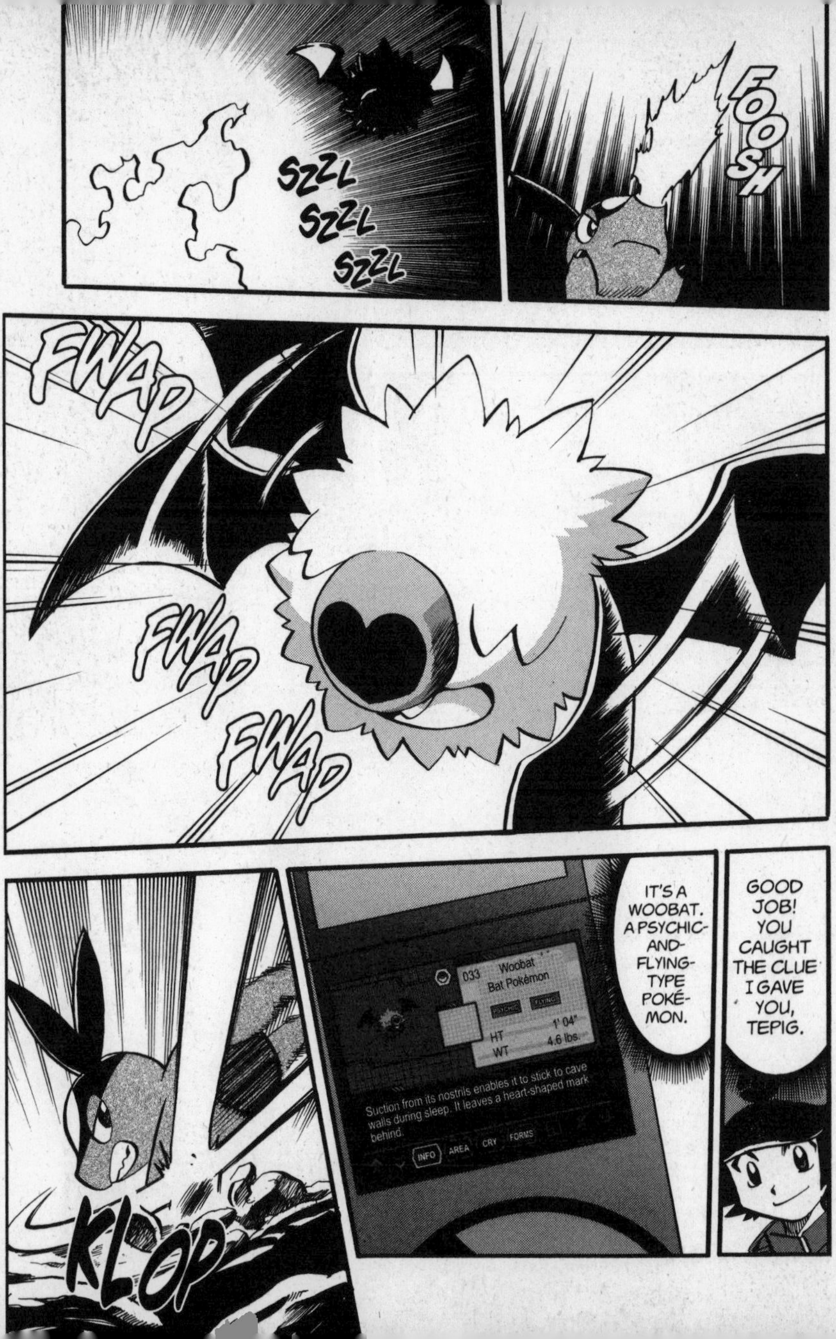
SZZL
SZZL
SZZL
FOOSH
FWAP
FWAP
FWAP
KLOP
033 Woobat
Bat Pokémon
PSYCHIC
FLYING
HT 1' 04"
WT 4.6 lbs.
Suction from its nostrils enables it to stick to cave walls during sleep. It leaves a heart-shaped mark behind.
INFO AREA CRY FORMS
IT'S A WOOBAT. A PSYCHIC-AND-FLYING-TYPE POKÉMON.
GOOD JOB! YOU CAUGHT THE CLUE I GAVE YOU, TEPIG.

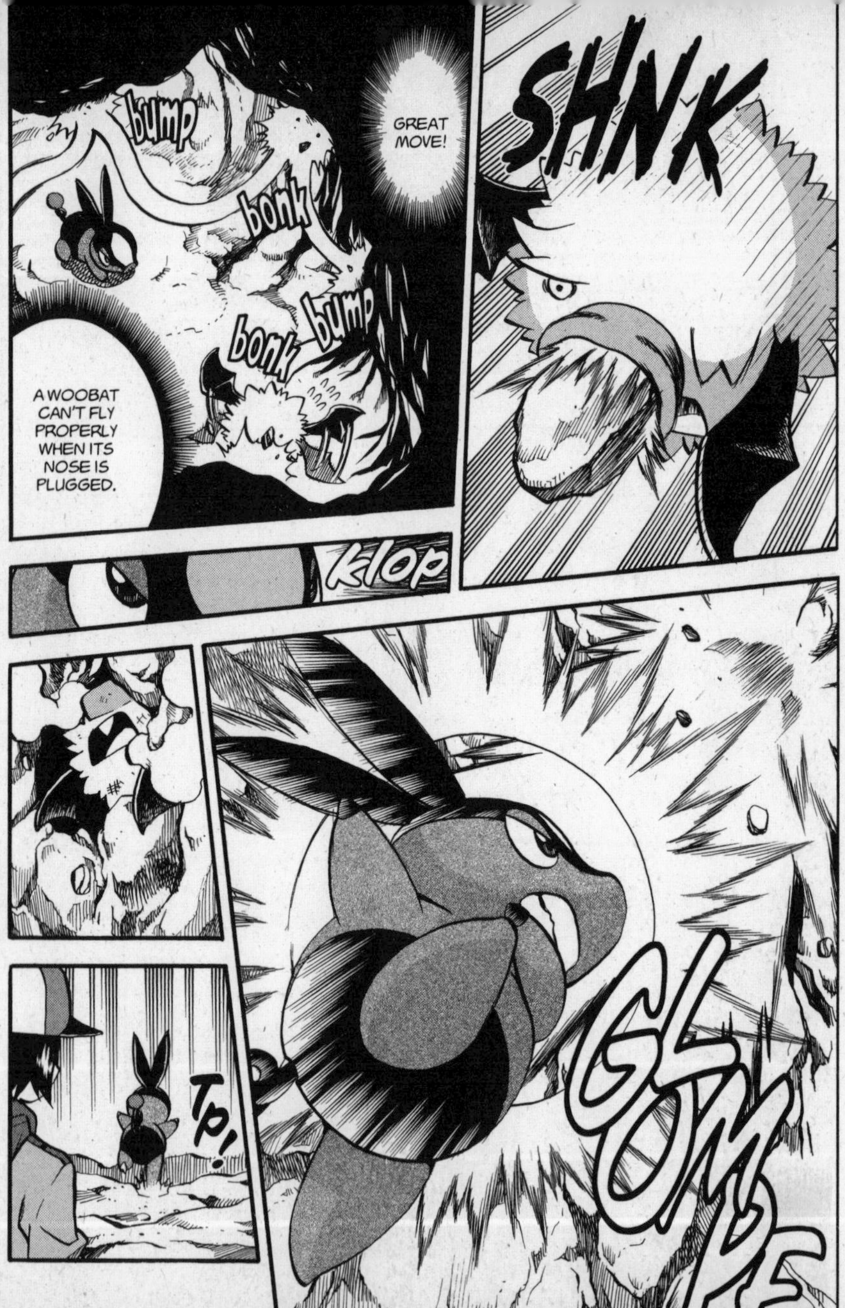
SHNK
GREAT MOVE!
bump
bonk
bump
bonk
A WOOBAT CAN'T FLY PROPERLY WHEN ITS NOSE IS PLUGGED.
klop
GLOMPF
Tp!

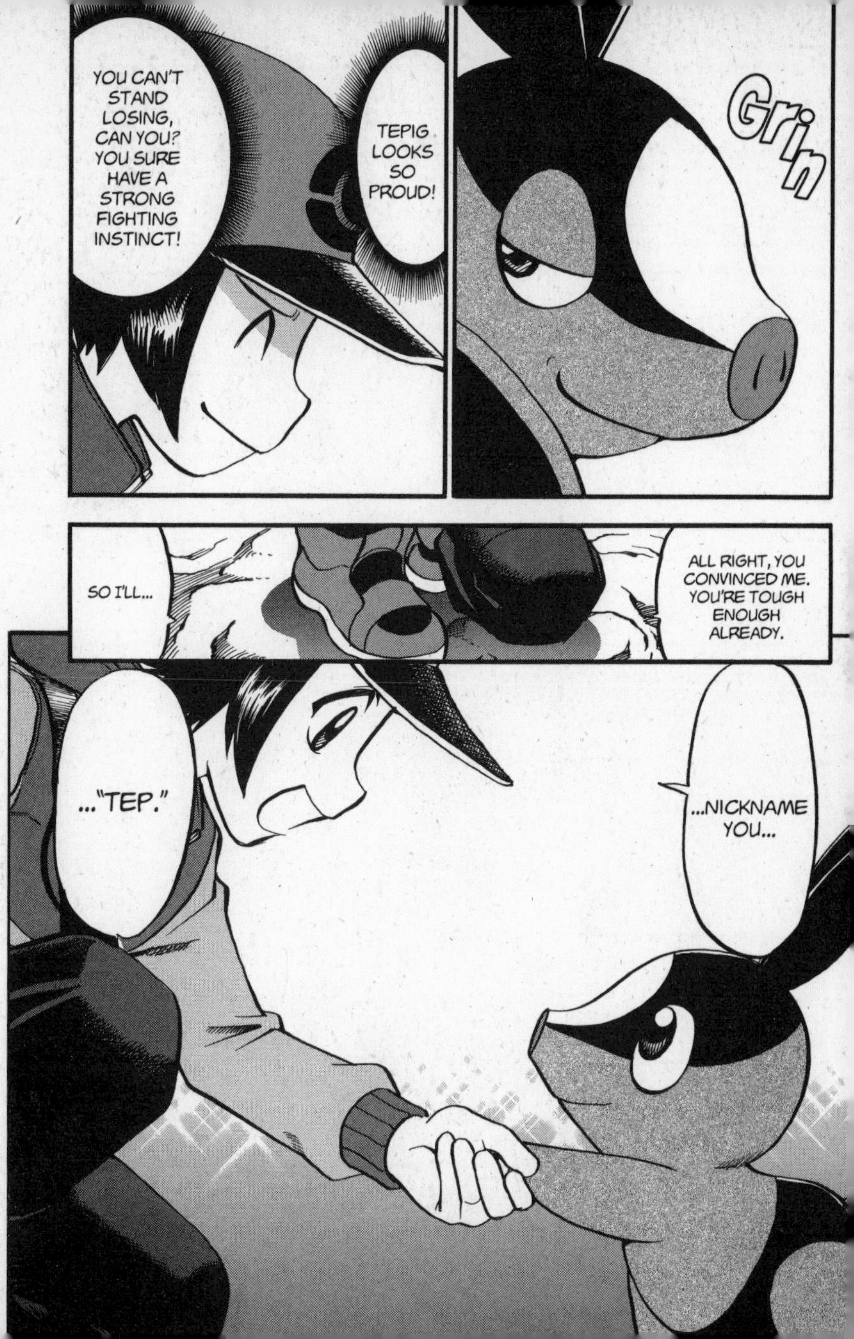
YOU CAN'T STAND LOSING, CAN YOU? YOU SURE HAVE A STRONG FIGHTING INSTINCT!
TEPIG LOOKS SO PROUD!
Grin
ALL RIGHT, YOU CONVINCED ME. YOU'RE TOUGH ENOUGH ALREADY.
SO I'LL...
...NICKNAME YOU...
..."TEP."

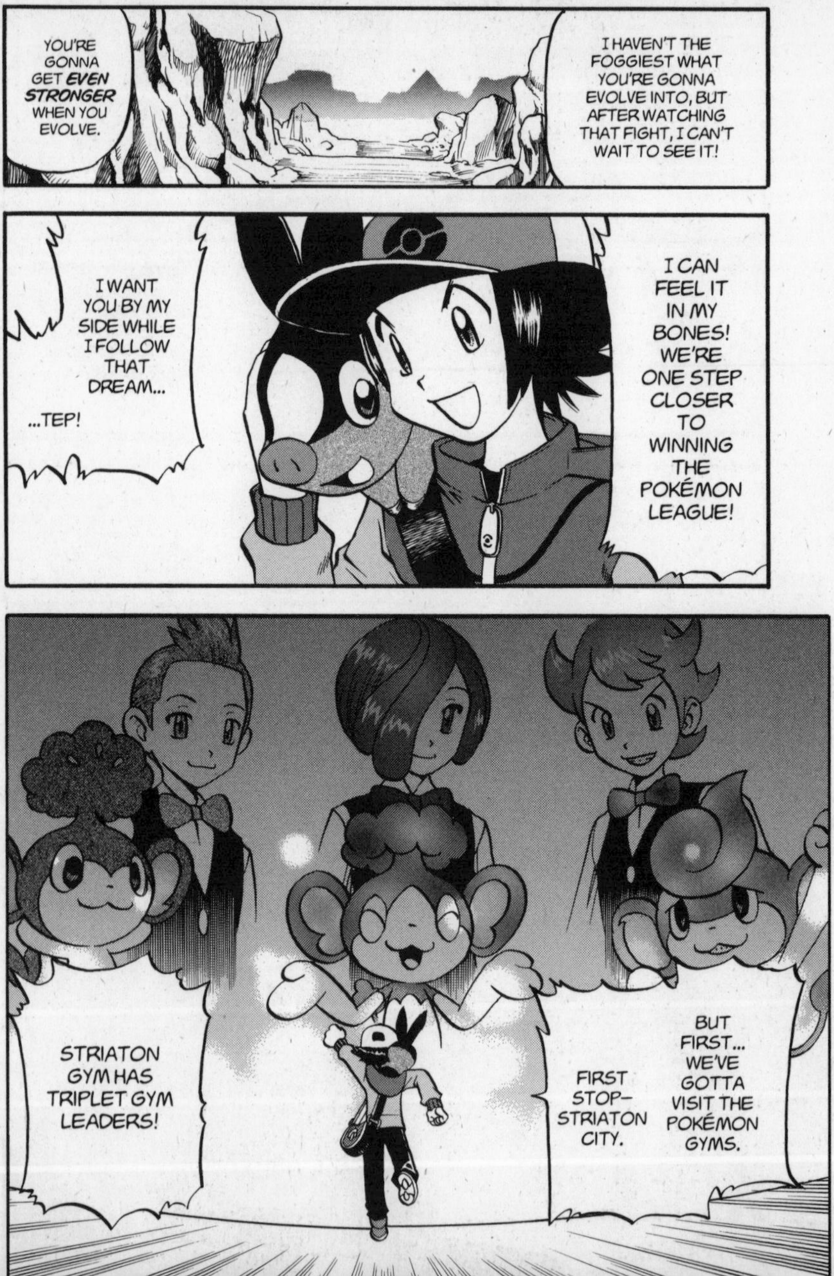
YOU'RE GONNA GET ***EVEN STRONGER*** WHEN YOU EVOLVE.
I HAVEN'T THE FOGGIEST WHAT YOU'RE GONNA EVOLVE INTO, BUT AFTER WATCHING THAT FIGHT, I CAN'T WAIT TO SEE IT!
I WANT YOU BY MY SIDE WHILE I FOLLOW THAT DREAM...
...TEP!
I CAN FEEL IT IN MY BONES! WE'RE ONE STEP CLOSER TO WINNING THE POKÉMON LEAGUE!
STRIATON GYM HAS TRIPLET GYM LEADERS!
FIRST STOP— STRIATON CITY.
BUT FIRST... WE'VE GOTTA VISIT THE POKÉMON GYMS.

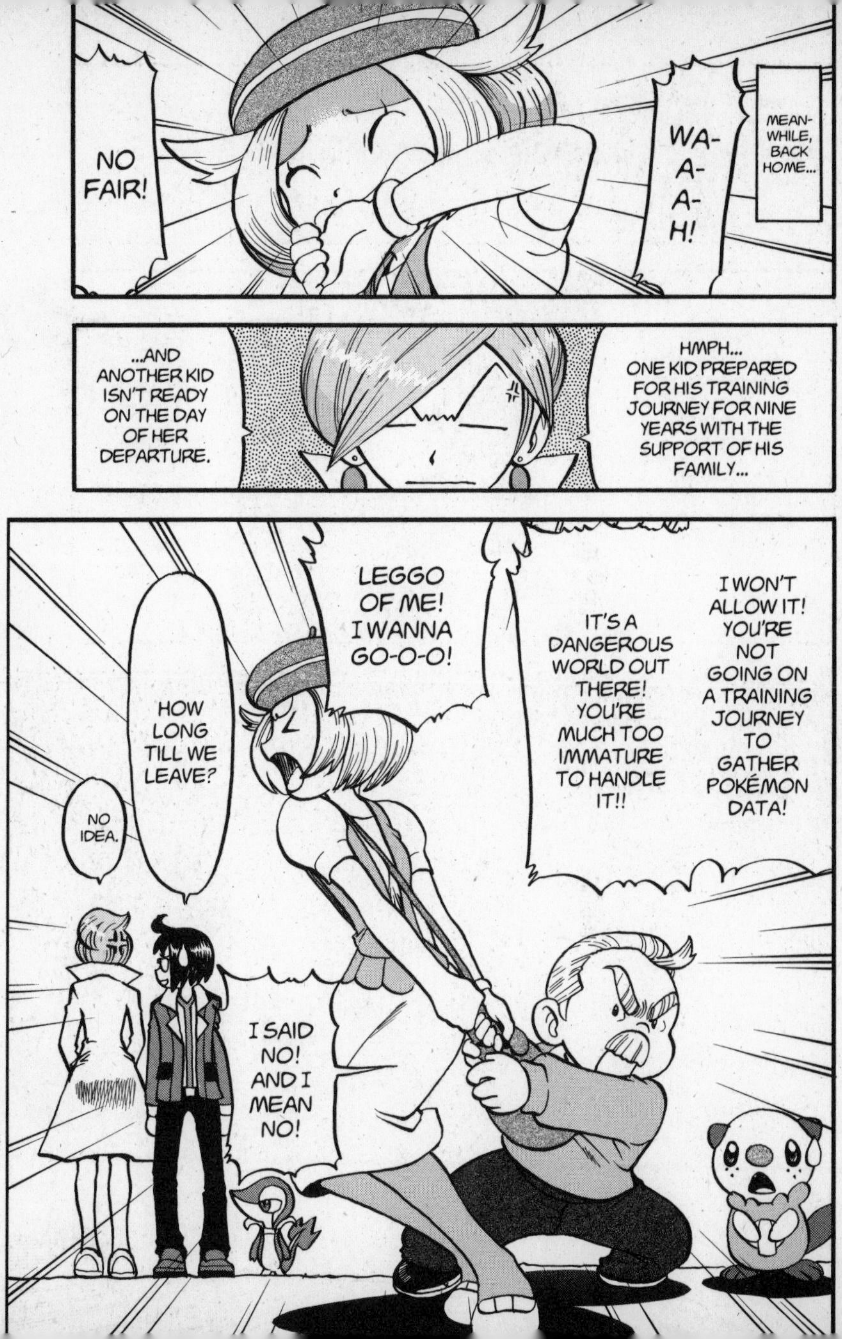
MEAN-WHILE, BACK HOME...
WA-A-A-H!
NO FAIR!
HMPH... ONE KID PREPARED FOR HIS TRAINING JOURNEY FOR NINE YEARS WITH THE SUPPORT OF HIS FAMILY...
...AND ANOTHER KID ISN'T READY ON THE DAY OF HER DEPARTURE.
I WON'T ALLOW IT! YOU'RE NOT GOING ON A TRAINING JOURNEY TO GATHER POKÉMON DATA!
IT'S A DANGEROUS WORLD OUT THERE! YOU'RE MUCH TOO IMMATURE TO HANDLE IT!!
LEGGO OF ME! I WANNA GO-O-O!
HOW LONG TILL WE LEAVE?
NO IDEA.
I SAID NO! AND I MEAN NO!

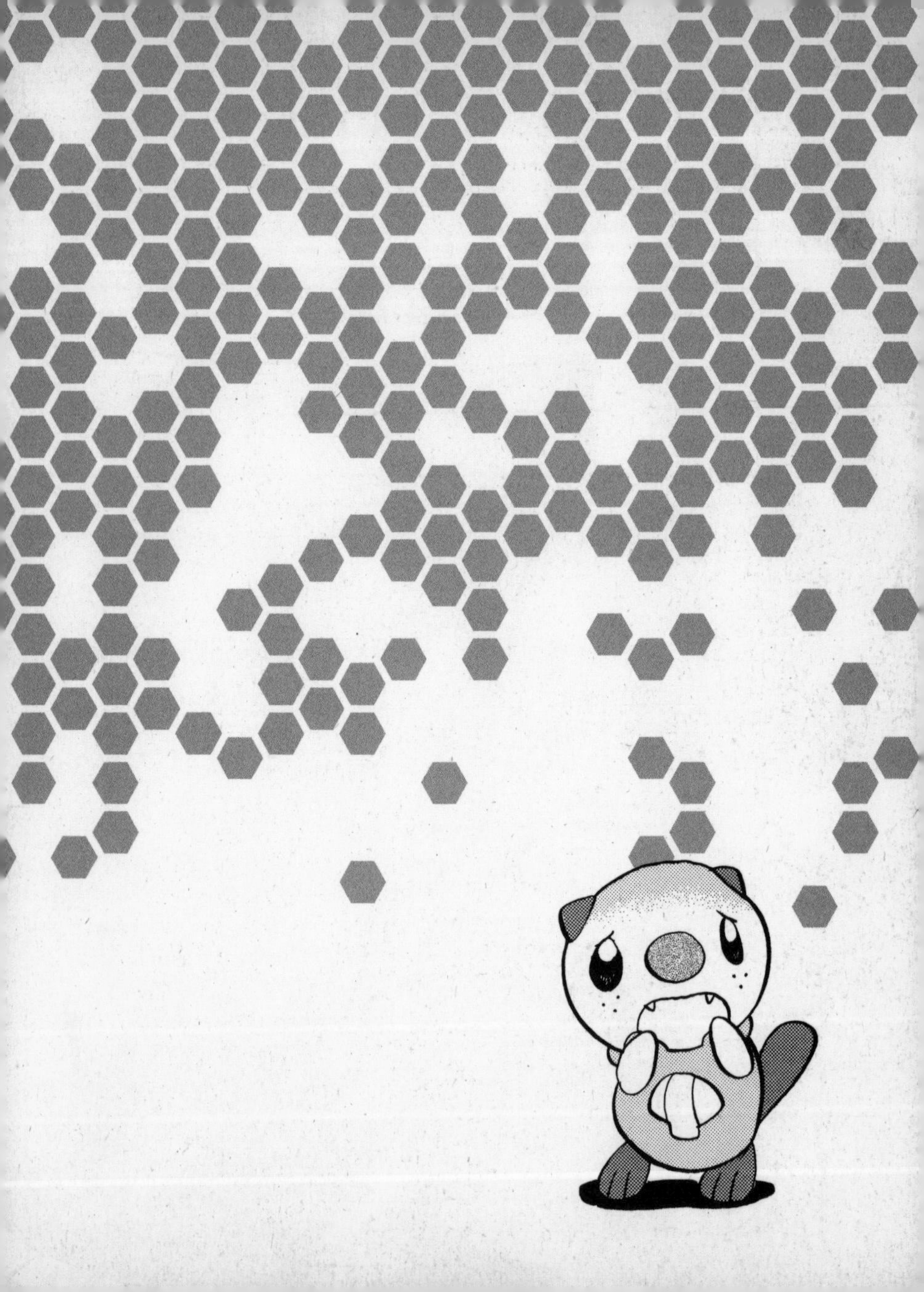

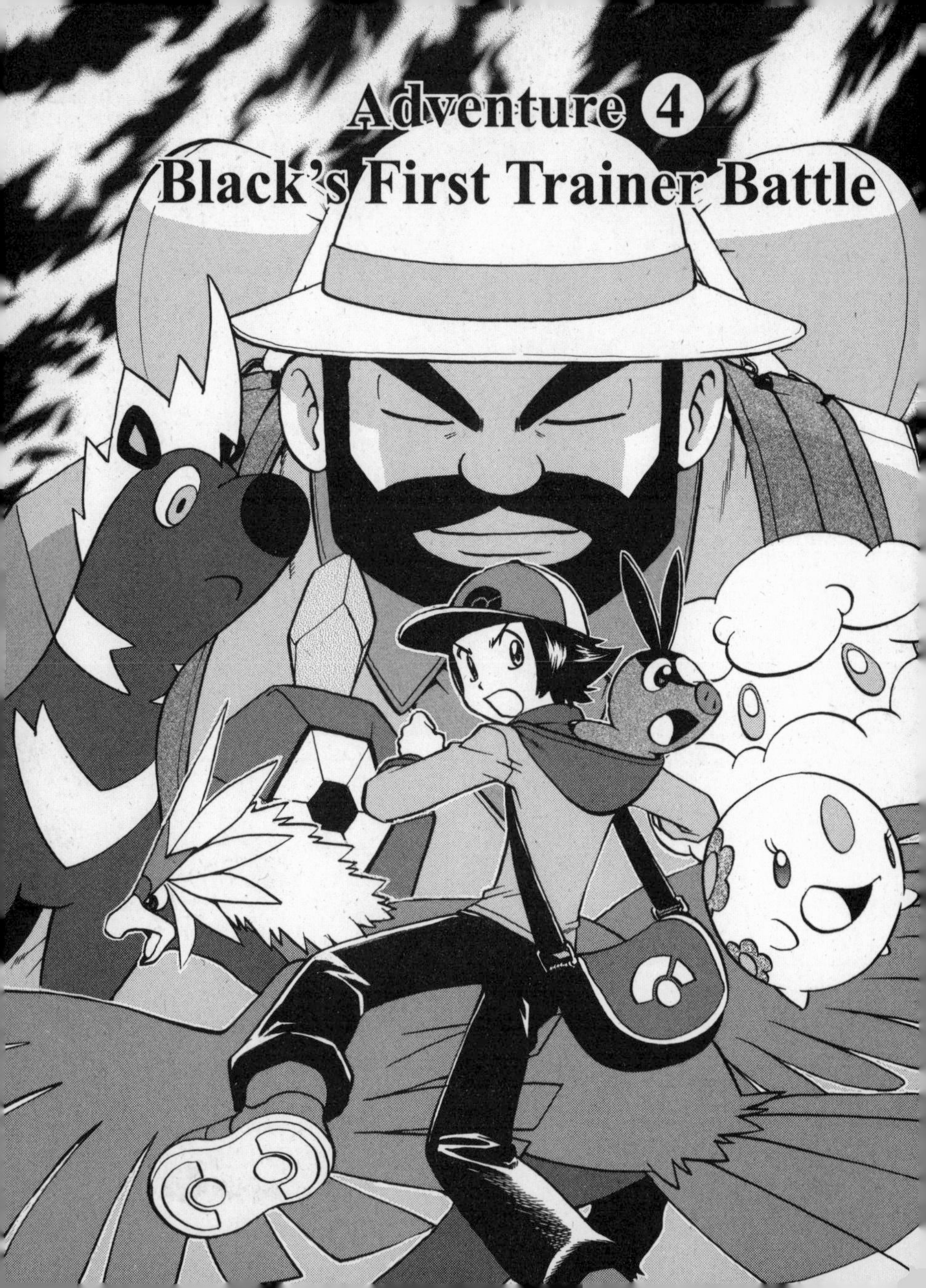
Adventure 4
Black's First Trainer Battle

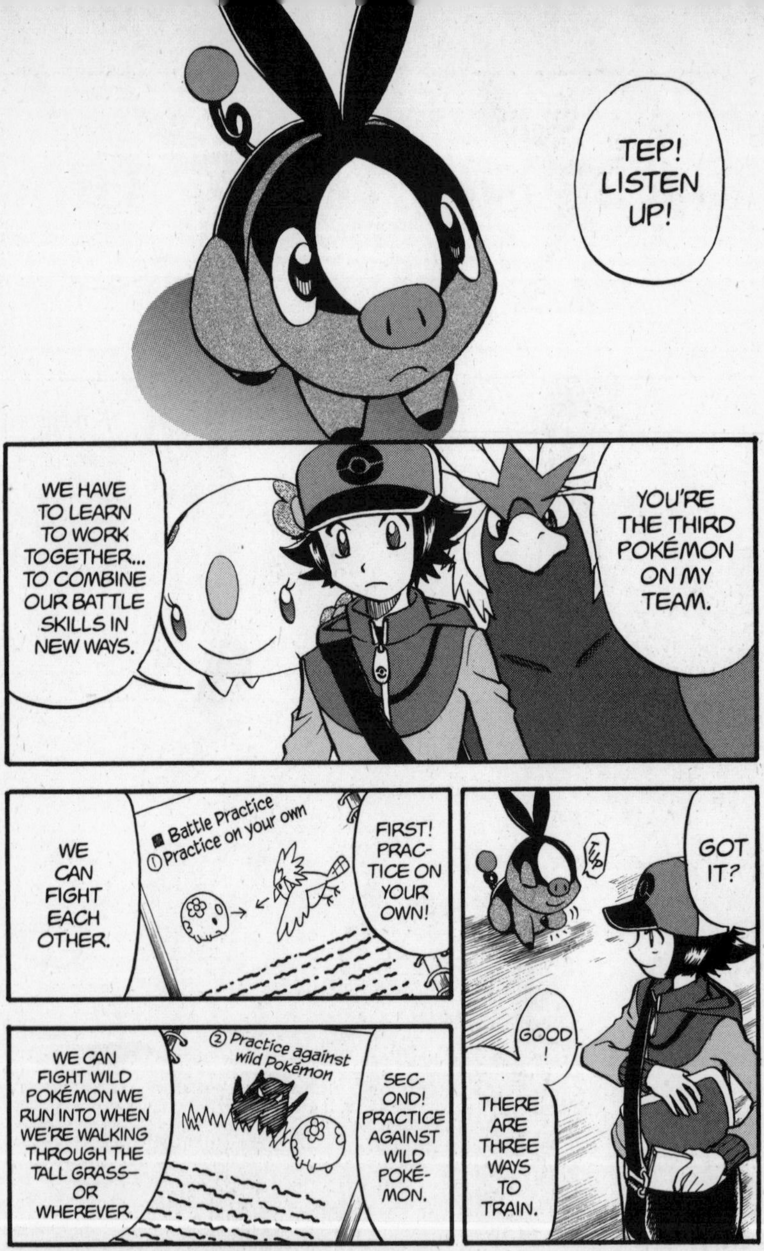
TEP! LISTEN UP!
YOU'RE THE THIRD POKÉMON ON MY TEAM.
WE HAVE TO LEARN TO WORK TOGETHER... TO COMBINE OUR BATTLE SKILLS IN NEW WAYS.
THERE ARE THREE WAYS TO TRAIN.
Battle Practice
① Practice on your own
FIRST! PRACTICE ON YOUR OWN!
WE CAN FIGHT EACH OTHER.
② Practice against wild Pokémon
SECOND! PRACTICE AGAINST WILD POKÉMON.
WE CAN FIGHT WILD POKÉMON WE RUN INTO WHEN WE'RE WALKING THROUGH THE TALL GRASS— OR WHEREVER.
GOT IT?
TEP
GOOD!

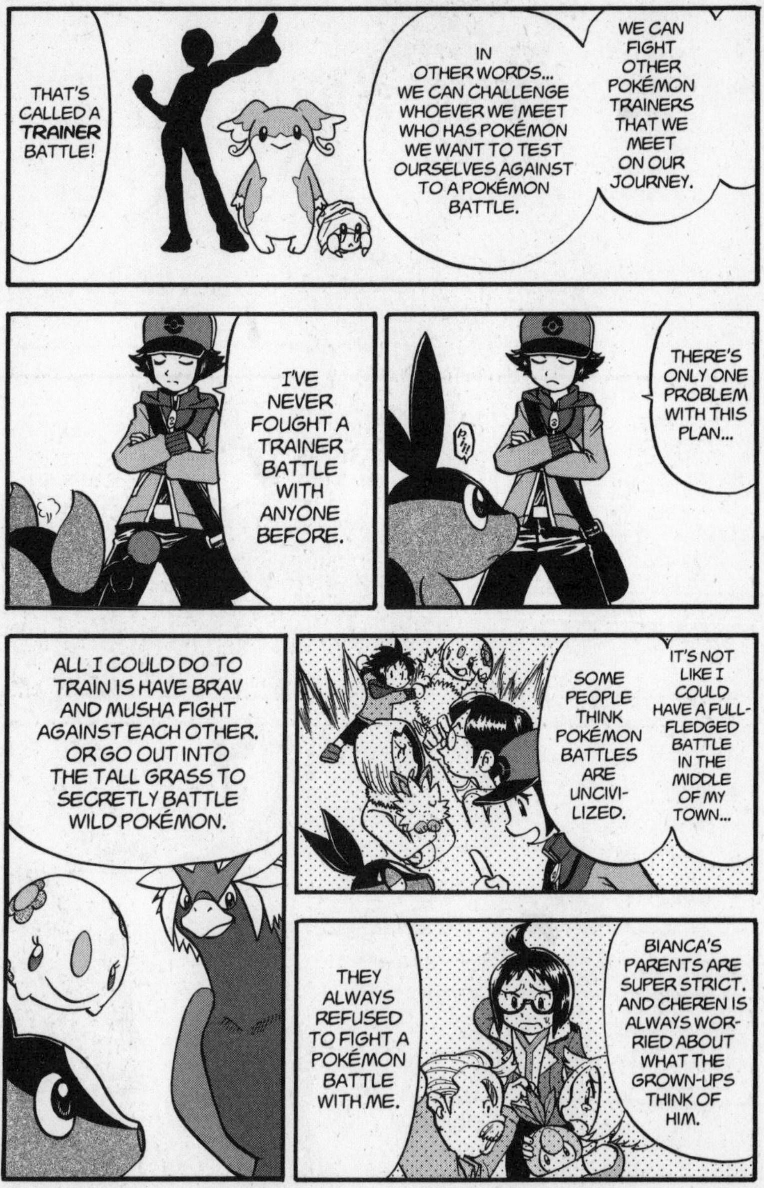
WE CAN FIGHT OTHER POKÉMON TRAINERS THAT WE MEET ON OUR JOURNEY.
IN OTHER WORDS... WE CAN CHALLENGE WHOEVER WE MEET WHO HAS POKÉMON WE WANT TO TEST OURSELVES AGAINST TO A POKÉMON BATTLE.
THAT'S CALLED A TRAINER BATTLE!
THERE'S ONLY ONE PROBLEM WITH THIS PLAN...
I'VE NEVER FOUGHT A TRAINER BATTLE WITH ANYONE BEFORE.
IT'S NOT LIKE I COULD HAVE A FULL-FLEDGED BATTLE IN THE MIDDLE OF MY TOWN...
SOME PEOPLE THINK POKÉMON BATTLES ARE UNCIVILIZED.
BIANCA'S PARENTS ARE SUPER STRICT. AND CHEREN IS ALWAYS WORRIED ABOUT WHAT THE GROWN-UPS THINK OF HIM.
THEY ALWAYS REFUSED TO FIGHT A POKÉMON BATTLE WITH ME.
ALL I COULD DO TO TRAIN IS HAVE BRAV AND MUSHA FIGHT AGAINST EACH OTHER. OR GO OUT INTO THE TALL GRASS TO SECRETLY BATTLE WILD POKÉMON.

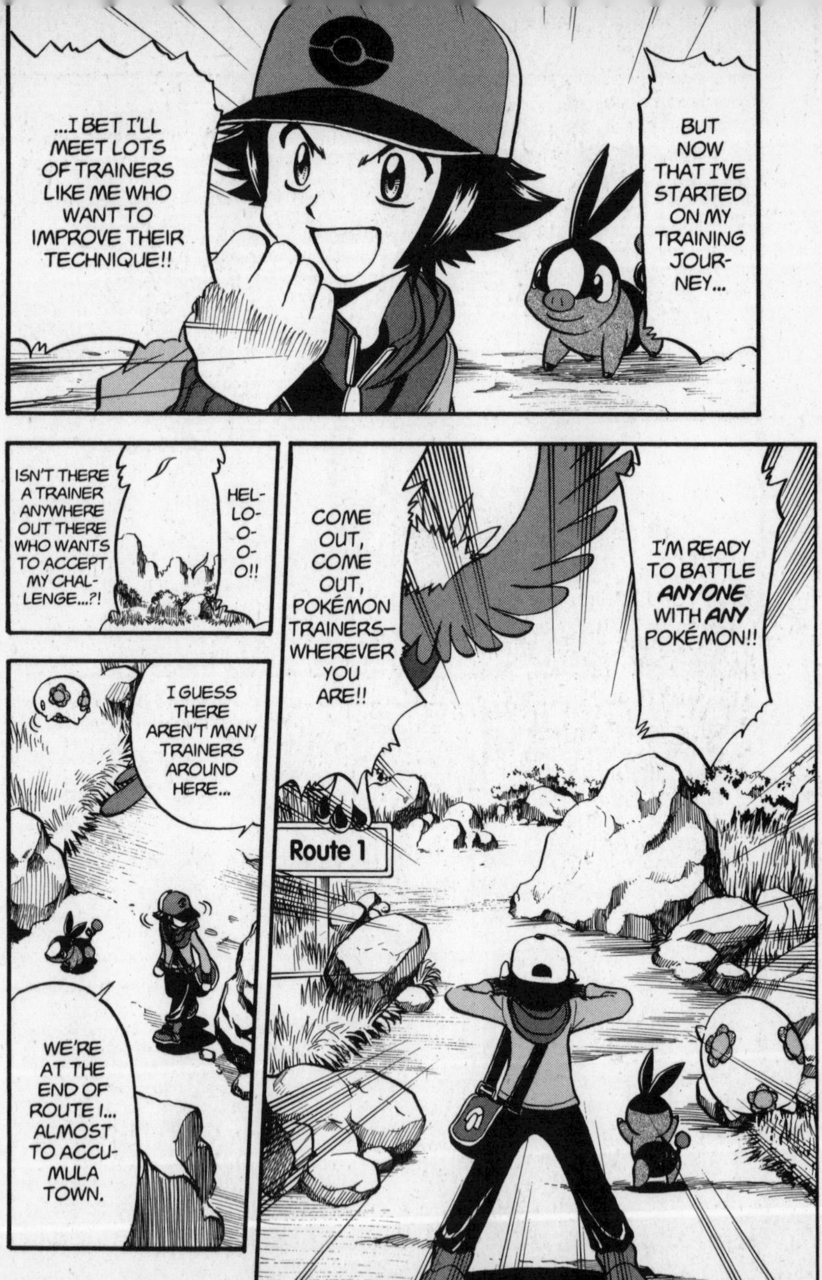
BUT NOW THAT I'VE STARTED ON MY TRAINING JOURNEY...
...I BET I'LL MEET LOTS OF TRAINERS LIKE ME WHO WANT TO IMPROVE THEIR TECHNIQUE!!
I'M READY TO BATTLE ANYONE WITH ANY POKÉMON!!
COME OUT, COME OUT, POKÉMON TRAINERS—WHEREVER YOU ARE!!
HEL-LO-O-O-O!!
ISN'T THERE A TRAINER ANYWHERE OUT THERE WHO WANTS TO ACCEPT MY CHALLENGE...?!
Route 1
I GUESS THERE AREN'T MANY TRAINERS AROUND HERE...
WE'RE AT THE END OF ROUTE 1... ALMOST TO ACCUMULA TOWN.

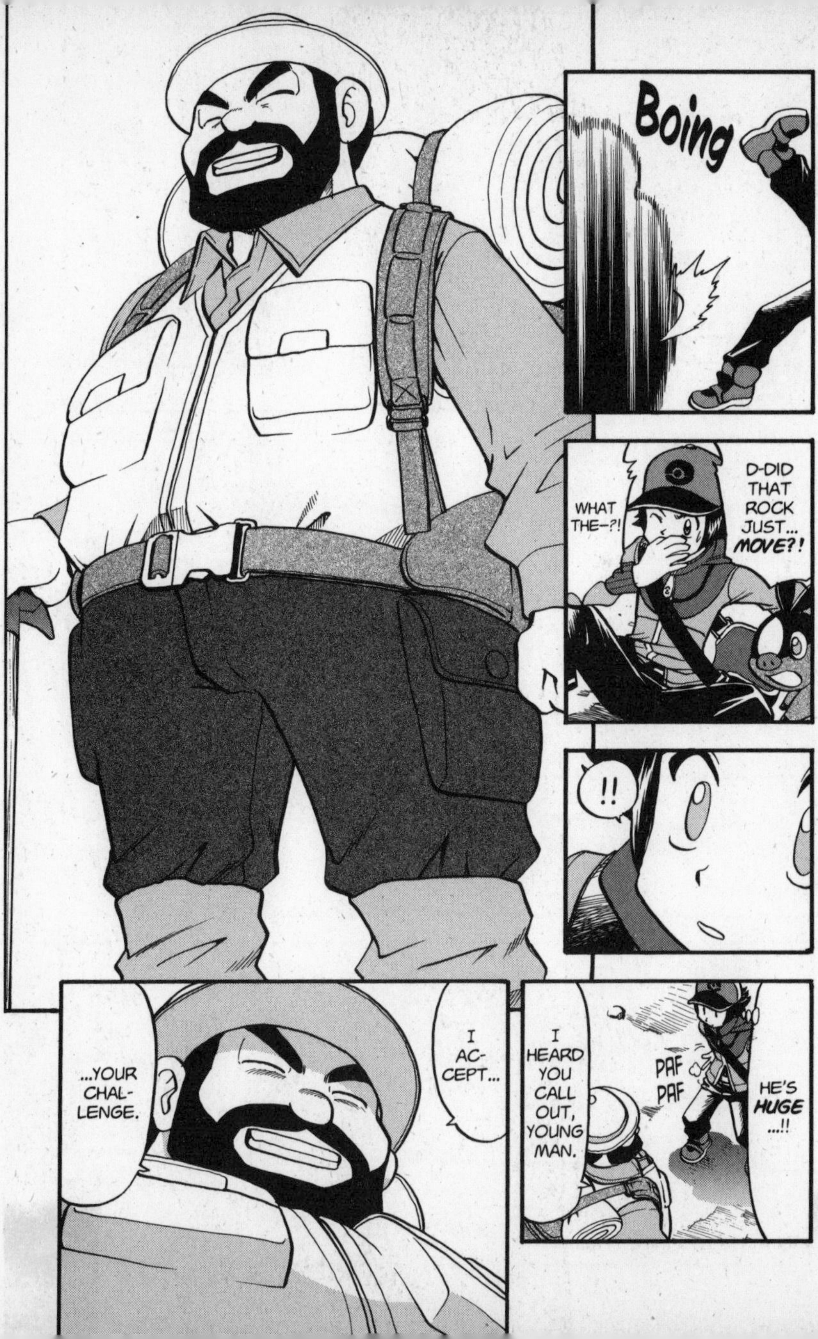
Boing
D-DID THAT ROCK JUST... MOVE?!
WHAT THE-?!
!!
HE'S HUGE ...!!
PAF PAF
I HEARD YOU CALL OUT, YOUNG MAN.
I AC-CEPT...
...YOUR CHAL-LENGE.

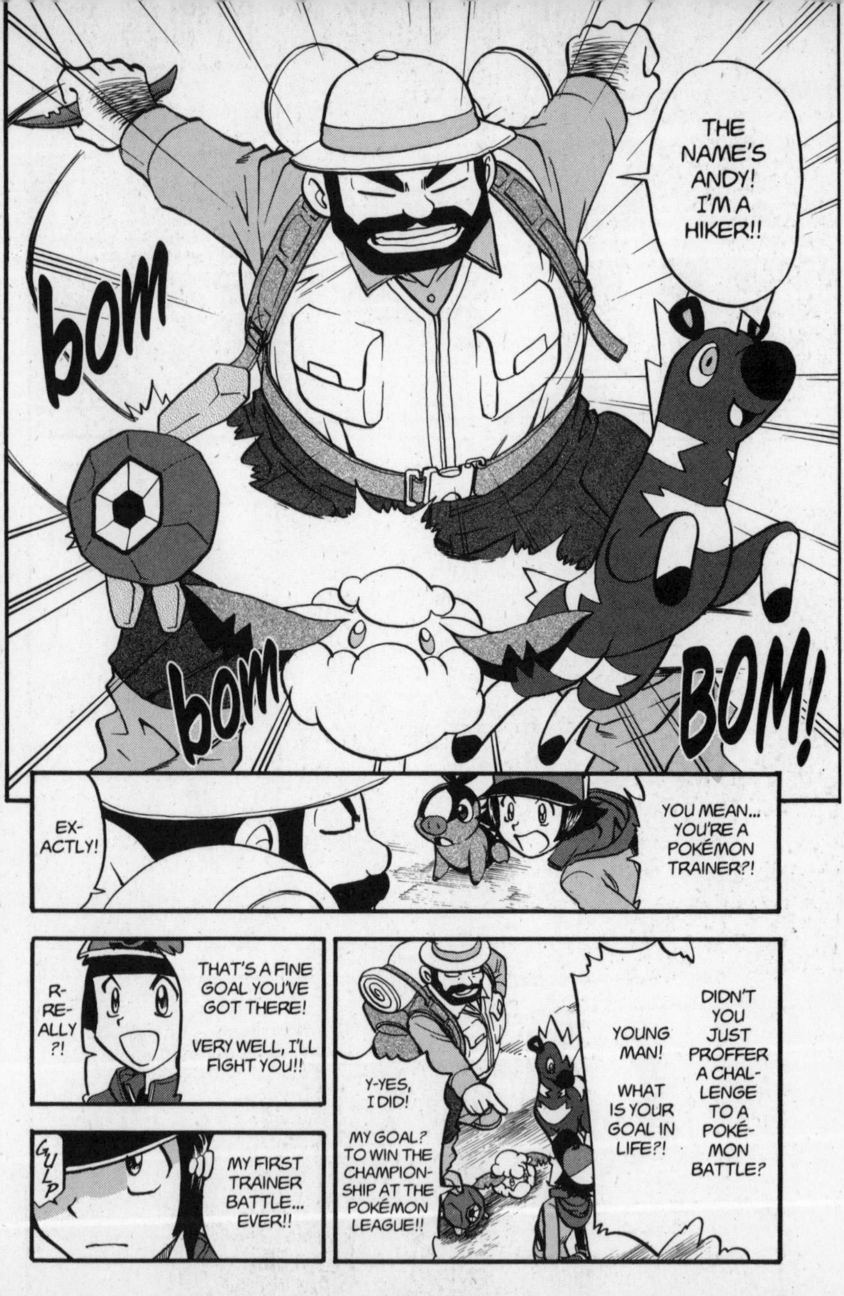
bom
THE NAME'S ANDY! I'M A HIKER!!
bom
BOM!
YOU MEAN... YOU'RE A POKÉMON TRAINER?!
EX-ACTLY!
DIDN'T YOU JUST PROFFER A CHAL-LENGE TO A POKÉ-MON BATTLE?
Y-YES, I DID!
YOUNG MAN!
WHAT IS YOUR GOAL IN LIFE?!
MY GOAL? TO WIN THE CHAMPION-SHIP AT THE POKÉMON LEAGUE!!
THAT'S A FINE GOAL YOU'VE GOT THERE!
VERY WELL, I'LL FIGHT YOU!!
R-RE-ALLY?!
GULP
MY FIRST TRAINER BATTLE... EVER!!

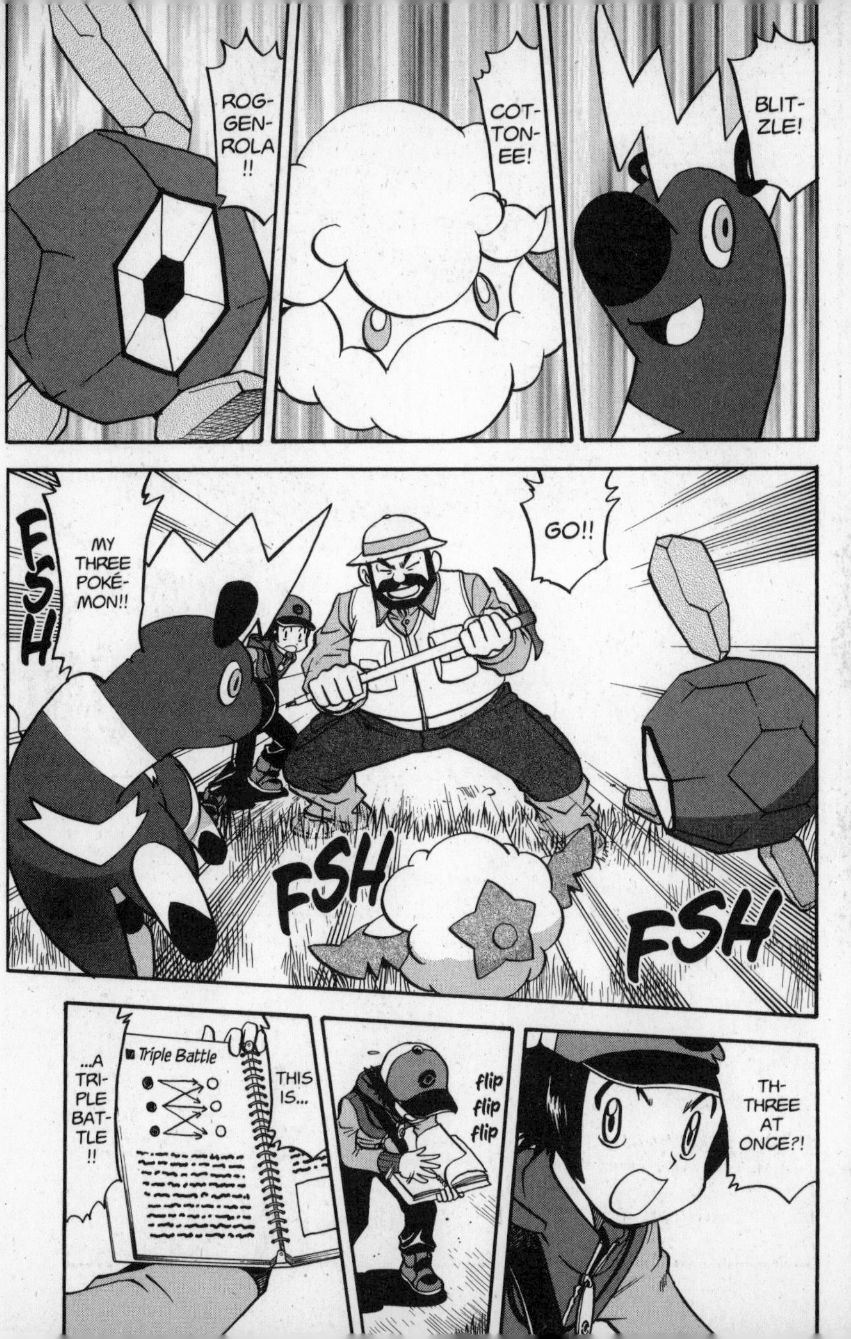
ROG-GEN-ROLA!!
COT-TON-EE!
BLIT-ZLE!
FSH
MY THREE POKÉ-MON!!
GO!!
FSH
FSH
...A TRI-PLE BAT-TLE!!
Triple Battle
THIS IS...
flip flip flip
TH-THREE AT ONCE?!

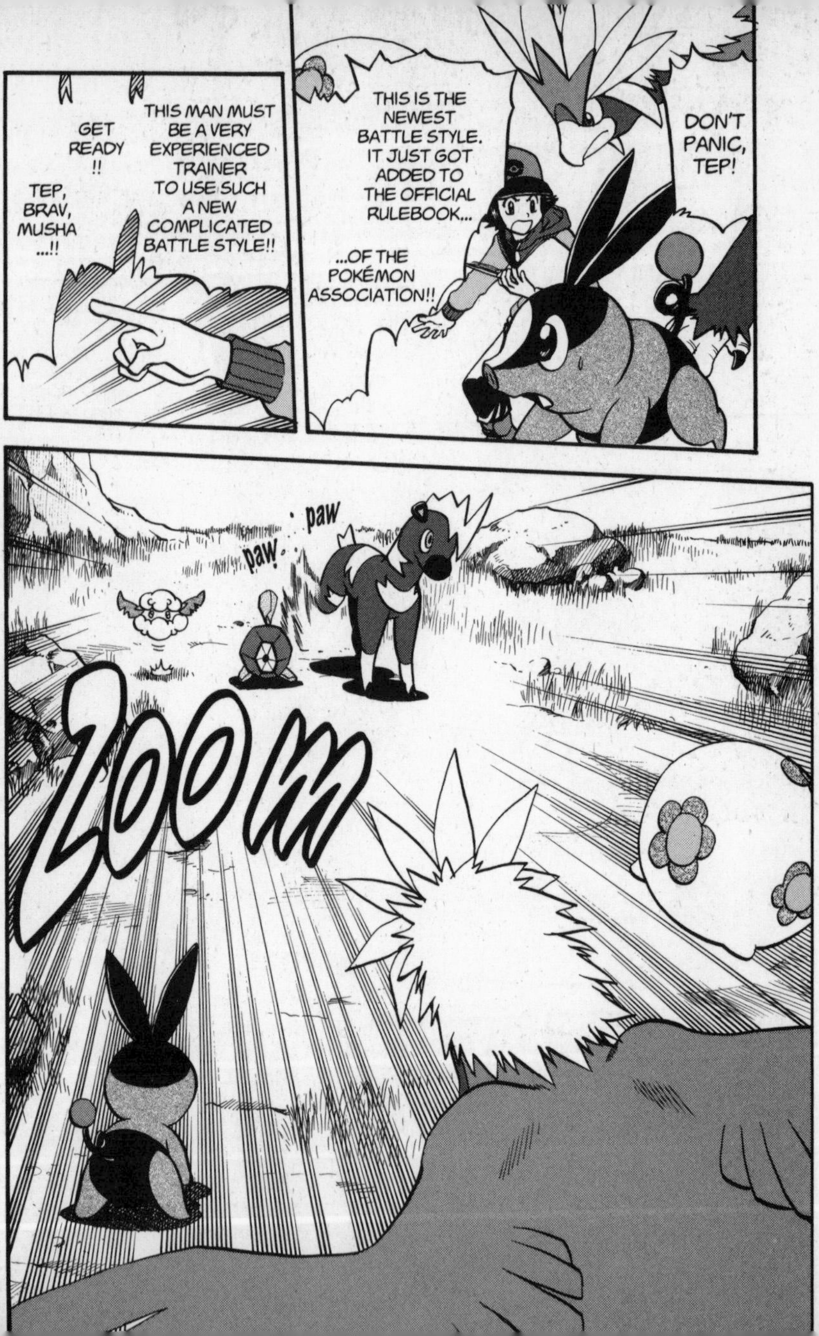
THIS MAN MUST BE A VERY EXPERIENCED TRAINER TO USE SUCH A NEW COMPLICATED BATTLE STYLE!!
GET READY!!
TEP, BRAV, MUSHA...!!
THIS IS THE NEWEST BATTLE STYLE. IT JUST GOT ADDED TO THE OFFICIAL RULEBOOK...
...OF THE POKÉMON ASSOCIATION!!
DON'T PANIC, TEP!
paw
paw
ZOOM

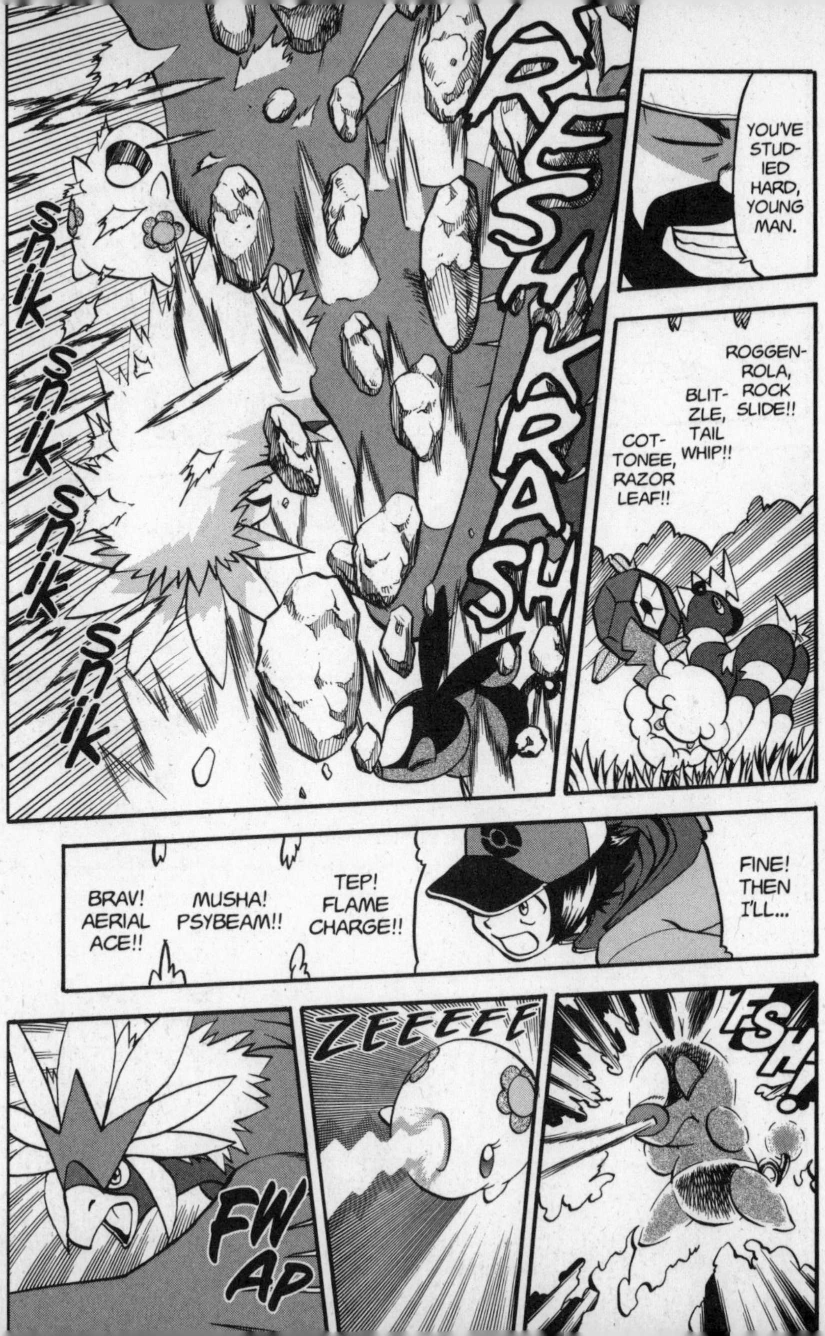

YOU'VE STUDIED HARD, YOUNG MAN.
ROGGENROLA, ROCK SLIDE!!
BLITZLE, TAIL WHIP!!
COTTONEE, RAZOR LEAF!!
KRASH
KRASH
SNIK SNIK SNIK SNIK
FINE! THEN I'LL...
TEP! FLAME CHARGE!!
MUSHA! PSYBEAM!!
BRAV! AERIAL ACE!!
FWAP
ZEEEEEE
FSH

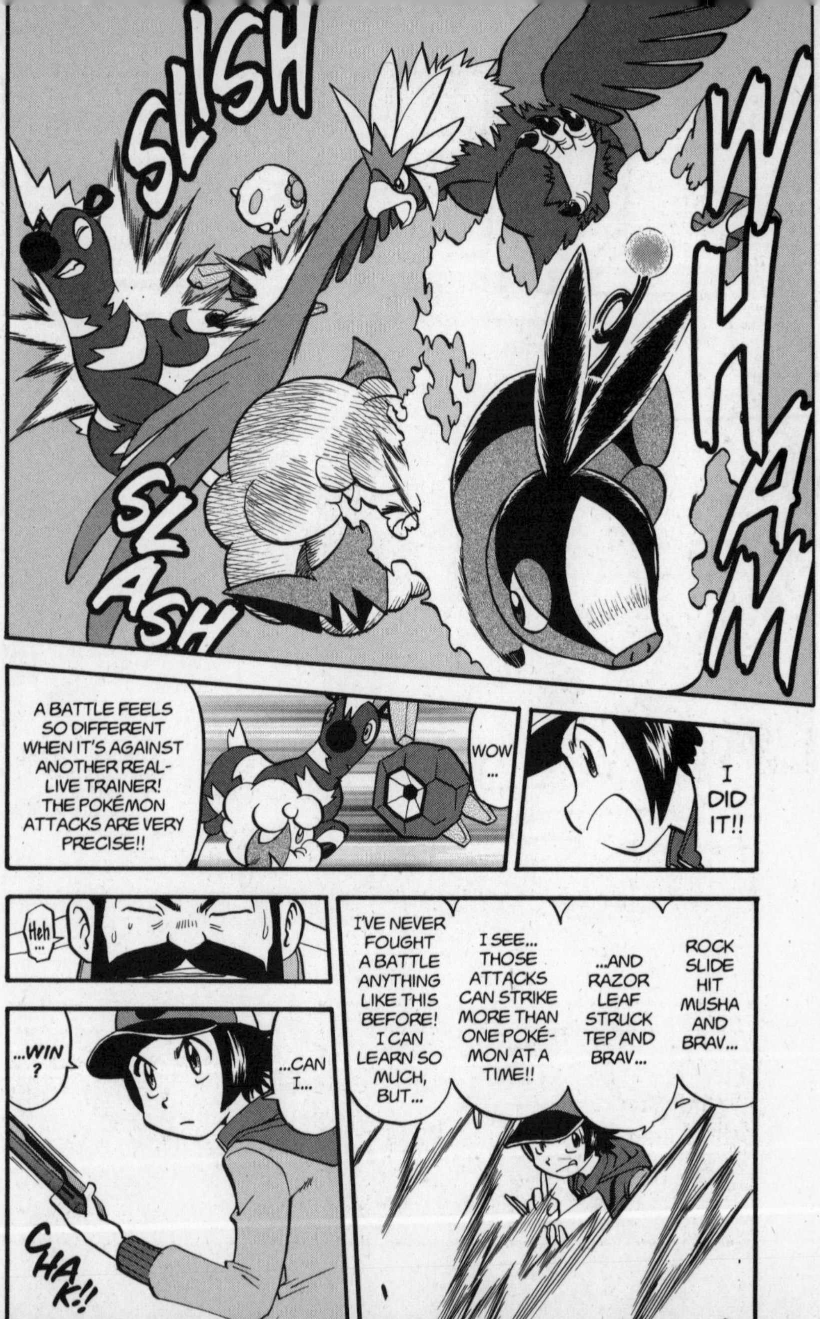
SLISH
SLASH
WHAM
A BATTLE FEELS SO DIFFERENT WHEN IT'S AGAINST ANOTHER REAL-LIVE TRAINER! THE POKÉMON ATTACKS ARE VERY PRECISE!!
WOW ...
I DID IT!!
Heh ...
ROCK SLIDE HIT MUSHA AND BRAV...
...AND RAZOR LEAF STRUCK TEP AND BRAV...
I SEE... THOSE ATTACKS CAN STRIKE MORE THAN ONE POKÉ-MON AT A TIME!!
I'VE NEVER FOUGHT A BATTLE ANYTHING LIKE THIS BEFORE! I CAN LEARN SO MUCH, BUT...
...CAN I...
...WIN ?
CHAK!!

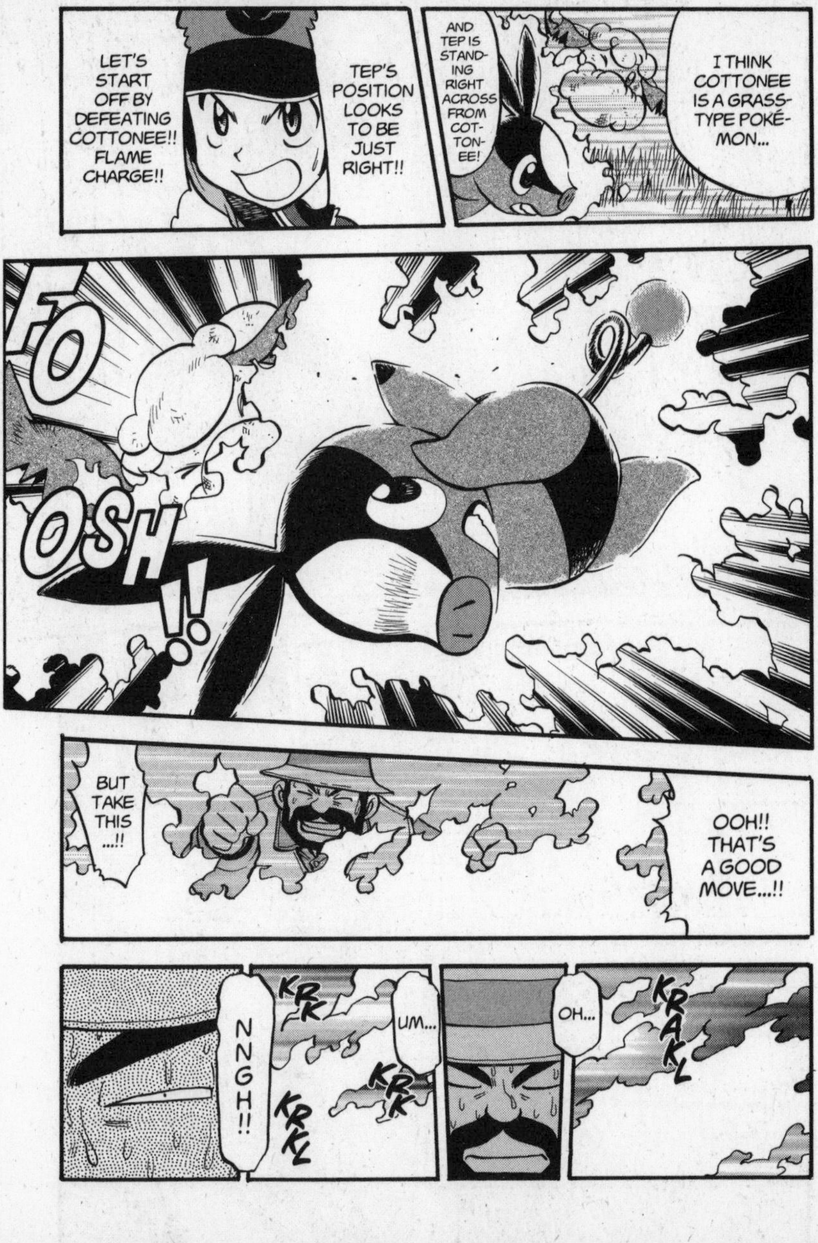
I THINK COTTONEE IS A GRASS-TYPE POKÉMON...
AND TEP IS STANDING RIGHT ACROSS FROM COTTONEE!
TEP'S POSITION LOOKS TO BE JUST RIGHT!!
LET'S START OFF BY DEFEATING COTTONEE!! FLAME CHARGE!!
FWOOSH!!
BUT TAKE THIS...!!
OOH!! THAT'S A GOOD MOVE...!!
KRAKL
OH...
UM...
KRK
KRK
KRKL
NNGH!!

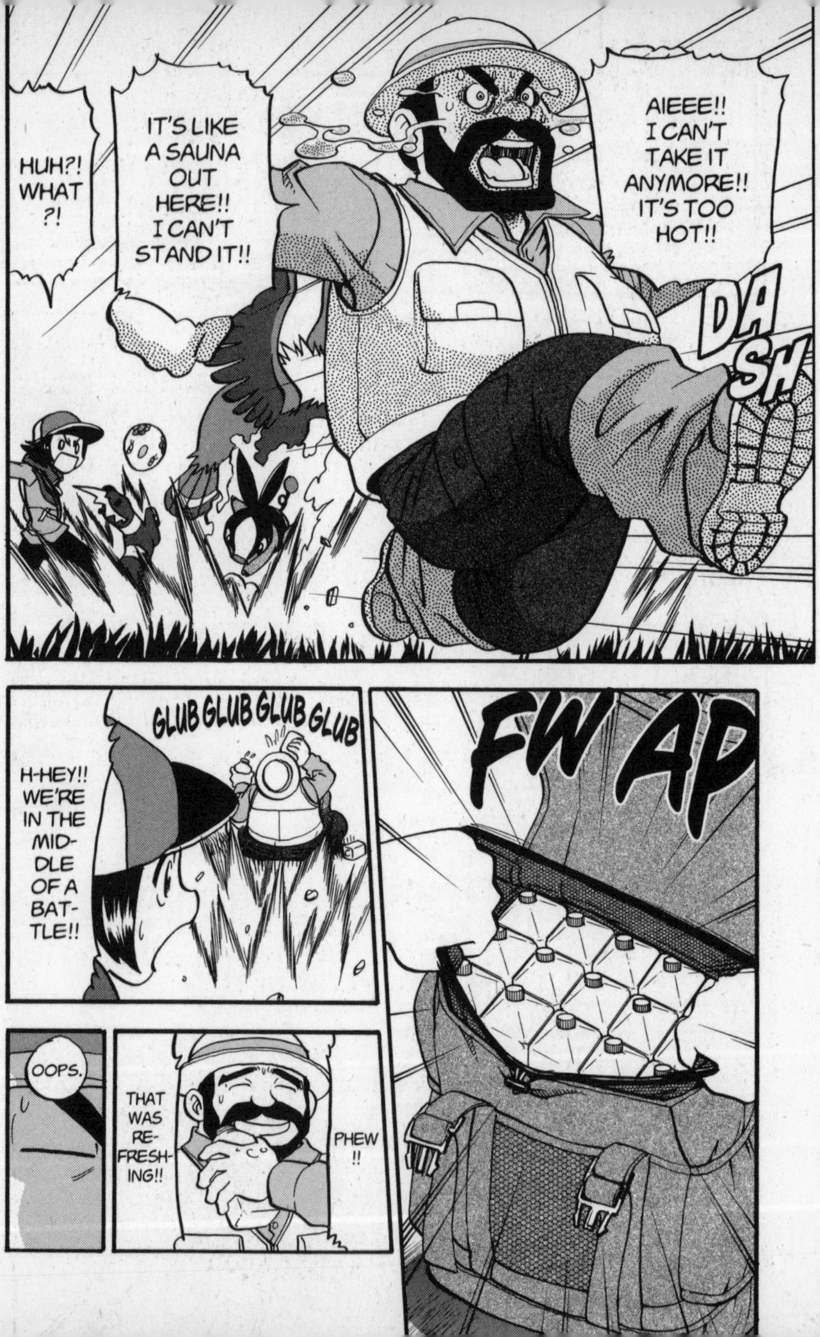
AIEEE!! I CAN'T TAKE IT ANYMORE!! IT'S TOO HOT!!
IT'S LIKE A SAUNA OUT HERE!! I CAN'T STAND IT!!
HUH?! WHAT?!
DASH
FWAP
GLUB GLUB GLUB GLUB
H-HEY!! WE'RE IN THE MIDDLE OF A BATTLE!!
PHEW!!
THAT WAS REFRESHING!!
OOPS.

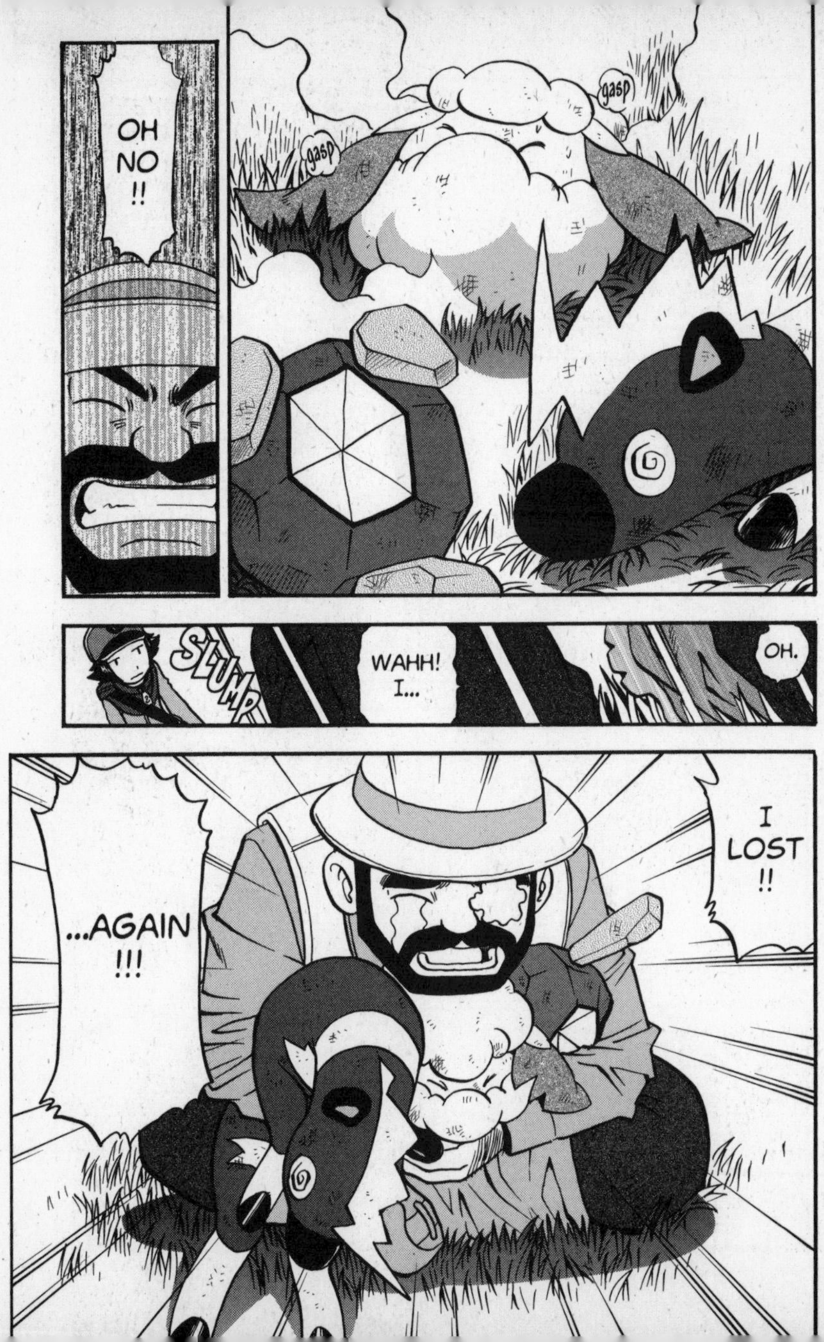
gasp
gasp
OH NO !!
SLUMP
WAHH! I...
OH.
I LOST !!
...AGAIN !!!

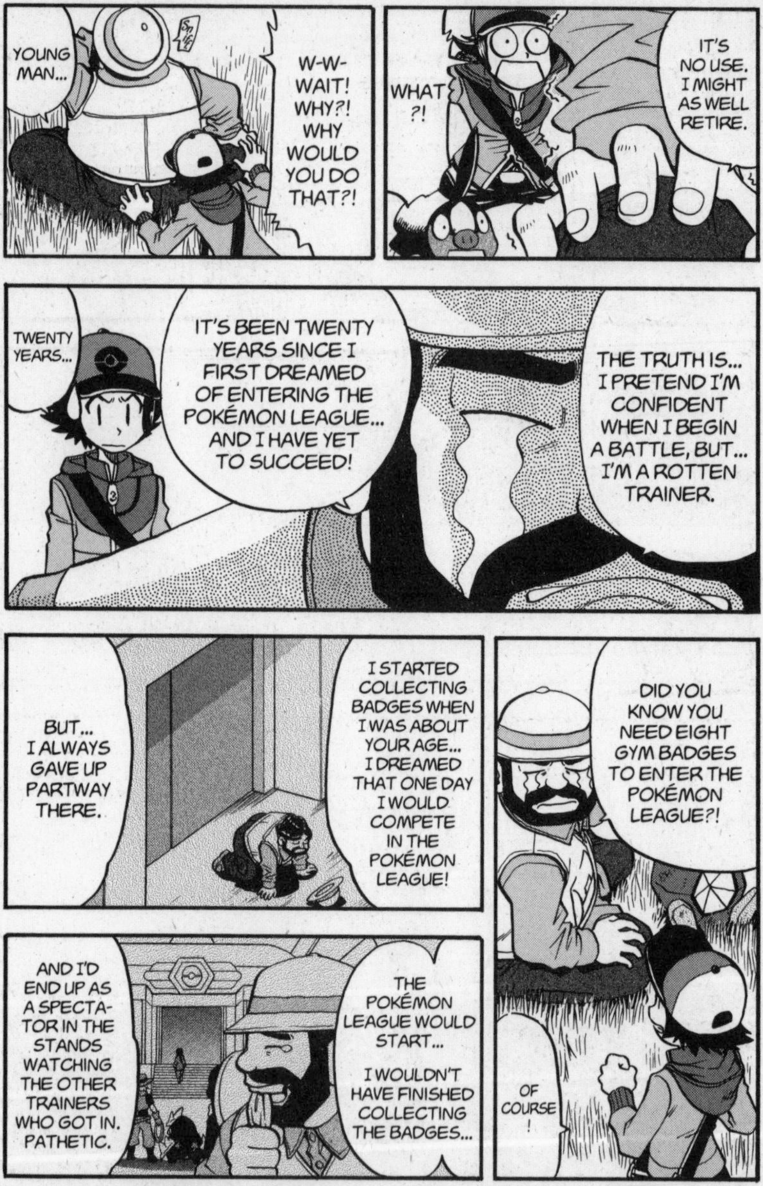
YOUNG MAN...
W-W-WAIT! WHY?! WHY WOULD YOU DO THAT?!
WHAT?!
IT'S NO USE. I MIGHT AS WELL RETIRE.
TWENTY YEARS...
IT'S BEEN TWENTY YEARS SINCE I FIRST DREAMED OF ENTERING THE POKÉMON LEAGUE... AND I HAVE YET TO SUCCEED!
THE TRUTH IS... I PRETEND I'M CONFIDENT WHEN I BEGIN A BATTLE, BUT... I'M A ROTTEN TRAINER.
DID YOU KNOW YOU NEED EIGHT GYM BADGES TO ENTER THE POKÉMON LEAGUE?!
OF COURSE!
I STARTED COLLECTING BADGES WHEN I WAS ABOUT YOUR AGE... I DREAMED THAT ONE DAY I WOULD COMPETE IN THE POKÉMON LEAGUE!
BUT... I ALWAYS GAVE UP PARTWAY THERE.
THE POKÉMON LEAGUE WOULD START...
I WOULDN'T HAVE FINISHED COLLECTING THE BADGES...
AND I'D END UP AS A SPECTATOR IN THE STANDS WATCHING THE OTHER TRAINERS WHO GOT IN. PATHETIC.

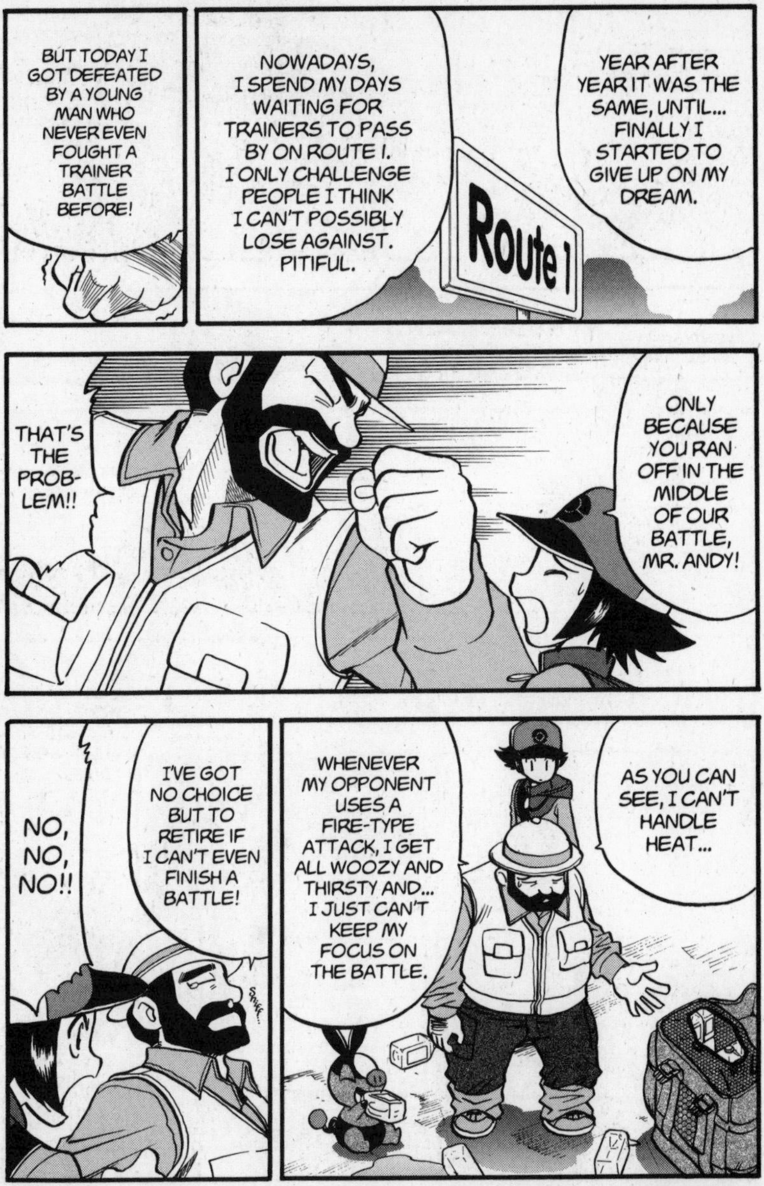
YEAR AFTER YEAR IT WAS THE SAME, UNTIL... FINALLY I STARTED TO GIVE UP ON MY DREAM.
Route 1
NOWADAYS, I SPEND MY DAYS WAITING FOR TRAINERS TO PASS BY ON ROUTE 1. I ONLY CHALLENGE PEOPLE I THINK I CAN'T POSSIBLY LOSE AGAINST. PITIFUL.
BUT TODAY I GOT DEFEATED BY A YOUNG MAN WHO NEVER EVEN FOUGHT A TRAINER BATTLE BEFORE!
ONLY BECAUSE YOU RAN OFF IN THE MIDDLE OF OUR BATTLE, MR. ANDY!
THAT'S THE PROB-LEM!!
AS YOU CAN SEE, I CAN'T HANDLE HEAT...
WHENEVER MY OPPONENT USES A FIRE-TYPE ATTACK, I GET ALL WOOZY AND THIRSTY AND... I JUST CAN'T KEEP MY FOCUS ON THE BATTLE.
I'VE GOT NO CHOICE BUT TO RETIRE IF I CAN'T EVEN FINISH A BATTLE!
NO, NO, NO!!
SNIFF...

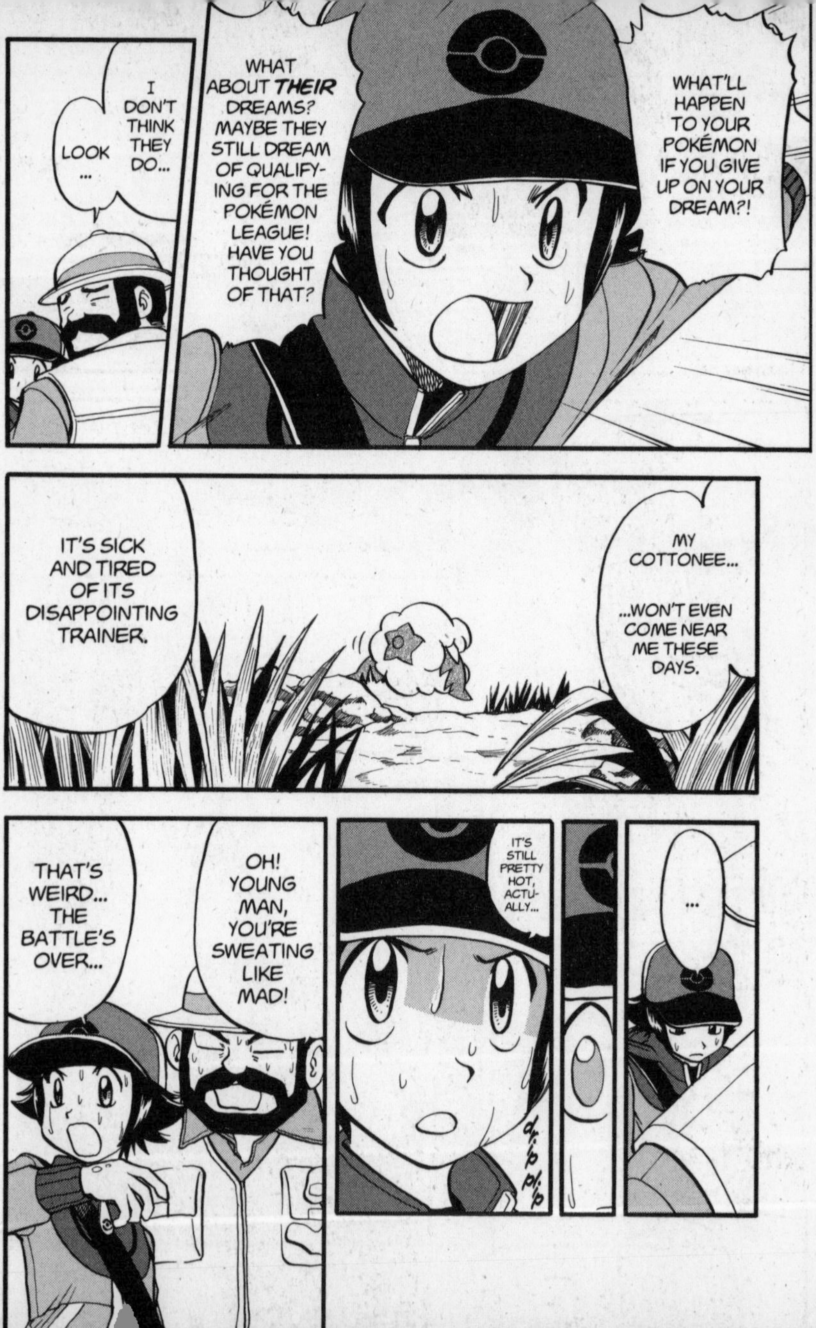
WHAT'LL HAPPEN TO YOUR POKÉMON IF YOU GIVE UP ON YOUR DREAM?!
WHAT ABOUT ***THEIR*** DREAMS? MAYBE THEY STILL DREAM OF QUALIFYING FOR THE POKÉMON LEAGUE! HAVE YOU THOUGHT OF THAT?
I DON'T THINK THEY DO...
LOOK...
MY COTTONEE...
...WON'T EVEN COME NEAR ME THESE DAYS.
IT'S SICK AND TIRED OF ITS DISAPPOINTING TRAINER.
...
IT'S STILL PRETTY HOT, ACTUALLY...
drip plip
OH! YOUNG MAN, YOU'RE SWEATING LIKE MAD!
THAT'S WEIRD... THE BATTLE'S OVER...

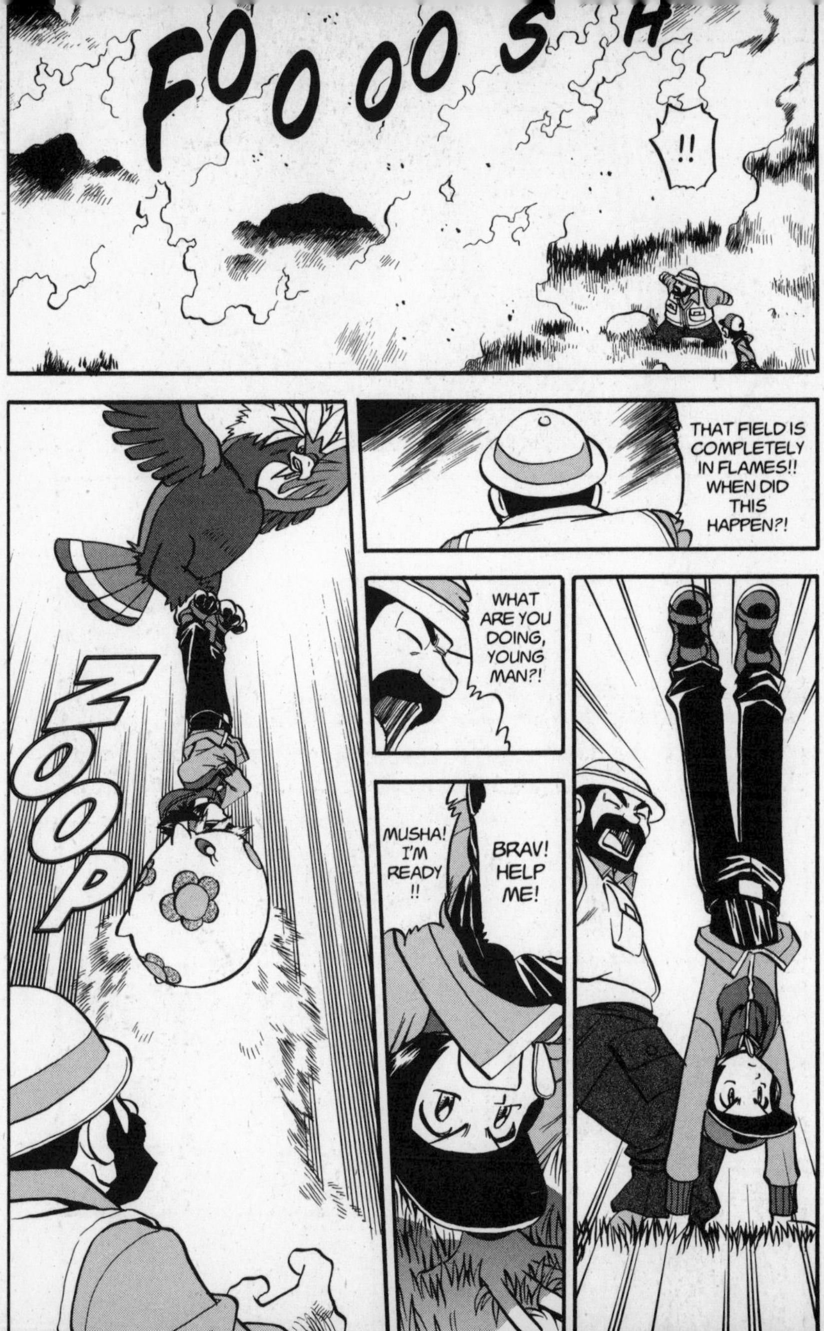
FOOOOSH
!!
THAT FIELD IS COMPLETELY IN FLAMES!! WHEN DID THIS HAPPEN?!
ZOOOP
WHAT ARE YOU DOING, YOUNG MAN?!
BRAV! HELP ME!
MUSHA! I'M READY !!

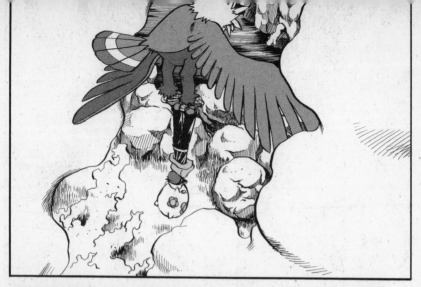

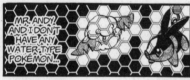

OKAY... THE SOURCE OF THE FIRE IS...
WAIT...! I BETTER FIND A WAY TO PUT IT OUT FIRST!
MR. ANDY AND I DON'T HAVE ANY WATER-TYPE POKÉMON...
!!
BUT THERE'S A RIVER NEARBY!! THAT'S IT!!
BRAV!! CAN YOU CARRY THAT BIG ROCK?!
YES!
YOU CAN DO IT!!
HOLD TIGHT!!
GRAB
tup
AFTER ALL, YOU'RE STRONG ENOUGH TO...
grk
grk

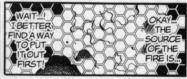

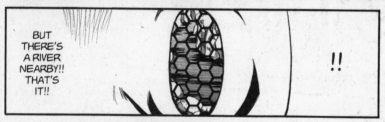

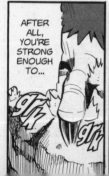

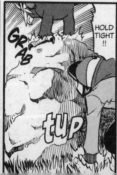

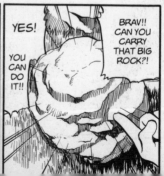

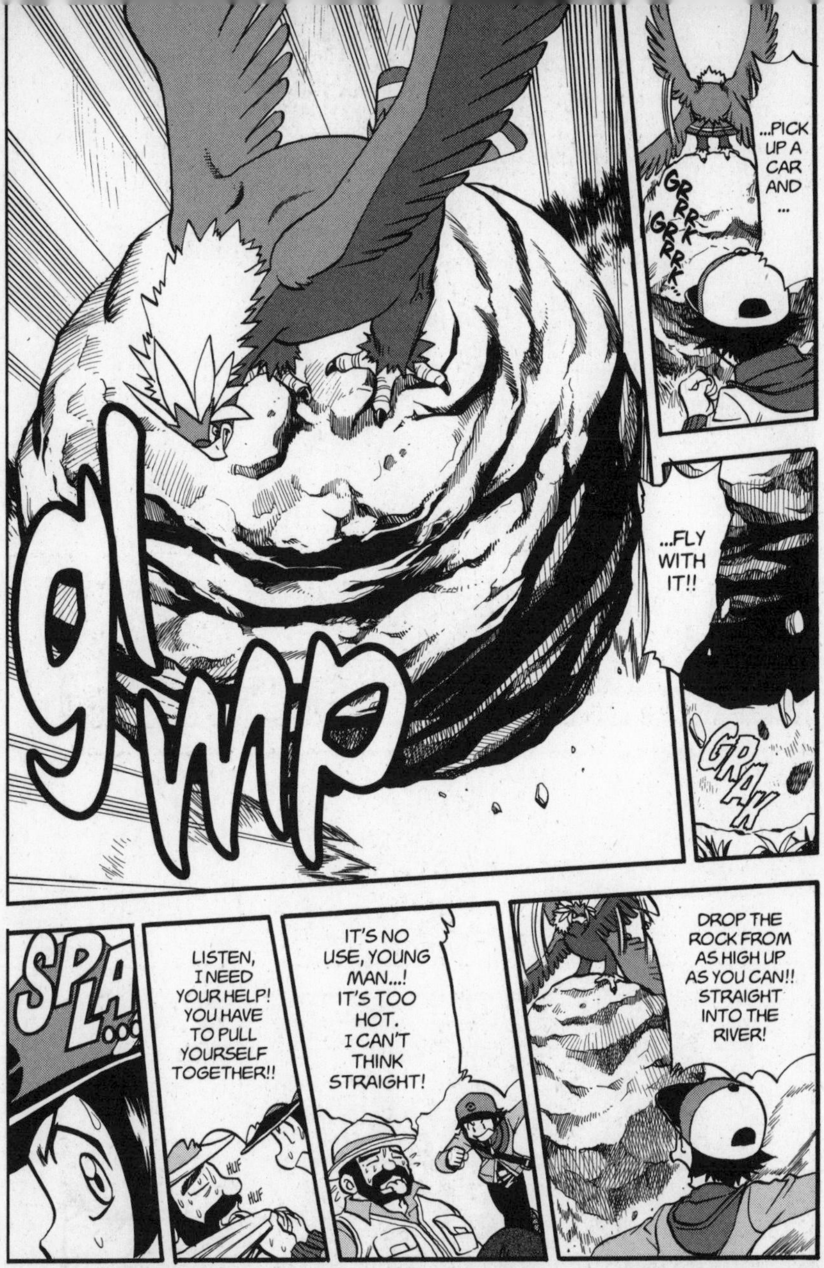
...PICK UP A CAR AND ...
GRRRK GRRRK
...FLY WITH IT!!
GRAK
glmp
DROP THE ROCK FROM AS HIGH UP AS YOU CAN!! STRAIGHT INTO THE RIVER!
IT'S NO USE, YOUNG MAN...! IT'S TOO HOT. I CAN'T THINK STRAIGHT!
LISTEN, I NEED YOUR HELP! YOU HAVE TO PULL YOURSELF TOGETHER!!
HUF
HUF
SPLA...

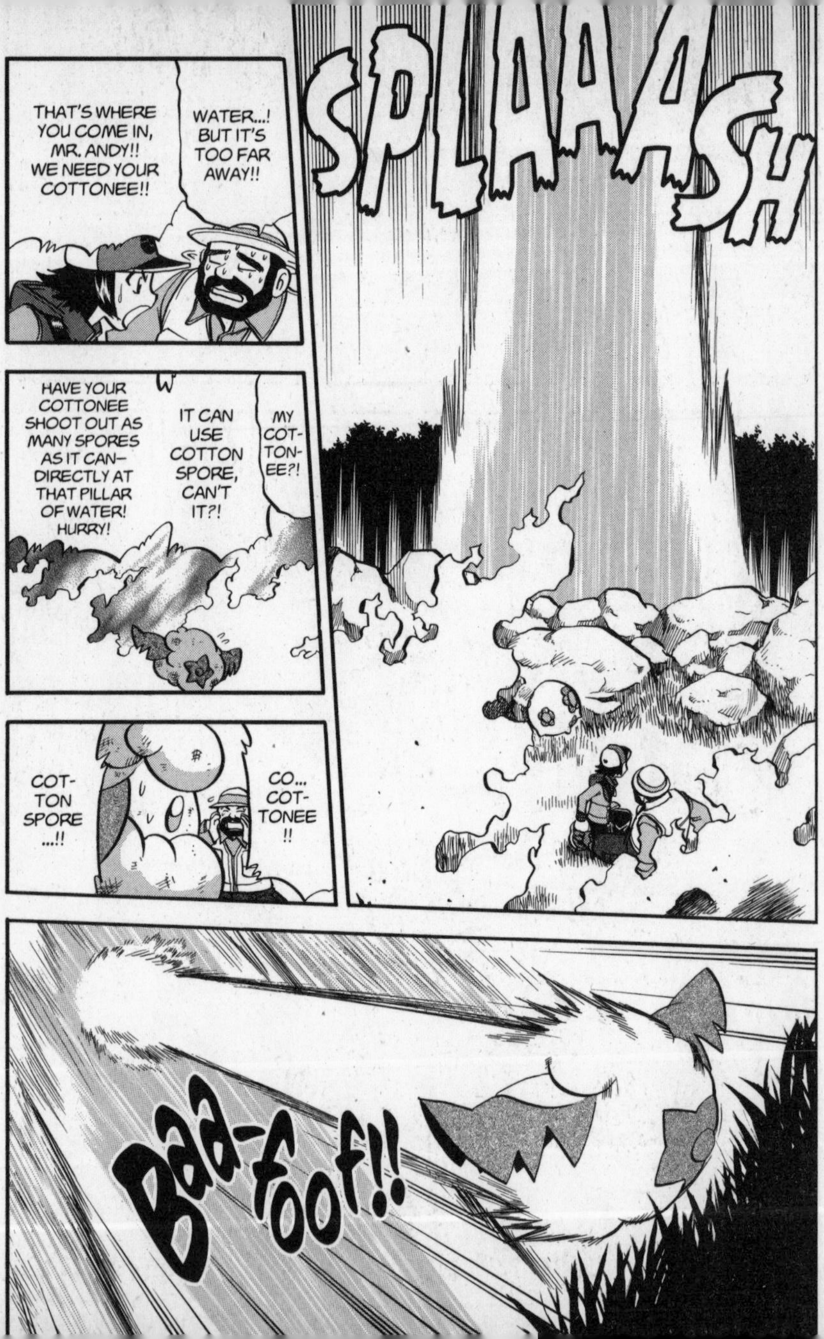
THAT'S WHERE YOU COME IN, MR. ANDY!! WE NEED YOUR COTTONEE!!
WATER...! BUT IT'S TOO FAR AWAY!!
SPLAAASH
HAVE YOUR COTTONEE SHOOT OUT AS MANY SPORES AS IT CAN—DIRECTLY AT THAT PILLAR OF WATER! HURRY!
IT CAN USE COTTON SPORE, CAN'T IT?!
MY COT-TON-EE?!
COT-TON SPORE ...!!
CO... COT-TONEE !!
Baa-foof!!

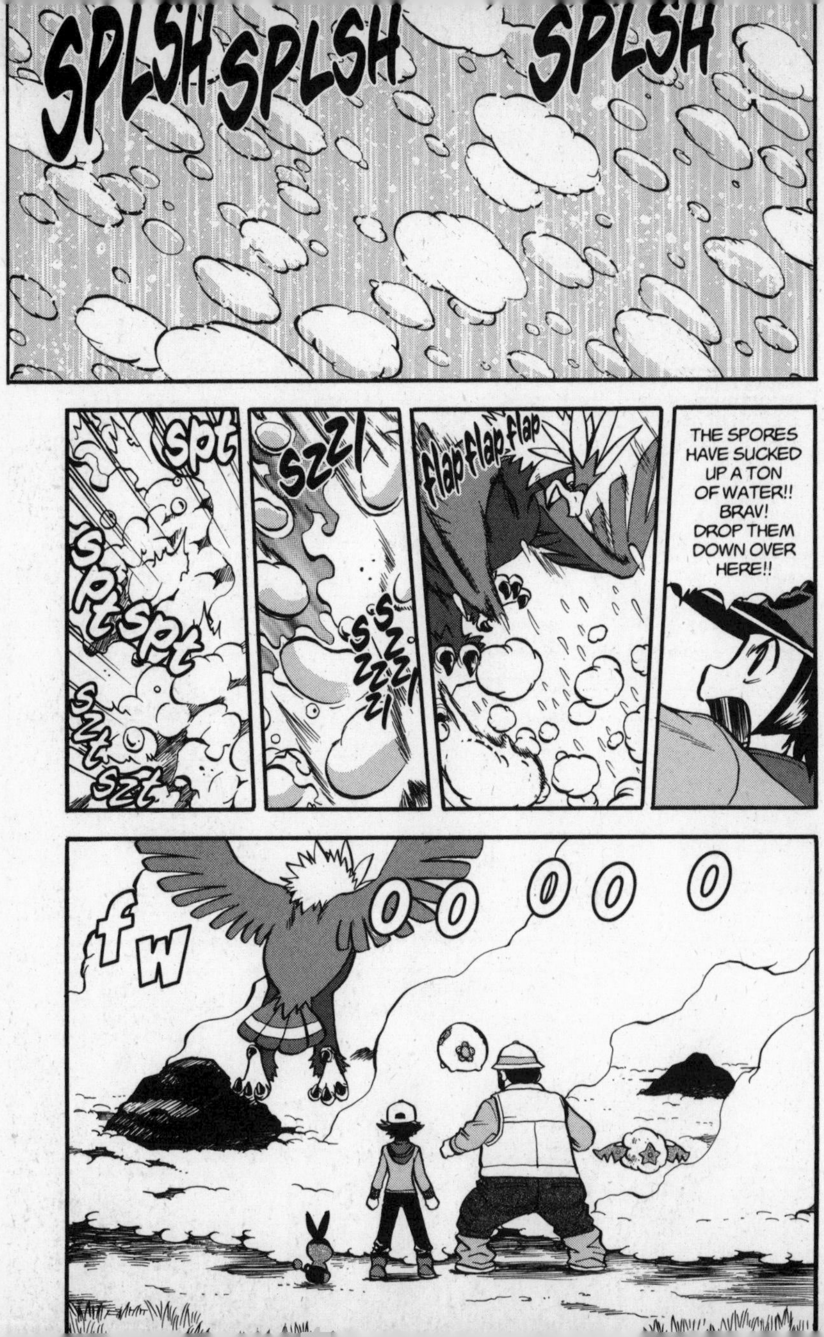
SPLSH SPLSH SPLSH
spt
spt spt
szt szt
szzl
s szzzzl
flap flap flap
THE SPORES HAVE SUCKED UP A TON OF WATER!! BRAV! DROP THEM DOWN OVER HERE!!
fw
OOOOO

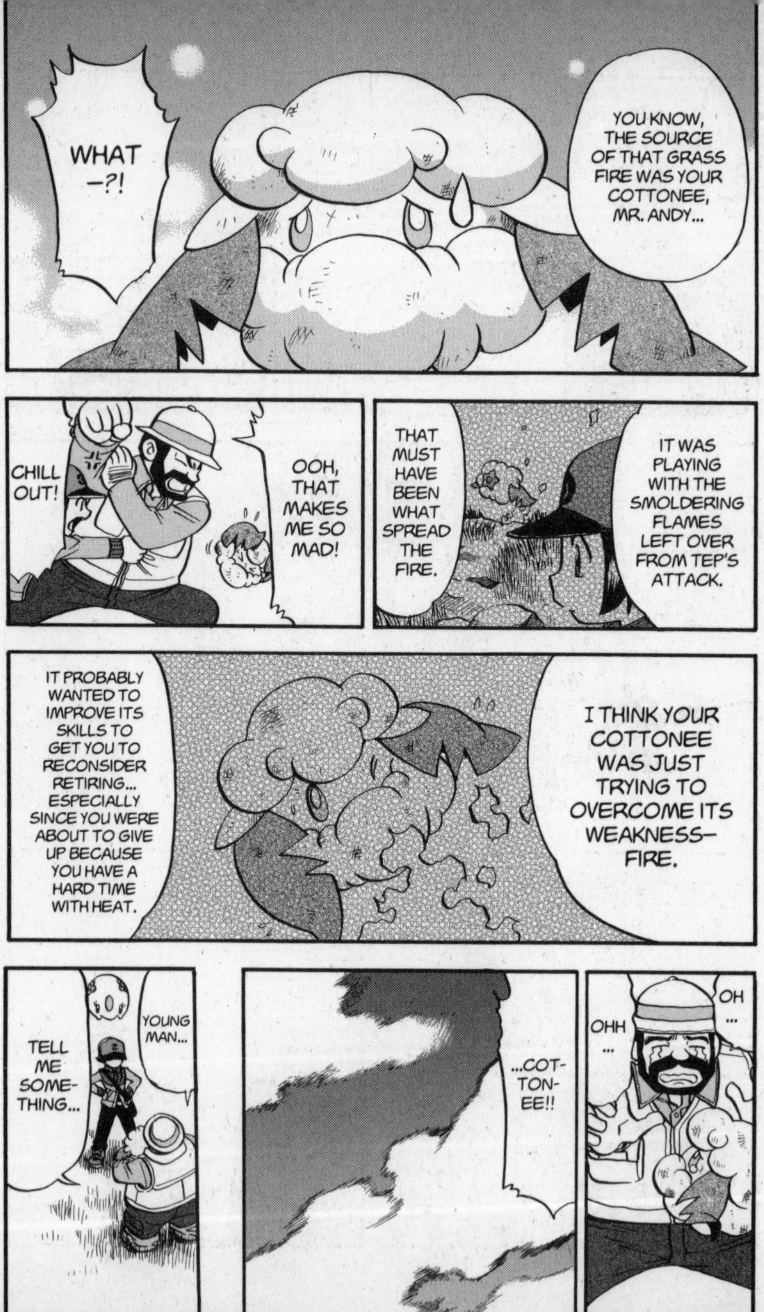
WHAT —?!
YOU KNOW, THE SOURCE OF THAT GRASS FIRE WAS YOUR COTTONEE, MR. ANDY...
CHILL OUT!
OOH, THAT MAKES ME SO MAD!
THAT MUST HAVE BEEN WHAT SPREAD THE FIRE.
IT WAS PLAYING WITH THE SMOLDERING FLAMES LEFT OVER FROM TEP'S ATTACK.
IT PROBABLY WANTED TO IMPROVE ITS SKILLS TO GET YOU TO RECONSIDER RETIRING... ESPECIALLY SINCE YOU WERE ABOUT TO GIVE UP BECAUSE YOU HAVE A HARD TIME WITH HEAT.
I THINK YOUR COTTONEE WAS JUST TRYING TO OVERCOME ITS WEAKNESS— FIRE.
TELL ME SOME-THING...
YOUNG MAN...
...COT-TON-EE!!
OHH ...
OH ...

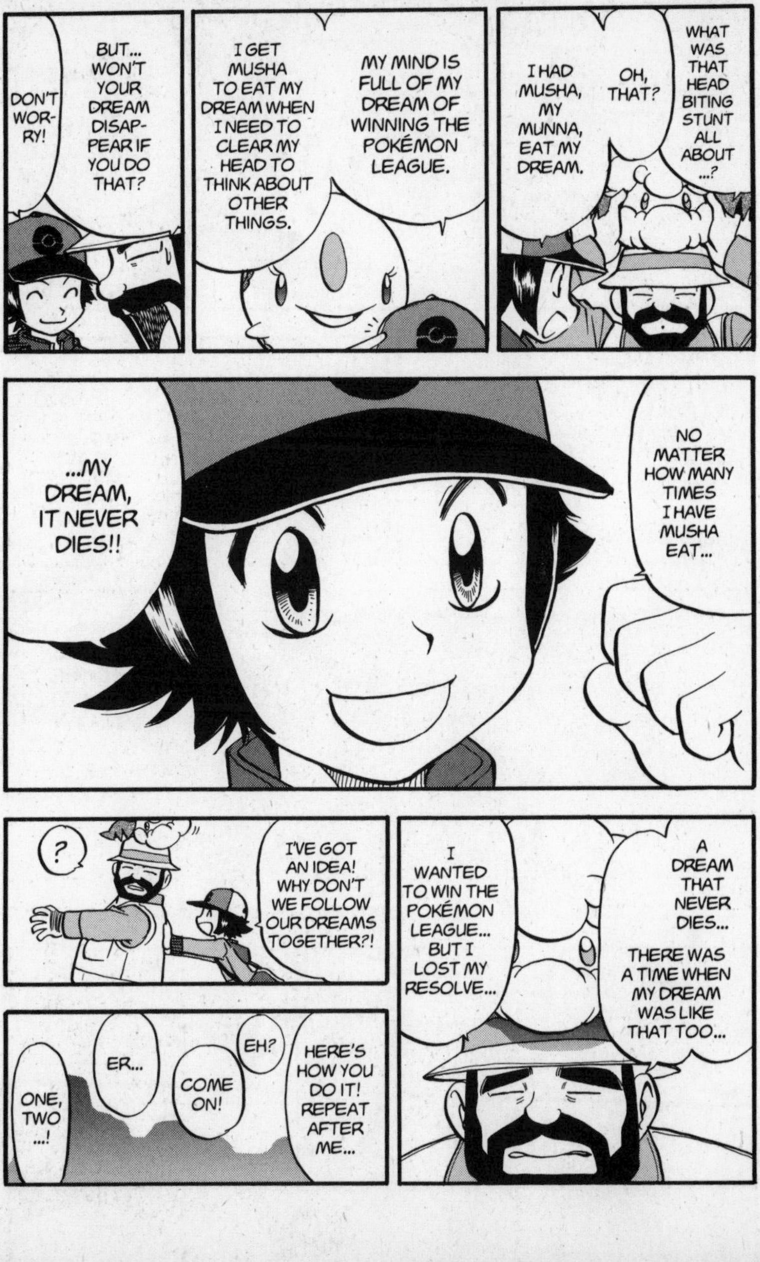
WHAT WAS THAT HEAD BITING STUNT ALL ABOUT ...?
OH, THAT?
I HAD MUSHA, MY MUNNA, EAT MY DREAM.
MY MIND IS FULL OF MY DREAM OF WINNING THE POKÉMON LEAGUE.
I GET MUSHA TO EAT MY DREAM WHEN I NEED TO CLEAR MY HEAD TO THINK ABOUT OTHER THINGS.
BUT... WON'T YOUR DREAM DISAPPEAR IF YOU DO THAT?
DON'T WORRY!
NO MATTER HOW MANY TIMES I HAVE MUSHA EAT...
...MY DREAM, IT NEVER DIES!!
A DREAM THAT NEVER DIES...
THERE WAS A TIME WHEN MY DREAM WAS LIKE THAT TOO...
I WANTED TO WIN THE POKÉMON LEAGUE... BUT I LOST MY RESOLVE...
I'VE GOT AN IDEA! WHY DON'T WE FOLLOW OUR DREAMS TOGETHER?!
?
HERE'S HOW YOU DO IT! REPEAT AFTER ME...
EH?
COME ON!
ER...
ONE, TWO ...!

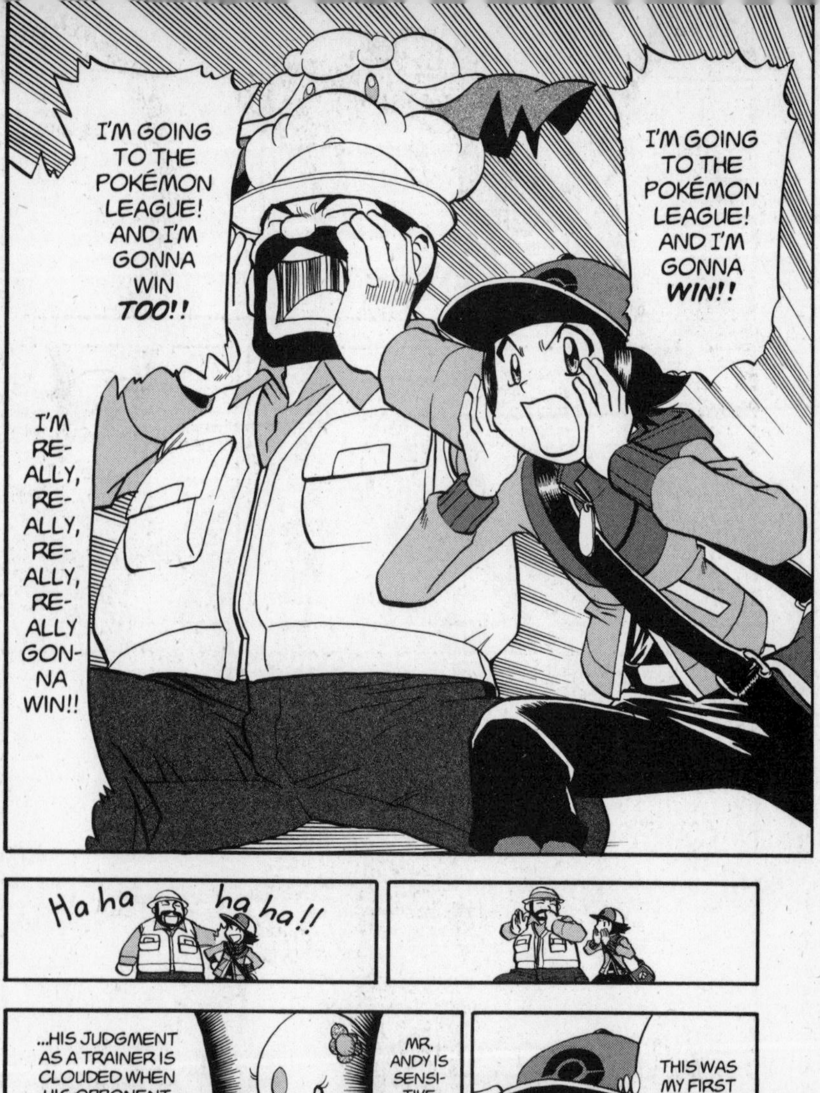
I'M GOING TO THE POKÉMON LEAGUE! AND I'M GONNA WIN!!
I'M GOING TO THE POKÉMON LEAGUE! AND I'M GONNA WIN TOO!!
I'M REALLY, REALLY, REALLY, REALLY GONNA WIN!!
Ha ha ha ha!!
MR. ANDY IS SENSITIVE TO HEAT, SO HE AVOIDS FIRE, AND...
...HIS JUDGMENT AS A TRAINER IS CLOUDED WHEN HIS OPPONENT ATTACKS WITH A FIRE-TYPE MOVE. EVEN A LITTLE THING LIKE THAT CAN AFFECT THE COURSE OF A BATTLE...
THIS WAS MY FIRST TRAINER BATTLE, BUT IT WAS SO MUCH FUN!

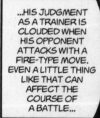

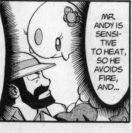

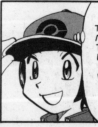

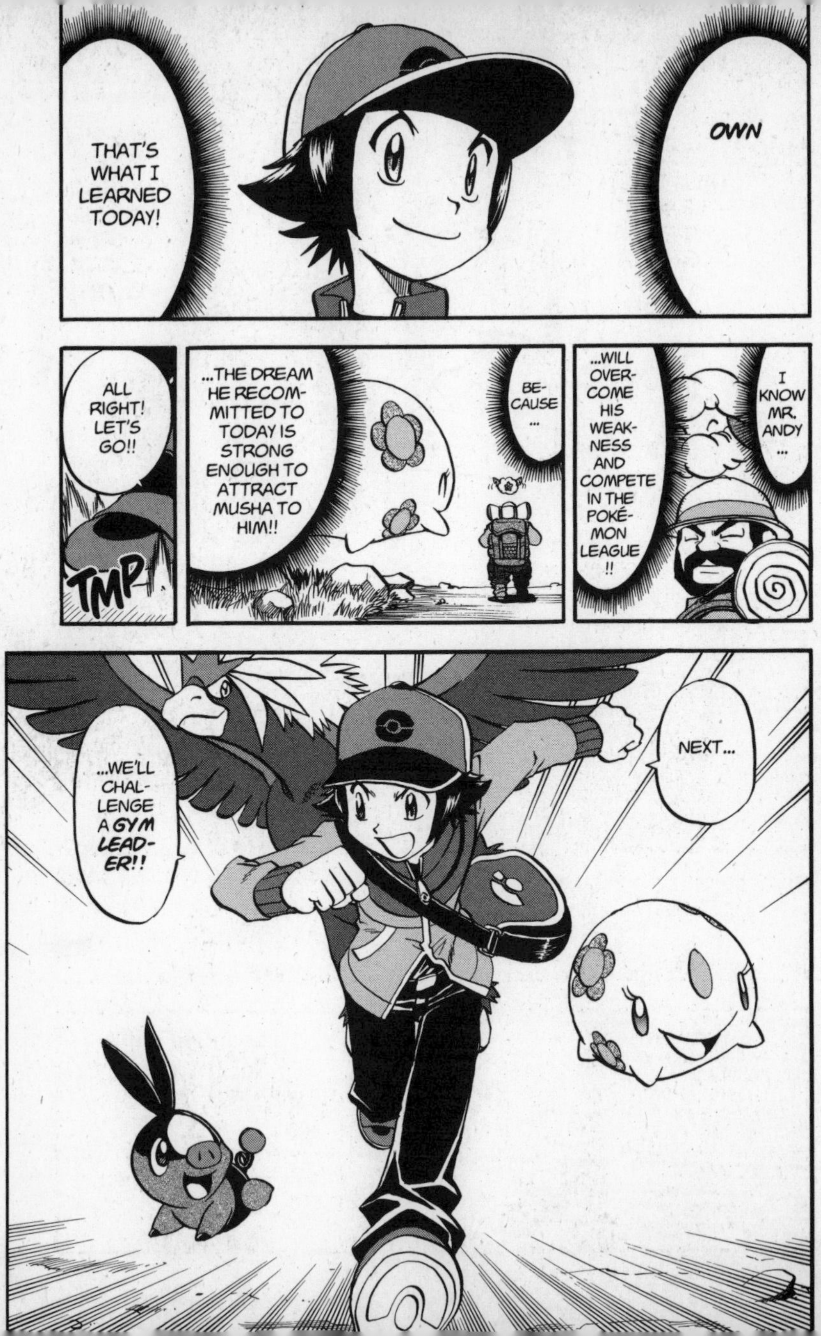
THAT'S WHAT I LEARNED TODAY!
OWN
ALL RIGHT! LET'S GO!!
TMP
...THE DREAM HE RECOMMITTED TO TODAY IS STRONG ENOUGH TO ATTRACT MUSHA TO HIM!!
BECAUSE...
...WILL OVERCOME HIS WEAKNESS AND COMPETE IN THE POKÉMON LEAGUE!!
I KNOW MR. ANDY...
NEXT...
...WE'LL CHALLENGE A GYM LEADER!!

More Adventures ON SALE NOW!

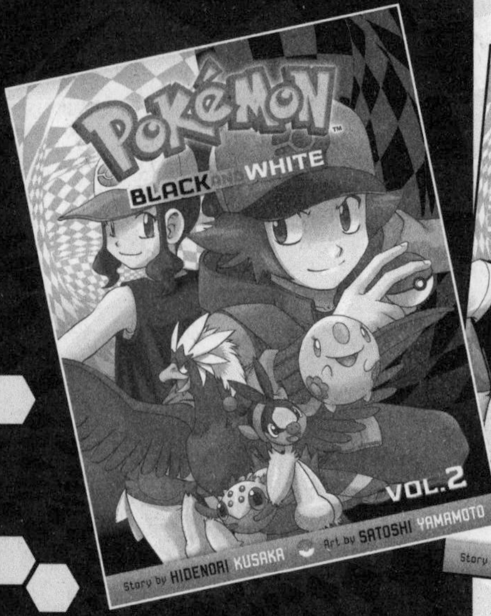
POKéMON
BLACK AND WHITE
VOL. 2
Story by HIDENORI KUSAKA
Art by SATOSHI YAMAMOTO

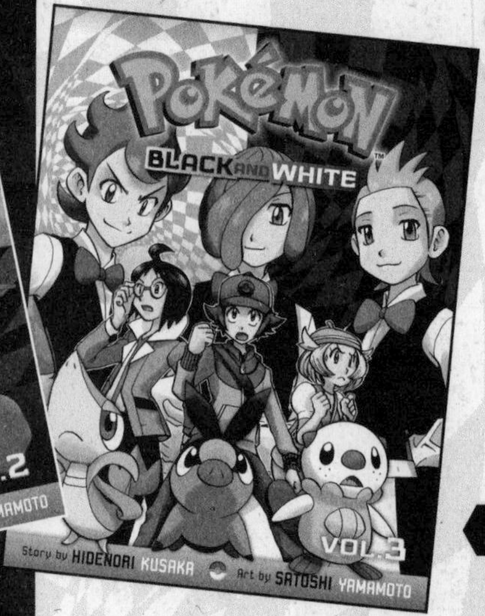
POKéMON
BLACK AND WHITE
VOL. 3
Story by HIDENORI KUSAKA
Art by SATOSHI YAMAMOTO

Black meets White, a Pokémon Trainer who runs a growing talent agency for performing Pokémon. Will Black catch show biz fever too? Then, mysterious Team Plasma urges everyone to release their beloved Pokémon into the wild.

IS THIS REALLY A GOOD IDEA? WHAT WOULD *YOU* DO...?

Team Plasma member N has the nerve to tell Black he isn't in touch with his Pokémon's feelings. Them's fighting words—literally! Which of the two Trainers has the best relationship with his Pokémon, and will that help him win a heated Pokémon battle...?

HEY! WHY WON'T WHITE HELP BLACK FIGHT...?